THE YOMIGAERI TUNNEL

Also by the author

The Lost Souls of Benzaiten

THE YOMIGAERI TUNNEL

Kelly Murashige

Published in the United States by Soho Teen
an imprint of Soho Press, Inc.
227 W 17th Street
New York, NY 10011
www.sohopress.com

Copyright © 2025 by Kelly Murashige
All rights reserved.

This is a work of fiction. Names, characters, places, and incidents either are the product of the author's imagination or are used fictitiously, and any resemblance to actual persons, living or dead, businesses, companies, events, or locales is entirely coincidental.

Names: Murashige, Kelly, author.
Title: The Yomigaeri Tunnel / Kelly Murashige.
Description: New York, NY : Soho Teen, 2025. | Audience term: Teenagers
Identifiers: LCCN 2024057042

ISBN 978-1-64129-703-5
eISBN 978-1-64129-704-2

Subjects: CYAC: Grief—Fiction. | Death—Fiction. | Legends—Fiction. | Tunnels—Fiction. | Fantasy. | LCGFT: Fantasy fiction. Novels.
Classification: LCC PZ7.1.M8385 Yo 2025 | DDC [Fic]—dc23
LC record available at https://lccn.loc.gov/2024057042

Interior design: Janine Agro, Soho Press, Inc.

Printed in the United States of America

10 9 8 7 6 5 4 3 2 1

EU Responsible Person (for authorities only)
eucomply OÜ
Pärnu mnt 139b-14
11317 Tallinn, Estonia
hello@eucompliancepartner.com
www.eucompliancepartner.com

*To those we lost,
those who grieve them,
and the person who gave me just enough BS to let me write this.*

A NOTE FROM THE AUTHOR

SO THERE WAS this boy.

No, I didn't date him. No, I didn't dump him. I just lost him.

It's been six years since a boy from my high school's graduating class passed away. By the time you read this, it might have even been seven.

Most times, though, it still feels like it was yesterday.

As two students in a K-12 school, this boy and I watched each other grow up. He was known to be a bit of a rebel, a bit of a punk, but it's like one of my first best friends told me, years after he passed: "He was different with you."

With me, he was kind. He was sweet. He was viciously witty and wickedly funny.

He was also my childhood. When he left, so did my hopes of one day seeing him at a reunion. Of reminding him of the time he asked me how to spell Eminem, and I was so unfamiliar with rap, I thought he was talking about the candy.

I still imagine him laughing sometimes.

The boy in the book may not be exactly like the boy I knew in real life, but it is still, in some way, about him. For him. Maybe even to him.

So though I took some creative liberties, I hope he understands. This book may be fiction, but the emotion is real. The grief is real. The heart is real.

Grief can be such a complicated thing. It can feel so dark and so isolating, much like walking alone in a tunnel. If you're lucky, the way Monika is, you won't have to walk it by yourself. My hope is that, by reading this book, you too will feel just a little less alone.

Please be warned that this book contains depictions of death, grief, dissociation, addiction, and a car accident. It also touches on emotional abuse and fear of driving. If reading about any of these subjects may be harmful to you, please take a moment and do what is right for you, even if that means setting this book aside for now.

There is a light at the end of this tunnel.

Thank you,
Kelly Murashige

THE YOMIGAERI TUNNEL

CHAPTER ONE
Most Likely to Have a Mental Breakdown in the Bathroom

YOU KNOW HOW they say there's a light at the end of the tunnel? Well, when I was little, I always thought it was *life*. There's a *life* at the end of the tunnel. In my childish mind, where stuffed animals could talk and unicorns were real and rainbows were more than mere tricks of the light, *that* was what we were being promised. We had to keep going, no matter how bad life seemed, because someday, we would reach the end of our darkness and be given a whole new life.

I believed a lot of dumb things when I was little, including the idea that swallowing a watermelon seed meant you were going to grow an entire fruit in your stomach, but I don't think hoping for life at the end of a tunnel is stupid. If you're sick of being the person you are, if you hate the people you're supposed to love and love the people you're supposed to hate, if you look in the mirror every morning and struggle to recognize the ghost reflected back at you, it feels like the only answer is to start a new life. How is some light supposed to help you? Wouldn't it be better if there *could* be life at the end of a tunnel?

Well, I'm older now. Too old to believe in all those childish fantasies. And I've decided I don't need the life to be literal. Just becoming someone else would be enough.

"Monika."

I raise my head. Natsuki, the former president of the Japanese Club, watches me through his thick-rimmed glasses, a cup of tea in his hands. We may have graduated together yesterday, but he already seems years ahead of me. Stanford-bound, just as he's been dreaming since he learned the difference between *college* and *collage*, he was always going to either wind up on some 30 Under 30 list or have a nervous breakdown. Par for the course for kids of our generation, really. I'm just glad he's willing to keep himself chained to our high school's Japanese Club long enough to organize and host this celebratory going-away brunch rather than leaving it to some of our classmates who—and I'm just being honest here—probably *still* don't know the difference between *college* and *collage*.

"Sorry," I say. "Did you need something?"

"No, nothing." Natsuki gives me a tight smile over the lip of his cup. "I just wanted to check up on you. You seem to be deep in thought."

I return his tense smile. "I'm just musing quietly."

It was impossible to think at that brunch table. Not just because some of the others were trying to see which of them could chug their miso soup the fastest, though that was an absolutely horrifying, mind-numbing, I-can't-believe-they-gave-you-a-diploma experience, but because everyone seemed so alive. And I just couldn't handle that.

So I excused myself for a moment, not that anyone had been paying me any attention, and sat on one of the lonely chairs by the glass-door exit. Cue quiet musing.

"Ah. Understandable." Natsuki glances over at the tables, takes a long sip of tea, then looks back at me. "I should check in with the Cultural Center's head of operations."

Probably a good idea. Natsuki may be just about the most well-mannered, levelheaded person I've ever met, but as the final act of his presidency, he invited the Japanese Clubs from some of the nearby schools too, and those kids can get rowdy, to say the least. Earlier today, two fellow grads were chastised for trying to steal the Noh masks from the Japanese Cultural Center's main display.

We were going to give them back, one said. *We just wanted to try them on.*

Uh-huh, Natsuki said. *Did you just graduate from high school? Or preschool?*

"Please tell her we're sorry," I say.

He grimaces. "Will do." After taking a peek at his phone, he glances at me, his expression cool. "Don't be a stranger, okay?"

I try not to read too much into it. He's only saying that because he has to, the type to seek people out on social media and follow them even if they never follow him back, wish them a happy birthday even if they never respond, and message them whenever he hears they've won an award or gotten an internship even if they leave him on read.

Before, our interactions were limited to the brief, obligatory exchange of tight-lipped smiles at club meetings.

Then Shun died, and everything changed. Every*one* changed. Our class both grew together and fell apart, and now, everyone's leaving again. Without him.

I'm convinced no one just dies. Even if they're alone when it happens, even if no one has spoken to them in years, even if they think no one cares, one person's death affects so many.

I watch, silent, as Natsuki makes a beeline for the head of operations. She stands in the little cubicle off to the side, the giant glass window giving her a perfect view of the chaos she's unleashed upon her beloved Cultural Center.

I reluctantly edge my way over to where the others are gathered. Avoiding the gazes of my classmates, I survey the students from the other schools' Japanese Clubs, my eyes snagging on the guy wearing a bright yellow shirt with a bunny-ear-toting anime girl, then the girl standing off to the side, her delicate fingers picking at the skin on her lips.

"If you try to ask for another color," Anime Shirt says, his eyes wide, "he grabs you by the collar and drags you into the underworld."

One girl tilts her head. "Then how are you supposed to escape him?"

"You have to either ignore him or say you don't want any kind of paper, then leave before he gets angry."

"He's a vengeful spirit. I'm pretty sure he'd be angry already."

Another girl narrows her eyes. "How are you supposed to ignore a spirit in the *bathroom*? There's no way I'm doing my business when there's a *guy* floating above me."

The first girl frowns. "I thought the spirit that haunted the bathroom was a girl."

Anime Shirt shakes his head. "That's a different story. Hanako-san."

I try not to roll my eyes. I used to be morbidly fascinated with Japanese folktales when I was little, but I've grown out of ghost stories. The scariest monsters are never actually fantastical beasts with shadowy faces and long claws; they're the very real truths lying beneath the surface.

"Fine," Anime Shirt says. "Someone *else* can tell a spooky story."

"Please," one girl says. "No more bathroom-related ones. I've had to pee for the past half hour, but now I'm too afraid to go."

Her friend laughs and takes her by the arm. "Come on. I'll go with you."

As they head for the bathroom, hands clasped, I find myself

thinking of Thea. My best friend is always willing to go on an adventure, even if our destination is just the bathroom or a teacher's cramped little cubicle. She offered to come here with me today, despite having not a single drop of Asian blood in her veins and no real interest in Japanese culture, but I let her off the hook.

At least one of us should enjoy the first official day of the rest of our lives, I said.

The rest of our lives, huh? She let out a monosyllabic laugh. *Well, that's depressing.*

"Enough with the ghost stories already," one of the remaining girls says, her hands raised like she's about to lay down the law. "Can't we talk about something else?"

"Like what?" Anime Shirt asks. "The fact that we're about to start college in a few months?"

"God, no. That's a million times scarier than the ghosts."

One of the guys raises a hand like he thinks we're still in class. "We're in the Japanese Cultural Center. Why not talk about cultural landmarks?"

The girl raises her brows, inadvertently matching the expression of the Hyottoko mask hanging on the wall behind her. "Uh, maybe because we don't have any?"

"Yeah, we do." Anime Shirt snaps his fingers and squints at the white-tiled floor like he's trying to make out the tiny letters on a microscopic cheat sheet. "What about that thing? The tunnel that's supposed to be around here? The—what was it called?"

"Yomigaeri Tunnel," his friend says.

A chill runs up my spine at the word *yomigaeri*. I'm far from a Japanese language expert, but even I know *yomigaeri* is related to resurrection.

Anime Shirt snaps his fingers one last time, the sound

echoing in the cavernous main room of the Cultural Center. "That's it. The Yomigaeri Tunnel. Anyone heard of it?"

"I thought we were done with the ghost stories," one girl whines.

"We are. A tunnel isn't a ghost. It's a tunnel."

"A *spoooooky* tunnel," another guy says with a wiggle of his fingers.

"A *fake* tunnel," one of the girls says. "I mean, that story doesn't even make sense."

"Oh, and the story of Hanako-san the bathroom ghost does?"

The girl shrugs. "Touché."

"Okay, so listen: There's supposed to be this underground passageway somewhere in this town. If you go into it, it makes you go, like, batsh—" Anime Shirt stops and glances at Natsuki, now in the middle of a forty-five-degree bow to the head of operations. "Crazy. It makes you go crazy."

"Dude," one guy says. "We just got out of high school. We're already crazy."

"No, seriously. It's supposed to show you all your worst fears. People have full-on hallucinated down there, like they're on acid or something."

"Maybe they *were* on acid," one girl says helpfully.

He shoots her a look. "*No.* They weren't."

"Why would you even go there?" one girl asks.

"It sounds awesome," one guy says. "Imagine getting high without having to pay for it."

"My brother ate some mushrooms from our yard once, and we didn't have to pay for those," another guy says. "We did have to pay for the hospital bills, though."

I have to suppress a smile. I'm going to miss this. Drop a bunch of high schoolers into one room and encourage them to talk about food, anime, and the creepiest ghost stories known to man, and there will never be a dull moment. Shun wasn't in the club, too much of a self-described loner to hang out with a bunch of kids Naruto-running from class to class, but I've always felt like he would have liked it here.

No, that's not true. I never even thought about him joining the club until it was too late. Until he had joined a club with a cost much higher than the fifteen dollars Natsuki had to squeeze out of us to cover all the Japan-exclusive Kit Kats and Hi-Chews the others had insisted he buy.

For the culture, they kept saying, as if all of Japan could possibly be contained in a shiny plastic wrapper.

"Why is it called the Yomigaeri Tunnel?" one girl asks.

When I turn to her, I recognize her as the one who kept picking her lip. She's rife with tension, her arms pulled close to her sides like she's trying to fit into a narrow vase. Her hair has been dyed a pale lavender, giving her the appearance of a withering flower.

I can't imagine how much bleach she had to use to get the color to stay. Thea tried to dye her hair once, but even after soaking the ends of the strands for hours, the change in color was almost too subtle to notice. She called it one of the greatest disappointments of her life.

It makes me want to DYE, she joked.

I laughed then. But it doesn't seem all that funny anymore.

"That's the cool thing," Anime Shirt says. "You aren't supposed to go to the tunnel just because you want the LSD experience without the LSD."

In the corner of my vision, I spot Natsuki side-eyeing us. He keeps his focus on the head of operations, but he can obviously hear us through the open cubicle door—which means the head of operations probably can too.

It's a good thing we've graduated. We're never getting invited back here.

"Supposedly, if you make it through to the other end, you get—"

"High," someone jokes.

I stare at the ground as another round of giggles bounces around the Cultural Center. I can't bring myself to laugh anymore.

Neither can the girl who asked about the tunnel's name. She may have seemed bored out of her mind earlier, but she's laser-focused on Anime Shirt now, her gaze so intense, I feel like she's staring at me too.

Maybe that—that look, as if she's seen straight into my soul—is what makes me do it. What makes me clear my throat, my eyes roaming along the walls, each one painted a deep scarlet, like an old wound, and say, "Doesn't 'yomigaeri' mean 'resurrection'? Does the tunnel have something to do with that?"

The others look over at me, their brows furrowed, as if they had forgotten I was even there. I suppose *I'm* the ghost in the room now.

"Yeah," Anime Shirt says after a moment. "They say—and this is just a rumor—the tunnel will let you resurrect someone."

We all fall silent again. I can feel people's gazes sliding around the room.

I wonder how much the students at the other schools know about Shun. He wasn't in the club, despite being part Japanese, but he was popular, at least at our school. They have to have heard something. Or maybe I just hope they have. I hope they know. I hope they care.

"But it's just a rumor. Plus, no one's ever gotten to the other side."

"How long *is* that tunnel?" someone mutters.

"It's not about how long it is."

"That's what she said," one guy pipes up, eliciting another wave of snickers.

The girl with the pale hair rolls her eyes and resumes picking her lip.

Ignoring the others, Anime Shirt says, "It's about what happens *in* there."

"That's what she said too," a girl says, earning her a high five from the other guy.

Pale Hair peels her lip, then brings the back of her hand to her mouth to stanch the flow of blood.

I look away.

"How would that even work?" another girl asks. "I mean, like, you get to the end of the tunnel, and God Himself is standing there? What if you go in from the other side?" She glares at the others. "Do *not* say, 'That's what she said.'"

"I don't know," Anime Shirt says. "It's just a story, and, like I said, no one has ever actually gotten through it."

"Where is it?" the girl with the bleeding lip asks. "The tunnel."

Anime Shirt exchanges a look with some of the others in the group. Scuffing his sneaker along the polished floor, he says, "I don't know. Again, it's just some scary story I heard from my cousin. It's not like it's real."

"It could be," someone says.

"I heard if you stay in there for too long, you suffocate," someone else adds, as if that's supposed to be reassuring.

"Probably just because there's a bunch of carbon monoxide in there," one guy says. "You go in there, pass out, and die. I read about it on Reddit."

"Of course you did," someone mutters.

"That's kind of the opposite of resurrection, though," someone else points out. "I mean, isn't that just dying?"

We tumble into a brief, awkward silence. It's probably because death isn't exactly the most pleasant post-brunch topic, but I can't help but think it's because they all know about Shun.

When I close my eyes, a flash of a white cross flickers in my mind like a lone candle.

"Well, *any*way," one guy says, waving a hand like he's shooing all thoughts of death out the glass doors of the Cultural Center, "did anyone ever hear of that seductive spider-woman thing? That sounds kind of hot, right?"

I turn away and start searching for the bathroom. That's enough Japanese Club for today.

Slowing, I take a moment to study the impressive array of kokeshi dolls and several strings of origami cranes in the glass displays along the back wall. I heard making a thousand cranes will grant you a wish. That certainly seems more likely than a magical tunnel pumped full of hallucinogenic gas. At least folding that many cranes would show how dedicated you are. I'm not sure what a bunch of acid trips are supposed to prove.

I step into the bathroom, relieved to see I'm the only one around. The bathroom stalls, like every public bathroom I've ever had the misfortune of being in, have gaps wider than the space in Shun's mouth that time he lost two adjacent teeth at once.

I had never seen anyone lose two teeth like that. Every time he caught me staring, he would grin, open his mouth, and run his tongue along his exposed gums, cracking up at my horrified reaction.

He had the type of laugh that drew everyone's attention. It didn't matter whether we were spread out in the classroom, in the middle of a lesson, or running around outside, swinging from trees and pretending not to hear the recess attendant's increasingly irritated warnings. Whenever he so much as snickered, we all had to look over to see what was so amusing.

It wasn't just that he liked laughing, though; he loved making other people laugh. He was what our classmates called *funny*, the parents called *trouble*, and the teachers called *the reason why I started packing extra-strength Tylenol in my purse*. I'm pretty sure he taught me, along with the rest of the class, half the swear words in the English lexicon.

We didn't give out superlatives at our school, but if we had, he would've been a major contender for Class Clown. I probably would've voted for him. I had always thought he was funny, even after we stopped speaking.

Maybe the no-superlative rule is a good thing. I don't know if any of us could look at our yearbooks now and see his picture under CLASS CLOWN.

Stop thinking about him, I tell myself as I wash my hands. I use too much of the sakura gel soap, leaving a thin, sticky sheen on my palms. I scrub harder, trying to rid myself of the coating, and by the time I turn the water off, my skin is red.

Just as I pivot to the paper towel dispenser—もったいない: DO NOT WASTE, the paper taped to the dispenser says—the door opens. I usually try to avoid eye contact with people, especially in the bathroom, but the movement startles me so badly, I can't help it. I look up just as the girl with the chapped lips glances my way.

Pale Hair.

I start to lift a hand to say hello, but before I can worry I'm about to inadvertently flick her in the face with water, she gives me a look so dark, I swear my life flashes before my eyes. Then she breezes into a stall and flings the door shut like she's locking out a ghost.

Look, I know what it's like to not feel like talking to people. To not even be able to smile at them. I *get* it. But I also have the manners to do my best and at least not look like I want to straight-up murder them.

I don't know what I could have possibly done to upset her. It can't be that she hates my school. I saw Natsuki talking to her not too long ago.

Then again, though, it looked more like he was talking *at* her. She never seemed to say anything back.

After glancing at myself in the mirror and fixing my bangs, I grab a paper towel, dry my hands, and head out. I consider yanking the door shut, just as payback for the way she closed the bathroom stall door, but that's petty. Besides, I'm not sure I can. The hydraulic door closer makes it impossible to slam.

Maybe I should be grateful for the brush-off. It's a nice reminder of what's to come, this brunch my last-ditch effort to contribute something to the Japanese Club, even if that something was just a five-dollar donation and a box of cookies.

After saying goodbye to Natsuki and thanking the Cultural Center's head of operations, who now looks somewhat placated, if a little weary, I push my way out of the Center. The switch from the air-conditioned room to the open air makes me shiver.

I want to forget this brunch ever happened. Write it off as something over and done with.

But as I take out my phone, I have a feeling that things have only just begun.

CHAPTER TWO
Most Nostalgic

ACCORDING TO THE bus schedule—which I check religiously, though it's wrong a good 50 percent of the time—the next bus home should be here in fifteen minutes. The one that would take me where I want to go won't arrive for another twenty.

Chewing the inside of my cheek, I open my text conversation with my mom. The last thing I sent her was a picture of the cookies I picked up for the brunch. Knowing exactly how rowdy the Japanese Club kids can get, she responded with an ominous **Good luck**.

Tapping out a message with one thumb, I ask, **Can Thea come over?**

When I was little, I almost never brought people to our apartment. My mother was convinced the place was in shambles and would therefore bring eternal shame upon our family if anyone were to see it. Even when I told her my friends were seven and had, that very day, eaten Oreos off the floor, she insisted the apartment was not ready for guests.

Things were different with Thea. At this point, she is practically my mother's unofficial second daughter. Starting in late middle school, after a couple of years of friendship, my mother said Thea could stay whenever she wanted.

Besides, my parents are actively pushing for me to talk to

people, even if it's just Thea. They're worried I'm going to slip into a depression because Shun's dead.

Joke's on them. I was al*ready* in a depression.

Yes, of course Thea can come over, my mother replies.

Thank you.

I swipe over to my text conversation with Thea. After a few seconds of deliberation, I tap her contact and call her. It takes a few seconds for her to pick up.

"Sorry," she says in lieu of a typical greeting. "I heard my phone ringing and instinctively ignored it until I realized it was you."

"How touching."

"It's summer," she says, as if that's an explanation. "So what's up? Is the Japanese Club thing over?"

"Yeah." I pause. "I know you were supposed to be relaxing today, but do you think I can coax you out of the house?"

"Can you *please* not make me sound like some kind of agoraphobic hermit crab? I'm not even home right now."

I frown. "What? Where are you?"

She pauses for a beat too long. "The mall. I may have gone to the bookstore. And to the library before that. It's been a rough summer."

"It's the first day."

"I got a lot of gift cards for graduation," she says, the indignation in her voice putting a grin on my face. "Plus, I'm going to miss the library."

My smile slips away.

That's right. Once summer ends, she'll be heading to New York.

"Hello?" There's a small burst of white noise as Thea pulls the phone away from her ear to ensure I'm still on the line. "Monika?"

Maybe I should hang up. Wait for the bus. Let her go back to daydreaming about New York, if it can even be called daydreaming when she'll be there in a matter of weeks. It would probably be better to keep her out of this entirely.

My fingers curl into my palm, a flower blooming in reverse. I could snap shut right now. *Should* snap shut right now. There's no point in involving her in this. We're not even classmates anymore.

"Monika. Are you being held hostage by the Japanese Club? Grunt once for yes and twice for no."

I can't help but laugh. And just like that, the tension breaks, my fingers going limp at my sides. "I don't think the club members like me enough to hold me hostage, to be honest. I was just wondering if you want to come over."

"Are you kidding?" she shrieks. "*Yeah*, I would. I'll be there in ten. Maybe not even ten."

"Don't speed," I say.

My mind drifts to Shun, the way it always does now. He was driving that night. He shouldn't have been. But it's not as if he ever paid much attention to the rules.

Thea hangs up without responding. And though I initially assume it's because she's thinking of Shun too, I soon learn it's because she's too busy doing exactly what I told her not to do, her old white Honda Accord screeching to a stop barely eight minutes after the end of our call.

"I said *don't* speed," I tell her as I fall into the passenger's seat.

"I didn't," she insists. "Traffic was light."

"Yeah, sure. When you started ripping down the road, that is. I bet pedestrians had to leap to get out of your way."

She rolls her eyes. "Not even. I'm a very responsible driver."

"Uh-huh." I glance at the backseat, where she's strapped in two giant bags. "Oh, God. Are those all books?"

"Yup." She pops the *P*. "The library's holding its summer reading program again, and I'm going *all in*."

She glances at me, expecting a smile, but I don't manage to flash her one until it's too late. Furrowing her brow, she says, "Okay, what is up with you? Why are you acting so weird?"

I try not to visibly cringe. I don't know what tipped her off—the look on my face, the awkward silences on the phone, or the way I can't stop fidgeting—but if my goal was to play it cool, I'm failing miserably.

Pulling myself out of my full-body wince, I take out my phone. "It's nothing."

"Yeah, right." She rests her wrist on the top of the steering wheel. "What is it? Was everyone getting all nostalgic about graduation or something, as if it didn't happen literally one day ago?"

I was never all that excited about graduation. To me, it was neither the end of something beautiful nor the beginning of something even greater. It was just an overblown accomplishment. Our school may have skimped on infrastructure and competent teachers, but it sure knew how to hold a commencement. From the moment spring break ended, we were in full Graduation Mode, strong-armed into practices for everything from sitting to singing. I didn't know I walked with my head down until one of the graduation directors shouted at me to *LOOK UP, FOR GOD'S SAKE.*

Sounds like a metaphor, I wanted to tell Thea. *"Look up. Those are your dreams out there, just waiting for you to reach out and grab them."*

But even in the moment, it felt much too big to say.

"Not exactly," I say to Thea now. "It wasn't about graduation, per se."

Or at all.

I didn't presume much about graduation, aside from the fact that my parents would be there, possibly crying, and it would be hot and overly long, and I would be stupidly nervous during my walk across the stage to retrieve my diploma.

I also assumed all four hundred of my classmates would be there. I think everyone in my class assumed so. And we were all wrong.

"What, then?" Thea asks. "What happened in there?"

When I swallow, it's all I hear. In trying to speak over the rush of blood in my ears, I end up half yelling. "It was Shun, okay?" Her eyes flick to me, and I force myself to lower my voice. "They were talking . . . about Shun."

Thea's face falls. "Oh."

Shun had a place in our class, even at commencement. The guys to the left and right of where he was supposed to sit left a space between them. Like a gap in a mouth. The graduation committee set a framed picture of him there, but even if it hadn't been there, no one would have taken his place.

We all cried when the dean called his name, his mother shakily mounting the stage to accept his diploma. It was the worst thing I had ever seen.

After the ceremony, the whole graduating class stayed back so our friends and relatives could unload envelopes and stuffed animals and celebratory inner tubes with crude messages scrawled out in black Sharpie onto us. Most families had a sign, a piece of cardboard or posterboard attached to a PVC pipe, to indicate where each graduate would be stationed.

Shun had a white cross.

Every time I had a lull in visitors, I found myself looking over at his family. Their eyes wet and their heads bowed, they burst into tears every time people offered up envelopes and placed candy lei beside the cross.

It felt wrong, leaving before them. I wanted to know if they would take the cross. If the deans would clean it up. If more people were coming. If the framed picture had been given to his mother or if the school would keep it someplace safe.

Shun wasn't the first person to ever die in his senior year, but he was the first person in the town, the first person in the school, the first person we *knew* to ever die in his senior year. It had also happened in January, right after he and all his friends had turned in their final college applications. What was supposed to have triggered full-on senioritis had instead brought on incurable grief.

I wouldn't say it was easy for anyone, but Thea handled it well. She claims it's because she never really interacted with him. They had been in a couple of classes together over the years, but they had never really held a full conversation.

I don't even have pictures with him, she said.

I don't either, I said, and the realization made me sick.

I know pictures aren't worth much. Even if our parents *had* pushed us together for a few photos when we were little, they wouldn't have meant much now. People would look at it and see two little kids forced to stand next to each other. They wouldn't know the whole story.

But at least it would have been *some*thing.

"They were talking about Shun?" Thea asks.

I nod.

But that's not true, is it? They weren't talking about him. They were talking about the tunnel. *I* was the only one thinking of him.

It feels like that's how it always is now. The school may have commemorated him at graduation, but in the moments before and afterward, it felt like I was the only one still consumed by thoughts of him, with no comprehensible reason why. I mean, I didn't even have pictures with him.

"What did they say?" Thea asks.

I stare out the window. "Nothing. I just want to go home."

Her eyes dart to me. That familiar feeling of shame, dribbling over my shoulders like water from a leaking AC, reminds me of how it felt to be a middle school kid in the back of my mom's car, my head turned away as I refused to answer her well-intentioned questions.

Thea, like my mom, decides to give me space. Until we reach the visitor lot on the bottom floor of my apartment building, there's only the *shoomp, shoomp* of her books shifting in the backseat, each one rearranging itself around the rest until eventually, they're all right where they belong.

CHAPTER THREE
Best Stalker

ONCE WE REACH the elevators—Thea hauling both book bags with her because she's afraid they'll get stolen if she leaves them in her car—I've calmed down enough to say, "Sorry. It's been a rough morning. Thank you for picking me up."

"It's fine. I just hope you're . . ."

Okay. As if I even know what that means anymore.

"I'm not the one toting an entire library around on my shoulders." I hold out a hand again, knowing she's going to decline my help.

"Nope. *My* books."

I grin. When we reach my floor, we head down the familiar hallway, the yellowish lights casting a sickly glow over the patterned, hotel-esque carpet.

"Sorry to have torn you away from your first love," I say as I stick the key into the lock.

She searches the hall, one hand over her brow. "My babysitter's son is here?"

I roll my eyes. Anyone who has spent even ten seconds with Thea knows she is a total romantic and has been ever since she set eyes on the dinky, towheaded kid sitting in front of the TV at her old babysitter's house. She may not have a crush on him anymore, but she's convinced there's some merit to the whole "love at first sight" thing. It's why she reads so many romance books, many of which I have attempted to read, only to fall asleep a few chapters in. I'm not much of a romantic, I suppose.

"*Reading*," I say, pushing the door open. "I meant *reading*."

"Oh. Okay, yeah. I love that too." She follows me inside, her bags banging her hips as she slides her way through the door. "But it's not like the books are going anywhere."

Yeah, well, neither am I. Thea may be heading to New York, but I'll still be here.

When Thea first started coming over to my place, she was painfully courteous, each step measured and each word quiet, as if she thought she was in an academic library with a power-hungry librarian stationed at the front desk. By now, though, she can grab a glass from the overhead cabinet, flick the faucet to the filtered-water setting, and grab herself a nice handful of ice cubes, all before I've even finished washing my hands.

Once we've reached my room, Thea's ice clinking against the insides of her glass, I take out my laptop and start searching up information about the origins of the word *yomigaeri*. As I thought, it's related to the concept of being brought back, rooted in *yomi*, or the underworld, and *kaeru*, to return. Nothing about a mythical tunnel, though.

Opening my millionth browser tab, I search up tunnels in my area. I'm not feeling all that optimistic, but to my surprise, there's an entire blog dedicated to the various highways, passages, and hiking spots in the area. When I scroll down, there's an old-school hit counter at the bottom to show how many people have viewed the page.

00000007, it reads.

Thea, sprawled out on the floor, rolls over and cranes her neck to take a peek at my bookcase. Letting out a little gasp, she reaches for one of the yearbooks lined up in chronological order on the lowest shelf. The last time I opened one, I cringed. I have never seen so many iterations of *HAGS* in my life. I hadn't even realized what it meant until someone said, *"Have A Great Summer."* Duh.

"Is this the one?" she asks.

My eyes don't leave my laptop screen. The blog's owner has documented every single oddity in the entire town. "Which?"

"The Operation 107 one, of course."

I groan and cover my face. "Oh, God."

Throughout most of eighth grade, I had a hopeless, pitiful, completely unrequited crush on someone four years our senior. A tutor at the middle school's writing center, Eli was said to be a gifted poet. I wouldn't know for sure. He hardly ever talked about his work and was much more comfortable focusing on how he could help others with theirs.

He was awkward, but that was why I liked him. He towered over everyone else, even most of the teachers, and it always took him a while to respond whenever someone asked him an unexpected question, as if he had, up until that very moment, been lost in his own headspace.

In retrospect, he must have known I was nursing a crush on him. I spent far too much time at the writing center, waiting to see if he would show up. He didn't seem to have any set schedule, so I would sometimes end up doing math homework in the corner, turning down other tutors' offers of help, only to leave disappointed at the end of the hour. Whenever he did appear, always with his laptop and a book or folder of scribbled notes, I would trip over myself trying to get to his table.

No, I guess that's not true. It would take me a painfully long time to build up the courage to approach him, even when it was clear I was only there for him.

I can't believe he's graduating, I said as our eighth-grade year drew to a close. *And he's going to some faraway school on the East Coast. I'm probably never going to see him again.*

Then you know what you have to do, don't you? Thea said.

I gave her a look. *I'm pretty sure kidnapping is illegal.*

Not THAT, you freak. She gently pushed my shoulder. A dangerous move, considering we were sitting on a wall near the bus stop. *You need to get Eli to sign your yearbook.*

My yearbook?

She nodded. *It's meaningful. A way of saying goodbye. Plus, if he ever gets famous, you can sell his signature for a ton of money.*

I put a hand over my heart. *If I were lucky enough to get his signature, I would NEVER sell it.*

Thea held up her hands in surrender. *I'm just saying. You should do it.*

Maybe I will, I said. Then, after thinking it over, I added, *But you'll have to help me.*

I thought that was a given.

"We thought we were so smart." Thea places a hand on the cover. "May I?"

I make a face. "Go ahead. Just don't make me look."

We spent our last days as eighth graders plotting how we would get Eli's signature. The biggest obstacle, aside from my waning confidence and tendency to humiliate myself in every way imaginable, was how to make sure we caught him at a good time.

"It was after school, wasn't it?" Thea says. "When we found him."

"Yeah. We took off running as soon as our classes finished."

Middle school got out a little earlier than high school, but we didn't know that then. As Thea and I ran, our yearbooks banging against our knees, one teacher called out after us, *WHERE'S THE FIRE?*

"It was like another world," Thea says. "It was actually pretty amazing how easily we tracked him down." She pauses. "Or, well, you. *You* tracked him down."

I would've known his cumbersome, loping gait anywhere.

THERE HE IS, I shrieked. We were roughly fifty feet away, hiding under the eaves of the high school's science wing.

WHERE? Thea asked, turning in every direction but the right one.

BY THE—HE'S—THE—TABLES, I said, my thoughts racing too fast for me to get out a coherent sentence. I took her by the shoulders and angled her toward the picnic benches just outside the science wing.

He was surrounded by his typical posse, of course. I could never shake the sticky coat of envy that fell over my shoulders every time I saw him with them. *I* wanted to be his friend. *I* wanted to talk to him every day on our way to class. *I* would let him copy off my homework.

No, on second thought, he would never copy my homework. He was the type to do it all on his own. Maybe even—*gasp*—early.

Well, now what? Thea said as we gaped at him. *Do you think you could just, like, ask him with all his friends around?*

NO, I snapped. *I could NEVER do that.*

"How did we even get that signature?" she asks now, flipping through the pages of my yearbook. "Weren't all his friends there?"

I nod. "So we did what any sane pair of middle school kids would do."

Thea frowns. "Used the power of friendship?"

"I said middle school kids, not anime protagonists."

She snorts.

"We held a stakeout."

"Oh, God. That's right." She shakes her head. "I'm pretty sure we only knew about stakeouts from, like, bad TV. I've never heard of a stakeout going well."

"Ours did," I say as she stops to study a black-and-white class picture. "Kind of."

She tosses me a skeptical look. "Did it, though?"

Thea and I snuck over to the staircase leading up to the picnic tables. I stood facing one way while she covered my blind spots. If one of us saw an opportunity to jump on Eli, we were to say, *107*. To our underdeveloped adolescent brains, this was an act of pure genius.

After a few minutes of waiting on the stairs, we found ourselves unbearably bored. We were in the middle of a heated debate—which was heavier: Thea's backpack or a small pony?—when something flashed in the corner of my eye.

One-oh-seven, Thea hissed. *ONE. OH. SEVEN!*

Eli was plodding down the stairs, his footsteps uneven. His mouth was the slightest bit open, as if he was tasting the air.

Gogogogogo, Thea whispered, shoving me into his path.

I skidded to a stop in front of him, my yearbook pressed to my chest and a marker clutched between my fingers, which were quickly losing feeling.

Oh, Eli said, his eyes on me. *Hey. What—what are you doing here?*

I, um. Not the most eloquent beginning, but I was just glad I hadn't reflexively thrown up on him. *Um, well—*

Thea and I had thought up the stakeout scheme and what to do if he said he wasn't willing to sign my yearbook. We had not come up with a plan for what to do if he asked what I was doing at his high school.

Just taking a tour, I said as casually as possible. By which I mean not casually at all. *But I was just wondering, um, if you, like, would maybe sign my yearbook? Maybe?*

Thea, who was doing her best to blend in, winced as I opened my yearbook with enough gusto to nearly send it toppling to the ground.

Your yearbook? he echoed.

Yes. I swallowed. *Because, you know, you're graduating—congratulations, by the way—and maybe it's just, like, you know, to remember you by.*

He hesitated, blinking, his eyes a deep, muddled brown. I was afraid I had deeply offended him, but he seemed more confused than anything, like he wasn't sure if I was real or a figure in a fever dream, sandwiched right between the part where he takes a test for which he didn't study and that strange scene where he speaks to a burning bush about whether flying fish can be classified as creatures of the sky.

I was in the middle of imagining my funeral when he said, *Yeah. Yeah, of course. I would love to sign your yearbook.*

Really? I shouted.

Behind me, Thea slapped a hand to her face.

I mean, that would be—thank you.

I had already collected signatures and notes from my classmates, but I had saved an entire section of a page for him. Still, I caught his eyes wandering across what had already been written. Smiling, he said, *You have a lot of signatures.*

Not that many, I said. I was careful not to add, *AND IT DOESN'T MATTER ANYWAY BECAUSE THE ONLY ONE I REALLY WANT IS YOURS.*

As he uncapped my marker—my favorite one, a beautiful shade of ocean blue—I was gripped with the sudden fear that I had flipped to the wrong page. Thea and some of our other friends had written *certain things* in the front pages of my yearbook, most of which had to do with my major crush on Eli. I'm pretty sure they had scrawled out his name and added hearts and everything. But considering he hadn't dropped the book like it had transformed into the aforementioned burning bush and taken off running, I figured I was safe.

He placed the tip of my marker to the page.

I had expected him to sign his name, maybe add a quick *Have a nice summer* or, God forbid, *HAGS*, but he just. Kept. Writing.

It couldn't have taken more than ten seconds, but it felt more like ten hours. I don't think I so much as breathed until Eli slid the cap back onto my marker, pressing it against the flesh of his palm to ensure it was all the way on. He fanned a hand over his writing, placed the marker on the page, and closed my yearbook.

Thank you so much, I said, careful not to get my hands anywhere near his as I took the book back. *I—you—thank you. And thank you for everything you did at the writing center. And I hope you have a lot of fun at college.*

Thanks. He had such a goofy, childlike grin. *See you around?*

I knew I never would, but I said something I hoped was *Yes* and not *I am insanely in love with you.* Then, before I could ruin the moment, Thea took me by the arm and dragged me away.

Thea's laughter, light and delicate like the sound of a soft mallet running along the spine of a xylophone, breaks into my thoughts.

"What?" I say. "What's so funny?"

"I forgot what he had written." Closing the yearbook but keeping one hand inside to mark the page, she uses her free hand to wipe her tears. "Oh my God. It's so funny. Oh my *God*. You have to read it."

"How painful is it?"

"Just read it."

She opens the yearbook. I spot his entry immediately, the blue just as vibrant as it was the day he wrote it. It's strange to think he was our age, and we were still middle schoolers. We must have seemed like such babies.

Hey, Monika, his message begins. *I really enjoyed getting to work with you at the writing center and wish you all the best as you go to high school and beyond. HOORAY!!! Okay, good luck. Eli.*

My cheeks warm. "Oh, God. He's so nice."

"And ridiculous." Thea throws her arms in the air. "'HOORAY!!!'"

"Okay," I say, closing the yearbook as heat crawls up my neck. "That's enough."

"Oh, man." Thea swipes a finger under her eyes. "Sorry, laughing that much made me really have to pee. I'll be back."

"Thanks for sharing," I call out as she heads for the bathroom.

As soon as she's gone, I resume browsing the niche website. By cross-referencing the tunnels listed with Google Street View, I manage to narrow my options down to just a few, all of which are relatively close by. The rest have all been closed off, either because of improved sewer systems, loitering wanderers, kids trying to get famous on YouTube for spelunking, or some combination of the three.

After marking the few open passageways on my map app, I put my phone away and drop my head into my hands for a moment.

What if I find the tunnel and never come back? I mean, I'm chasing after a ghost. I have no idea what could be waiting for me. Even if I don't find some top-secret entrance to the land of the dead, I still shudder to think about all the different nightmarish scenarios I could get myself into: getting mugged;

breaking my ankle; succumbing to carbon monoxide poisoning; falling into a pit of quicksand, the way I always thought I would after playing one too many action-adventure games; going on an acid trip and emerging convinced I'm the Second Coming of Christ; or, God forbid, getting roped into some hippie's multilevel marketing business.

The toilet flushes. As the water runs, Thea starts humming to herself, the song catchy but unfamiliar.

And just like that, I know I can't bring her with me.

It's not because I think she's susceptible to pyramid schemes. Thea's one of just two people in our class to have gotten into Columbia and the only person not to brag incessantly about it. If anything, she would talk the hippie out of her own scam, convincing her it isn't very business-savvy of her to try to #GirlBoss her way out of abject poverty.

But I can't drag Thea into this. This isn't some wacky adventure, like our infamous Operation 107. This could literally be life or death. It could also just be proof that I need to stop listening to ghost stories, but still. I'm not going to chance it. She has to get to Columbia.

Setting my teeth on my lower lip, I close out of the website. I think I've pinpointed the most likely suspect—and it just so happens to be one ten-minute bus ride away from my house. It's almost like the universe is telling me to go.

Or maybe our town is just that small.

I'll have to say goodbye to my parents. I have the feeling Shun never said goodbye to his. And I bet that haunts his mother every single day.

Thea turns the water off, still humming like a happy little songbird.

Abandoning my laptop, I stumble off my bed and land beside the still-open yearbook. Sliding it back into place, I take out another one. One from the third grade, the year I met Shun.

The glossy pages smell heavenly, like fresh paper and ink. My fingers skim the surface as I scan the names and messages. I don't remember what color Shun used or if he left a message. I'm not sure he even signed it at all.

My eyes snag on his name just as the bathroom door opens. I keep my hand on the page for a second, my fingers spread along the bottom corner.

Thea steps back into my room. "What are you looking at?"

I swallow.

"Nothing," I say.

Then I close the yearbook.

"I DON'T UNDERSTAND," Thea says as I walk her back to her car, her expression so serious, it's hard to believe she was in mirthful tears over Eli's message not even half an hour ago. "What are you doing?"

"Investigating," I say. "We can call it the second secret operation of my life, after the one with you. But this time, I'm flying solo."

She doesn't smile. "I don't like this. If you're going to make me cover for you, you should at least tell me what you're actually planning to do."

I wish I could have left Thea out of this entirely. If something *does* go wrong, I don't want to burden her with the guilt.

No, officer, I imagine her saying, her hands shaking around her glass of water. *Nothing seemed off to me before she disappeared.*

"Please. Just trust me. I need some time to do something. It's not illegal"—debatable; it might be trespassing—"and it's not danger—"

The word snags in my throat.

It *is* dangerous. In a lot of ways.

Every time I've done something stupid, Thea has been by my side. Whether we were trying to grab the cup all the way at the back of the cupboard, with me clambering onto the counter and Thea holding out her arms, ready to brace my fall, as if that wouldn't have given us both concussions and enough medical bills to rule out her Columbia matriculation for good, or running our disastrous yet ultimately successful Operation 107, she's been there for me. This will be the first time I'm doing something this big alone.

But it's better this way. It's not like I'll have her for much longer anyway.

"It's fine," I say. "I'll be fine."

Thea blinks. "Wait, wait, wait. Monika. *What are you doing?*"

I don't know.

"I'm looking for this tunnel. That's all I can tell you."

"What? A tunnel?" She steps forward and places her hands on my shoulders. "What is going on with you?"

"I need to do this," I say. "If I ever want to get closure, I need you to let me go. So can you do this for me? Please? Let me tell my parents I'm going to be with you tomorrow. You don't have to reach out to them. You don't have to tell them anything unless they ask you directly. Please. *Please.*"

She holds my gaze for a good five seconds. Then, slowly, she lets out a breath. "Fine. But if anything goes wrong, you're calling me immediately. I'll pick you up no matter when it is. If I don't answer the first time, call again. Then again. Just keep calling. Got it?"

I open my mouth, ready to crack a joke, but when I catch a glimpse of the gravity in her expression, all my witty words turn to grit. "Okay. Thank you." I take her hand. Her fingers are warm. "I really love you, you know."

"DO NOT," she says, snatching her hand back. "I don't know if I'm just overreacting or what, but you're freaking me out. I don't like how much this sounds like a goodbye."

"It isn't," I say.

And I pray I'm not lying.

IT'S FUNNY. SHUN never once appeared in my dreams before he died. Yet for a month after his death, up until the beginning of February, he appeared at least once a week.

Sometimes, it was like nothing had changed. He was just there, somewhere in the background, as I raced from class to class. I noticed him, though, the way I never had in all the years after elementary school. When I awakened, I could see him, his mouth set in neither a frown nor a smile, just as it often had been in life, once we got older.

Most of the time, though, my dreams were some monstrous combination of sadistic and sweet. In one, we were in the third grade again, seated beside each other because I was still quiet, unsure of how to speak to people my own age, and the teacher wanted to minimize the amount of trouble Shun caused. People said Shun seemed calmer around me. I was afraid he was just bored. But then, right as I turned to him to ask if he had finished the homework, he let out this sound, too soft to be a scream and too low to be a squeak, and crumbled into dust. Even when I swiped a hand through the empty air, even when I called his name, even when I dropped to my knees and ran my hands along the sickly yellowish-beige tiles, he wouldn't come back.

In another dream, we were in the fourth grade, and I was disappointed to learn he wouldn't be in my class anymore. I searched for him, passing the pickup area and sweeping through the cafeteria, but no matter where I went, he wasn't there, and I could never tell him there was a part of me—a stupid, tiny part—that missed him.

Once, I dreamt I was at a college fair, university banners of all colors hanging from poles. All Shun did, even in my dream, was walk past me. But just as he passed, I remembered he was dead. I whirled around to take another look at him, my heart in my throat, but he was already gone.

I used to tell my mother about my dreams, crying and choking on my own tears. She would always weep with me. She had known him too.

At some point, I stopped mentioning my dreams, and she stopped asking. She probably didn't want to bring him up, just to avoid triggering something. Maybe she even truly believed I had moved on.

For a while, I believed it too. But the night before I make my way to the rumored Yomigaeri Tunnel, I dream I'm running. To him. Away from myself. And the entire time, I hear his voice, echoing in my head: *I'm waiting.*

CHAPTER FOUR
Most Likely to Disappear

IT'S NOT TOO late to go back, the tiny voice in my head keeps saying.

But it kind of is.

I've already done all the preparations. This morning, I checked and double-checked the location of the tunnel. I said goodbye to my parents. Not in a suspicious way, like I did with Thea, but in a casual, if-this-is-the-last-time-I-see-you-I'm-glad-we-had-this-talk kind of way.

I really don't think anything bad will happen. That one guy said some people he knows went into the tunnel, and they came back fine. Afraid and possibly high, sure, but fine.

The tunnel, just past one of the rivulets connected to the town's canal, looks like it belongs in an entirely different town. The surrounding dirt is a rusty red-brown, ferns, weeds, and graffiti coating every available surface. It looks like a place where nothing good ever happens.

Once I've passed the majority of the underbrush, I find myself at the mouth of a tunnel.

I didn't expect it to be so easy. I didn't think I was going to have to fight an army of the undead or anything, but it feels kind of anticlimactic. Even my high school's commencement had more buildup than this.

"Are you going in?"

At the sound of a vaguely familiar voice, I jump. Like, *actually* jump, my feet lifting off the ground and my nerves catching fire.

"Or are you just going to stand there and stare?"

I watch, frowning, as a girl emerges from the ferns. Barefaced and armed with a heavy jacket, jeans, and a backpack with a clip at the front, she has a gleam of defiance in her eyes.

It's her again. Pale Hair, the girl who kept asking all the questions about the tunnel at the Japanese Club get-together.

I stare at her for a moment, wondering if the hallucinations are beginning already.

"Cat got your tongue?" she asks.

"What are you doing here?" I ask. Then, realizing that's a stupid question, I correct myself. "I mean, that's obvious. But why were you, like, *crouching* over there?"

"I can crouch if I want to," she snaps.

My eyelashes flutter. "I mean, yeah. Sure. It's a free country. I'm just trying to ask why."

"I don't have to explain myself to you," she says, crossing her arms.

I say nothing. Despite her classic adolescent sass, she seems a lot younger now, both because her jacket is a little too big and because she's scrubbed her face clean. She looks ready to film an episode of *Survivor*.

"So you believe it," she says. "You think if you get through the tunnel, you'll be able to revive someone."

For a split second, all I see is Shun's white cross, just the slightest bit crooked.

"I don't know." I glance at her. "Do you?"

She rolls her eyes. "Well, I didn't spend hours looking up tunnels for *fun*. This whole thing sounds like something sad, depressed, desperate people believe in when they have no other options."

"Well, but you're still here, aren't you?"

She presses her lips together. When my eyes drop from her haughty expression to the clear water bottle in the mesh pocket on the side of her backpack, I notice a quarter of the water is already gone. It's possible she only filled it three-fourths of the way, but based on the way she places a protective hand over the bottle, as if she's trying to block my view, I have the feeling she's been here for a while, waiting for someone else to show up.

"So?" She keeps her hand on the bottle. "Who's your person? The person you want to bring back."

I hesitate. Realizing there's no simple way to explain what Shun was to me, I say, "My classmate."

"Your classmate." She says it like it's the stupidest thing she's ever heard. "Your *classmate*? Were you dating or something?"

"No," I say quickly. "It wasn't like that."

No, we hadn't been dating. No, we had never even thought about it. He had been a classmate. That was supposed to be all.

But things are never that simple. No one is ever just a classmate. Not when you lose them like that.

"So what, then?" The girl frowns. "You're feeling all sappy and nostalgic? Over a classmate?"

"Why can't I?" I swallow. My heart is pounding so hard, I bet she can hear it. "Who's *your* person?"

For the first time, discomfort shows on her face, tugging at the sides of her mouth. In a quiet voice, she says, "My mother."

My gaze drops to the red dirt beneath my boots. That makes so much more sense. A girl taking the plunge into a tunnel of delusions to save her mother? Sounds like the plot of a teen dystopian novel. So what am *I* doing here? What makes me think *I* can save some guy I barely know anymore?

I don't need to have an answer. I just need to have the will. Am I the person people expect to bring him back? No. Not at all. But I was the one who heard the rumor of the tunnel. I was the one who made it down here. I have the power to do something, and for once, I'm going to do it. I don't care what this girl thinks of me. I'm not doing it for her anyway.

She's still human, though. Still hurting.

"I'm sorry," I say about four seconds too late.

"Yeah, well." She eyes me. "I'm sorry for your loss too, I guess."

We look at anything but each other.

"Do you think this is stupid?" I ask. "Is this just, like, completely stupid? For all we know, nothing's there. Or worse, something's there, but instead of saving lives, we're going to lose our own."

"The thought has occurred to me," she says flatly. The material of her jacket makes a *shick-shick* sound every time she moves. "But at this point, I don't have much to lose."

I do. Don't I? That's why it was hard to say goodbye to my parents, hard to make Thea cover for me, hard to get myself on the bus when I didn't know how different life would be by the time the next bus pulled up at my stop.

The girl lets out a long breath. "Look, are we going to go in there? Or are we going to stand out here and stare at each other?"

"Hey," I say. "You were the one skulking around in the ferns."

"I wasn't *skulking*."

"Then what were you doing?" I ask, because she still hasn't answered my question.

She hesitates. Her lavender hair actually washes her out, leaving her skin sallow. Her cheeks are hollow. Her eyes are dull. She looks a little like a ghost herself. But maybe that's to be expected. She didn't lose some boy she knew once; she lost her mother.

"I was waiting," she says, "to see if anyone else was going to come."

My eyes slide over to her. "How long were you going to wait?"

"Not long," she says. But she's avoiding my gaze. "It's not like I was planning on holding a stakeout or anything."

I can't help but think of Thea and Operation 107. If I make it out of this place, I'm calling her first thing.

Of course, if I *do* make it out, that probably means I'll have Shun with me. I have no idea how she would react to that. I don't even know how *I* would react. Every time I even start to imagine it, the illusion dissolves like mist.

"So can we go?" the girl says, throwing out an arm and gesturing to the tunnel. "We've been standing here for, like, forever."

I swallow. "You mean we're just going to, like, walk in?"

She drops her arm to her side, the material of her jacket swishing. "As opposed to what? Skipping? Prancing? Belly dancing?"

I do not have the body for belly dancing. Or the flexibility. Thea once filmed us dancing to a pop song sometime in middle school, and when I saw us on the screen, I realized two things: (1) Thea is much, much prettier than I am and (2) I dance like a wet noodle.

"Oh my God," the girl says. "Are you seriously considering belly dancing in there?"

Heat explodes in my cheeks. "No."

She purses her lips. "Look, if you're not going in there, tell me now so I can ditch you and head in there myself."

She lifts her chin, as if to challenge me, but I can see the tension in her neck. She's not fooling me. If she wanted to abandon me here, she would've done so a long time ago.

I stare back at her. The longer I stare, the more obvious it becomes.

She's just as nervous about this as I am.

"How long have you been here?" I ask.

She shoots me a look, suspicion casting a dark veil over her face. "Why does it matter?"

I don't know why she acts like every question is a personal attack. Given how hard she's chewing on her bottom lip, I have the feeling she doesn't know why either. Or maybe I'm reading too much into things, like all those body language experts who claim these two celebrities are secretly feuding because one had her hip cocked the wrong way.

"Fine," I say. "We don't have to make small talk."

She turns her head. "Thank God. I hate small talk."

"But don't you think we should at least know each other's name?"

"Why does it matter?" she asks. Then, pulling her arms even closer to her chest, she sighs. "I'm Shiori. I guess since we're both former members of our schools' Japanese Clubs, you should say it the right way. *She-oh-ree*, with the flip on the *R*." She waves a hand. "Not that I care. And again, not that it matters."

"It matters," I say. "Shiori."

I swear her eye twitches. "Yeah. And you?"

"Monika. With a *K*." It's surprisingly easy to write in Japanese characters. That's the only reason my parents spelled it that way.

"Of course it is," Shiori says.

Okay, well. I never thought we would be friends, and it's not like that's our goal here, but still. It's not like I chose my name.

"Come on, Monika-with-a-*K*," Shiori says. "Let's go."

She grabs me by the wrist. Her skin is cold, and I can feel the slight calluses pushing out of her palm. I open my mouth and start to yank my arm back, but at the last second, I change my mind and let her pull me into the unknown.

At first, it seems like a regular, run-of-the-mill, cylindrical tunnel, far from the portal to hell I had been expecting. Then, just as I'm turning to Shiori, expecting her to be mid-eye roll, as if to say, *I can't believe we actually thought this was a magical tunnel*, we're plunged into total darkness.

"HOLY CRAP," SHIORI says, those three syllables bouncing off walls we can't see and knocking back into us.

"Don't let go," I say, not even the slightest bit embarrassed to hear the shake in my voice. If it weren't for Shiori's fingers, still clamped around my wrist, I would be lost entirely.

"Trust me, I wouldn't dream of it." She shakes my arm, presumably flinging her other arm out in her frustration, though I obviously can't see or appreciate the dramatic gesture. "Oh my *God*. It can't be this dark all the way through, can it?"

When I swallow, I'm pretty sure it echoes. "Do you think we can use flashlights? Or would that be breaking some kind of rule?"

"What rule?" I can hear her rummaging around in her jacket pockets. "Common sense?"

"Wait," I say, tugging on her sleeve. "I'm serious. What if we're not supposed to use a light? Maybe this is part of the test. It's a test, right?"

I can practically hear her rolling her eyes. "Or a great way to end up face-planting and knocking ourselves unconscious before the 'test' can even begin."

"Yeah, but—"

That's when the entire world falls away.

A scream builds in my chest but never manages to leave my throat. The darkness yanks at my clothes and whispers along my neck, pulling me down. I don't know if I accidentally shake Shiori off or if she releases me in her panic, but even as I try to swipe for her, I feel nothing.

So this is how I die. I can't say I didn't see it coming. Or, well, I guess I can. I can't see much of anything. Ha, ha. But I knew this was a possibility. I can't be that upset about it. More than anything, I'm glad I was able to say goodbye. Not everyone gets that privilege.

I'm just about to give in and let go when I hit something solid. The pain takes my breath away, little shock waves spitting out of my shoulder and leaving me stunned. It takes me a few seconds to recover from the impact, and when I sit up, I find myself alone in the dimness.

"Shiori?" I call out. The effort makes my ribs throb. "Where are you?"

No answer.

I'm not surprised. That would be too easy.

"Okay," I say to myself. I glance over my shoulder, but there's no light coming from that way. It seems I'm supposed to continue forward.

I take a small step, the sound of my boot against the gritty tunnel floor reverberating around me. I stretch out a hand and study my palm. Tiny black crystalline particles coat my skin. Rubbing my fingers together, I take a breath and keep walking. I can hear my heartbeat in my ears, but I guess that's a good thing. At least I'm still alive.

At the sight of something in the distance, I slow to a stop. I squint, trying to make it out, but the dusty light of the tunnel obscures it.

I reach for my phone. Maybe I can use the flashlight, or at least text Thea to say I'm pretty sure I'm losing my mind.

My fingers have just brushed my denim pocket when a light explodes in the center of my vision. I try to raise a hand to shield my eyes, but my arms are so heavy, I can't even lift a finger. My entire body seems to be collapsing in on itself.

If this is what people describe as an LSD-like trip, I'm glad I never touched drugs. There's nothing fun about this.

That's not what my uncle said, a tiny voice says. I think it's in my head at first, but as silence falls around me, I realize it came from somewhere too far ahead for me to see.

I blink hard as the light around me fades. The first thing I see is a set of stairs beneath my sandals. And they're moving.

I try to whirl around to see if Shiori's crouching behind me, just as she was at the beginning of the tunnel, but I can't seem to turn. I can only face forward.

Dropping my head, I study my legs. My kneecaps are the size my elbows usually are. My sandals, which I remember having for years when I was a child, aren't even as big as my normal hands.

I'm an elementary school kid again.

What's not what your uncle said? someone says.

I look up. At the top of the stairs, a few girls lean on the railing, their neon-colored shirts bright even in my hazy memories. I recognize them, but they look so strange, almost alien, their faces squished and their bodies like sticks.

He said, one girl continues, *it's supposed'ta rain tomorrow. For, like, a lot of days.*

How many? another girl asks.

I try to raise my hands to cover my ears, partly to test if I can move and partly because their voices are freakishly high, like they've been huffing helium. But I still can't get my arms to do anything.

Then I'm falling again.

For a second, I'm weightless. Floating. My eyes take in everything around me: the gray cement steps; the dark metal railing smelling of coins and hands; the rock wall to my left; the cafeteria at the top of the stairs; and, all around me, hungry children on their way to lunch.

I remember this now. In the days to come, it *will* rain, for forty days and nights. Our parents will send us to school in rainboots and ponchos, umbrellas tucked under our arms and lunches wrapped in plastic to keep out the moisture. In the evening, it will storm hard enough to shake the buildings and wipe out electricity grids. At one point, I will say, *Maybe the torrential rain will just wash us all away*. I will secretly hope it will, because in my child mind, getting swept down a river of stormwater, floating in the inner canopy of an umbrella, is like something out of a cartoon. I will enjoy the rain, for the most part, but water will keep soaking my socks, leaving my toes shriveled like umeboshi.

Right now, though, I don't know any of that. All I know is how it feels to fall.

My knee hits the steps, splitting my skin. A sharp pain explodes in my bones as my elbows scrape against the cement.

Oh my God, someone says from behind me. *Are you okay?*

My cheeks are burning even worse than my elbows. *I'm fine. Thank you.*

Somewhere behind me, someone is laughing. I instinctively try to pivot, even though I know I couldn't a few seconds earlier.

I can now, though, my body twisting until my eyes land on a boy with short, dark, spiky hair. He stands at the base of the staircase, his eyes sparkling as he laughs. After a second, his friends join in. One even points at me, as if they all need a reminder: *There she is. The target of our mockery.*

My eyes flick back to the guy who first started laughing. The one with hair like a Chia Pet.

My skin is still prickling, both from embarrassment and from my fall in the stairwell. I want to shout, *IT'S NOT FUNNY*, but I can't make myself speak.

With the boy's laughter ringing in my ears, I turn back around and continue up the stairs, clinging to the railing like a ninety-year-old lady.

This is the first time I ever see Shun.

CHAPTER FIVE
Most Empathetic

IT TAKES ME a good few seconds to open my eyes, and even when I do, I'm not quite sure where I am. I turn my hand over, waiting for the pain from my fall on the stairs to rush back in, but it never does. I glance down and find my small sandals have been replaced by my sturdy boots. All around me, there is only the dim light of the tunnel.

The tunnel. Right. That guy from the Cultural Center said people had hallucinations in here. I just assumed they were trippy visions, not memories of things that actually happened.

No, they weren't even memories. They were experiences. *Re*-experiences. I was forced to live through that moment on the stairs all over again.

The guy at the Cultural Center said the tunnel shows people all their worst fears. I guess public humiliation is one of mine.

Public humiliation . . . or Shun.

I forgot he had witnessed my tumble. I didn't see him again for another two years, after all, and by then, we had both probably fallen up or down the stairs a couple more times. I know I did. I hated that stairwell. I thought if I ever became rich, I would fund its destruction. I wouldn't have even asked for a metal plaque or anything. Knowing it was gone would have been enough.

I turn. If I squint, I can just make out the blocky staircase in the distance, translucent and floating a foot or two off the floor. It's as if the memory is clinging to existence.

I check over my shoulder for signs of Shiori. After a few seconds of silence, I face the stairs. If I get too close, will I get sucked back into the memory again?

My steps are slow and silent, as if I'm tiptoeing around a sleeping monster. The staircase is gossamer, golden light pouring over it like resin. Leaning forward, I try to place my hand on the bottom step—only for my fingers to go straight through.

So I can't reenter the memory.

What if I really *am* hallucinating? What if, in real life, I'm still standing at the mouth of the tunnel, my jaw dropped and my eyes wide? What if Shiori is slapping me across the face, partly to snap me out of it and partly because she's always wanted to slap someone, K-drama style? Would she even stay to make sure I'm okay? Or has she left me behind, writing me off as a lost cause?

I stop and scan my surroundings. I still haven't heard from Shiori. I slide my hand into my pocket, only to remember I don't have her number.

Not that it matters. My phone is gone.

God, Thea's going to be so mad.

Maybe if I head back to the stairs, I'll be able to find it. But what if I trigger the memory again? What if I get trapped in it? I'm not even sure I had my phone by the time I reached the staircase. With any luck, it'll be magically returned once I'm out of here. I mean, if the tunnel can bring a *human* back from the dead, it can surely return my phone.

I'm still doubling back, biting my tongue and hoping I'll find my phone conveniently duct-taped to the wall, when I hear soft sobs from somewhere in the distance.

"Hello?" I call out. My voice is raspy, as if I've been breathing in smoke. "Shiori?"

No answer.

Maybe it's not Shiori after all. Maybe I'm still in a memory.

I force myself to my feet and take another look around, but all I see is the tunnel wall. "Shiori? Is that you?"

The crying stops, punctuated by a final sniffle. "Who's there?"

I step forward. "It's Monika. Can you keep talking? I don't know where you are."

"I'm here," she says.

Not helpful.

"Did you see them? The memories?" I edge my way closer to the voice, one hand running along the tunnel walls. "Can you say something so I can find you?"

"I don't know what you want me to say." She pauses. "But yeah. I saw them."

"What did you—"

We round the corner at the exact same time. The first thing I register, after the fact that we were *this* close to banging heads, is the puffiness of her eyes.

"Oh." She takes a shaky breath. "You scared me."

"You scared me too." I inch backward, giving her some space. Her eyes are watery, and her nose is red, but she looks otherwise unharmed. "Are you okay?"

"I don't know. Am I?" She tugs at her sleeves. "I feel like I'm going crazy."

"Me too." I glance at her jacket. "You don't still have your phone, do you?"

She slides her hands into her pockets. "No. I have no clue where it went. I know I had it when I got here." She lets out an impressively long sigh. "You don't think they're *gone*, do you? I can't afford to buy a new phone right now."

I glance over my shoulder, half expecting our phones will magically appear, but it seems the tunnel specializes in summoning memories, not mobile devices.

"You're going to judge me for this," Shiori says, "but I'm kind of relieved."

I slide my eyes over to her. "What do you mean?"

"At least the tunnel's doing *some*thing, you know? It *isn't* just a normal tunnel."

I think of that momentary flash of Shun, his eyes so full of life.

"No. It's not." I shift my weight from one foot to the other. "What have you seen so far?"

"I don't know." She chews her lip. "Embarrassing things."

"Me too."

We're quiet for a minute. I spend the first few seconds staring at the ground, tiny rocks hissing beneath my soles. When I look up, Shiori's swiping a sleeve along her eyes.

"Are you okay?" I ask.

"I'm fine," she snaps. Then, bringing one hand to her eyes, she clears her throat and says it again, more calmly this time. "I'm fine."

We lapse back into an uneasy silence.

"Do you want to talk about it?" I ask. "Whatever you saw?"

"Why?" She places one hand against the tunnel, then turns around and leans against it, her arms still crossed. "What could telling you possibly do?"

I find myself thinking of Thea. She always listens when I need to rant, even when it's about something as insignificant as a lost point on a quiz when I clearly should have gotten at least partial credit.

I never told her about that memory on the staircase, though. I haven't thought about that for a long time.

"I don't know," I say to Shiori. "Sometimes it helps to talk about it."

She brushes her lavender hair over her shoulder. It looks gray in the filthy light. "Why don't you go first, then?"

I give her a look, my eyes narrowed. "Why? It's not like I'm going to use your embarrassing moments against you."

"Well, but how do I know I can trust you?" Shiori asks.

Oh my God. This girl is almost as maddening as the tunnel.

"If you tell me what you saw," I say, "we might be able to figure out this tunnel's game."

She rolls her eyes. "This is *not a game*."

It takes all my self-control not to lie down on the ground and scream as loudly as I can.

"That's not what I meant," I tell her. "I'm just saying I've played a lot of games, and—"

"No. Don't you dare give me that whole 'life *is* a game' spiel. It's not. I always hated that board game anyway."

I never played it. I've always been more of a video-game person. But I haven't picked one up for a year, if not longer. Ever since Art Harris and *Bitter Mouse*, every game I've even watched gameplay footage of has felt haunted.

"I didn't mean 'game' like that," I tell Shiori.

Besides, games aren't always fun. Sometimes, games are experiences. Opportunities to see things from another perspective. In that way, the games I play aren't so different from the books Thea borrows in bulk from the library, corners poking out from her bag like the limbs of a baby in a womb.

"I'm just trying to understand this place," I say, "and I think it would help if you told me—"

"Why don't *you* tell *me* first?" Shiori suggests, her eyes narrowed.

"All right. Fine. I saw myself tripping on the stairs." I cross my arms. "Okay, now you."

"What, so you didn't see your"—she pauses for a moment longer than necessary—"*classmate?*"

My jaw twitches at the word.

I don't have to answer her question. She hasn't answered any of mine. But I can't shake the feeling that we're missing something here. It's like we got tossed into the heat of battle without so much as a tutorial. If we can talk things through and share what little we've learned so far, we might be able to make some progress.

"I did," I admit. "He was there when I tripped."

She stares at the dark wall, her jaw working like she's pushing a piece of gum around the bottom of her mouth.

"Why? Did you see your person too?" I wait until her eyes flick to mine. "Your mother?"

She breaks eye contact so suddenly, I feel the slightest twinge of pain, as if she just jabbed me in the ribs with her elbow. "Not really. It was just this memory from, like, elementary school. The teacher called on me, but I hadn't been paying attention, and I think he knew it. I kept looking to my friends for help, but they wouldn't give me a hint."

"And you knew, didn't you?" I move to her side and set one shoulder against the wall. "You knew it was a memory, even when you were reliving it."

She nods. "I just didn't have control. And that has to mean something, right? We need to keep going?"

I hesitate. "I mean, I guess. But don't you think we should talk about this a little more?"

"No." She kicks off the tunnel wall, the heel of her boot making a sharp *clack* against the ground. "See you later. Or not."

"Wait. Hold on."

"Nope. We're wasting time."

She tries to dodge me, but I step in front of her, barring her way. We're roughly the same height, though without those heels on her boots, she would probably be an inch or two shorter. At five-three, I'm not used to being the taller one in any given comparison, unless the other person is a literal child.

"Listen," I say. "I realize I'm not your ideal adventuring partner. Trust me. You're not exactly mine either."

I would like it much better if Thea were here. Sometimes, when I'm upset, she'll ask me, *Do you need a distraction, comfort, advice, or space?* and no matter what I choose, I know she'll understand and do whatever it takes to help me heal. It's a privilege to be her best friend. One I hope I haven't abused by asking her to cover for me while I'm hallucinating in a tunnel.

But Shiori's the one here with me, and as annoying as she may be, there's something just a little comforting about having her around. I'm not the only one fighting my memories in the hopes of altering someone's present and future. I'm not even taking it as hard as she is—which, strangely, makes me feel just the tiniest bit better, like I'm not the only one losing my mind.

"I know this isn't the way you expected things to go," I say. "I'm just trying to help."

Shiori narrows her eyes. "I didn't *ask* for your help."

"Yeah, well, you were crying."

Her hand twitches at her side. "Can you stop bringing that up? We're not going to accomplish anything by standing around and talking about our *feelings*."

I don't know why *that's* what gets me, but before I can rein myself back in, I take a step back and hold my hands up in mock surrender. "Fine. You're right. I'm *so* sorry to have caused you trouble by being an empathetic human being. Let me robotically walk beside you until we inevitably get hauled off and pulled back into our memories."

"Fantastic," she snarls.

The anger burns in my stomach for a few more seconds, but as we start heading down the tunnel, I feel it fading, leaving a deep, post-outburst void.

Maybe I shouldn't be so hard on her. Her mom died. I can't imagine how hard that must have been. How hard it must *still* be.

Shun lost a parent too. His father passed away when he was young, before we ever met. He never told me, but my mom heard about it after meeting his mother at parents' night.

In the time it took for the rest of our graduating class to reach voting age, Shun's mother had lost both her husband and her son.

People tended to go easier on Shun because his father had died. He wasn't the only one whose parent had passed away, but while some people grew distant and others held their other loved ones close, Shun did a strange combination of both, spinning people around, pulling them in, then pushing them away. He interrupted and talked back to teachers, clamored for attention, and swore like he got paid for each curse word he managed to throw out before a teacher inevitably sent him to the principal's office.

Maybe it's not because his dad died, someone muttered one day. *Maybe he's just a jerk.*

He wasn't, though. I know he wasn't. He was a jokester. He was a rebel. He was a musician. He was a hurting little boy. He was someone I knew a long time ago. He was the first person in our class to make me laugh, to make me uncomfortable because I wasn't sure I could find some of his jokes funny, to make me question if someone could do bad things and still be a good person.

He was Shun. And that was always enough.

"Hey," Shiori says.

She never gets the chance to finish her sentence. Because just as that single word lifts off her tongue, the ground falls out from beneath our feet, sending us plummeting back into the unknown.

CHAPTER SIX

Most Addicted to Slushies

WHEN I HIT the ground, all the wind is knocked out of me. I stay there, stunned, waiting for the pain to rush in, but there's nothing but an uneasy stillness, as if I've stepped into a graveyard.

I slowly push myself up onto my hands and knees. With the help of the tunnel wall, I get back onto my feet. In searching my surroundings for something familiar, I discover the area behind me has become shrouded in eerie shadows.

Okay, well, I'm not going *that* way.

Facing forward, I take a few cautious steps. I always figured if I ever got up to any movie-worthy hijinks, it would be more about my trials and tribulations as a girl gamer, or a painful friendship breakup story. I'm not brave or witty enough to go on a life-or-death adventure like this.

I lift my head as something silver flashes in the distance.

Silver. What would have been silver? A fork? The metal legs of our chairs? Something on the playground?

I slow to a stop as the next memory pulls me in.

No. None of the above.

A metal hook hangs on the wall, clinging to a cracking, staticky, off-white phone.

Swallowing, I take one last step and immediately feel myself shrinking. When I look down, I'm dressed in a flowery frock, the bodice crimped and the sleeves a little too big. I keep having to pull them back onto my shoulders.

I look down to see I'm holding my mom's hand. Her palm is sweaty. I made sure to tell her so.

It's chilly. Usually, when I'm this cold, my mom notices the goose bumps rising on my skin and gives me her jacket, draping the too-large sleeves over my shoulders, but this time, she's not going to notice. She's focused on one person and one person only, and he's on the other side of the glass.

She takes a deep breath, sits on the creaky plastic chair, and pulls me onto her lap. I raise my head and study the transparent sheet in front of us. It's smeared with fingerprints. I strain against her and reach out to touch it, but she catches my hand and pulls it back. She doesn't have to, I realize as she settles me back into her lap. My arm is too short. I never would've been able to press my palm to the glass, even if she hadn't stopped me.

I can feel my throat opening as I prepare to raise an objection, but I already know I won't. My mom has been nervous all morning. The last thing I want to do is make things worse.

The man on the other side of the glass won't meet my gaze.

There's no doubt he saw me. As soon as we entered, his eyes flicked to me, then darted to my mom, then fixed themselves to the far wall, and I may only be a first grader, but even I know an angry expression when I see one.

My mom's hand trembles as she picks up the battered phone and sets it to her ear. On the other side, the man crosses his arms.

Come on, she whispers.

I tilt my head up to look at her. *Huh?*

No, not you, baby. She keeps her eyes on the man. Then, almost unthinkingly, she raises a hand and knocks her knuckles against the glass.

Don't touch the barrier, ma'am, a guard says from behind us. She stiffens. *I'm sorry.*

On the other side, the man's mouth quirks. After another brief pause, he takes the phone from its cradle and sets it to his ear.

Hi, my mom says to him.

If I listen closely enough, and if I watch the movement of his lips, I can piece together what he's saying: *Why did you bring her?*

She recoils, then glances at me. I look back at her. She does her best to smile and sets a hand on my hair. Over the years, it will thicken and lighten, more brown than black, but right now, it's thin, slippery, and darker than night. I look like the Japanese dolls I will, years later, see trapped behind glass at the Cultural Center.

She wanted to see you, my mom says into the phone. She's trying so hard to sound chipper, her voice nearly cracks.

HERE, though? The man still can't face me. *I don't want my niece to see me like this.*

My heart breaks a little.

Back then, my understanding of what had happened to my uncle was limited. I knew he was doing things he shouldn't. Things my parents told me I should never do. But they told me not to do a lot of things, from dropping a paper towel on the floor to wipe up a spill with my foot to eating my dessert before my entrée. I wasn't sure what my uncle had done to get him in trouble, but it seemed a lot worse than sneaking a spoonful or two of pudding before dinner.

In the memory, I swivel around and take another peek at the guard. He looks bored, his eyes half closed. I shyly wave to him, but he doesn't notice, and that only makes me more embarrassed. I turn back and nestle closer to my mom's rib cage.

She loves you, my mom says to my uncle. *She just—*

Well, she shouldn't, he says, his voice so loud, I don't even have to read his lips.

My mom pulls back. I hear a tiny *tink* as she swallows.

He sighs and mutters something I think is an apology. As he and my mom tiptoe around each other, I take the time to study him. He looks different here, and it isn't just because of the pale fluorescent light. The last time I saw him, he was gaunt, more skeleton than living being. Wounds in various stages of healing ran along his arms and neck. He always smiled when he saw me, but there was a bone-deep exhaustion in his eyes.

Now, behind the glass, he looks a little more like a regular person. His cheeks are hollow, and his skin is sallow, but there's still something about him. Something alive.

Mommy. My hand grasps the brisk air. *I wanna talk to him.*

Trepidation skitters across her face. *What?*

I want, I say, stretching out my fingers. They look so stubby and small.

I try to catch a glimpse of my uncle's expression, but I can't turn my head. I guess I'm too focused on grabbing the phone to consider maybe my uncle doesn't want to talk to me.

Honey, my mom says. I realize now she's trying to slow me down, trying to think, trying to find a way out of this without upsetting my uncle or hurting my feelings. *No, no. This is more of a grown-up thing.*

But I miss him, I hear myself say.

The atmosphere shifts. I may not have recognized it in the memory, but I feel it now. I can practically hear the sound of their hearts cracking.

My mom lifts her eyes to my uncle. His lips are pressed tightly together as he gives her the smallest nod. Air slips through her lips as she exhales. One inch at a time, she edges the phone down to my head.

Hi, I say into the transmitter. *Hi, it's me. Hi.*

Hey, kiddo, he says.

My reaction is visceral, and though I can't move the muscles in my child body, I can still feel the chill up my spine.

Kiddo. That's right. He used to call me that all the time. It always made me giggle.

Right on cue, I let out a tiny laugh, the sound floating out of me like an invisible butterfly. Behind me, I feel my mom relaxing, the tightness in her chest easing. Even my uncle cracks a grin, pressing the phone against his cheek like he wants to capture all the threads of my laughter between the receiver and his ear.

Hi, I say again. *What are you doing in there?*

My mom tenses. I don't think I noticed it in the moment, but her discomfort is blatantly obvious to me now, all these years later.

Well, kiddo, your uncle did some not-so-great stuff. But he's working on doing better.

But why are you there? I ask. *Can you come out? I'm in the Christmas play.*

He lowers his head. I would too, if I could. *No. No, I can't. I'm sorry. If you tape it, I'll be sure to ask your mommy if I can watch it later.*

I feel myself frowning. *Okay. But I'll save a ticket for you, just in case you CAN come.*

My uncle glances at my mom. I don't know what she does, whether she mouths something to him or tells him something with her eyes or refuses to look at him, but after a moment, he says, *Sounds good, kiddo.*

Honey, my mom says. *Can mommy have the phone back?*

Okay, I say, and when she takes the phone from me, I notice it's the tiniest bit sticky. For the next few minutes, I focus on getting the stickiness off my fingertips, wiping it on my thumb, then the back of my hand, then the chair. Yet it stays, clinging to my skin, as if it's now a part of me.

I'll come back again, my mom says, and this time, I don't catch what my uncle says in return. Nodding, she whispers an *I love you*, then a *goodbye* and hangs the phone back on the hook. She swipes a hand along her cheek and sets her hands on my sides, preparing to lift me off her lap. *Come on, baby. Say goodbye.*

Bye-bye, I say, flapping a hand.

As my uncle waves back, his eyes sad, my mom places me on the ground.

I look up at her. *Mommy, can he come home with us?*

Her eyes jump to the guard. Not because she genuinely believes he has the power, authority, or will to release my uncle, obviously. Simply because he's the only other adult around.

My heart aches for her. I wish I could tell her I'm sorry. I get it now. I see how hard this was for her, and even if I didn't mean to, I made it that much harder.

No, she says, her tone leaving no room for argument. *He has to stay here.*

I glance back, but someone in the same outfit as the guard on our side steps out of the corner—had he been there the whole time?—and grabs my uncle's shoulder. I flinch at the rough way the guard pulls my uncle up and shoves him to one side.

Come on, my mom says, her voice sharp. Her grip on my hand tightens until it hurts. To the guard on our side, she says, *Thank you.*

For what? I want to ask. He didn't do anything but stand

there. If he really wants to help, he can let my uncle come home with us.

Funny how I remember what I was thinking, even now.

My mom takes me back to the car. Once the doors are closed and locked, she lets out a sigh, her hands crimped over her steering wheel.

Mommy? I crane my neck to see her from the backseat. *Are you okay?*

Yes, baby, she says, even as her head hangs down. *I'm okay.*

Already bored, I look out the window. The block has been sapped of color, nothing but grays and beiges remain. I make a face. If I could repaint it, everything would be pink and blue. Maybe green and yellow too.

My mom lifts her head and checks the rearview mirror. As she pulls out of the lot, she says, *We should get something yummy. What do you want?*

Slushy, I cheer. *Slushy, slushy, slushy!*

She laughs. *Okay. I think they have a machine in the drugstore.*

I jump every time she says *drugstore*. It makes me feel like I'm wrong for going there to get colored pencils or glue sticks or, yes, even slushies. Because drugs are bad.

I wish I could close my eyes.

By the time we enter the parking garage, my strawberry slushy has already started to thaw. Whenever I move my straw, it leaves a gaping hole in the frost. I don't like when it does that. A perfect domed slushy is, in my six-year-old opinion, the best thing in the world. Even better than puppies. And I really like puppies.

Oh, crap, my mom mutters.

My head snaps up. *You said a bad word.*

My mom doesn't seem to hear me. Her eyes are trained on the car beside her empty stall. Around the steering wheel, her fingers are white. In the moment, I can't understand why my mom seems so tense. It's Friday, I saw my uncle, my dad is home early for once, and I have a slushy. By my standards, today is the best day ever.

You said a bad word, I repeat as she parks the car.

She still ignores me.

We walk in silence. When we get to the front door of our apartment, my slushy has almost fully melted, red dye leaking out and pooling at the bottom. I poke the few remaining ice crystals with my straw, evidently and justifiably disappointed by its unslushiness.

My mom opens the door and kicks off her shoes, the heels clattering against the tile. I wince at the sound and take an anxious sip of my slushy. Slipping out of my sandals, with my straw poking the inside of my cheek, I start racing into the den.

Don't run with a straw in your mouth, my mom calls out.

I slow to a fast-walk, sucking in so hard, I feel like a fish. The second I spot my dad, my lips spread into a smile.

Hi, I say, flinging my arms out. *We got a slushy.*

Ooh, slushy, my dad says, spinning around in his chair and reaching for the cup. I dutifully hand it over and watch as he takes a sip, smacking his lips to make me giggle. *What's the occasion? Where's Mommy?*

We went to see Uncle, I say.

My dad blinks. *You what?*

The memory stutters. Coldness spreads from my hand, still dripping with condensation from the slushy, and floods the rest of my body as my dad fades into the background. I don't even have time to panic. The next thing I know, I'm sitting beside the door to my room, covering my face as my parents argue in the den.

It was just a quick visit, my mom says.

Yeah, my dad says, his voice icy. *A quick PRISON visit.*

He's my brother, my mom snaps. *What am I supposed to do? Leave him there to rot? We're not like YOUR family, okay? He doesn't have anyone else.*

That's fine, but—

That's FINE? I'm telling you my brother and I don't have parents or family friends, and you say that's FINE?

Well, no. It's not FINE. I mean—you know what I mean.

I don't, actually. Why don't you tell me?

I've reached the hiccupping stage of crying. I try to hold my breath to make it stop, but that only leaves me dizzy.

I'm sorry about your family, my dad says. *Visit your brother if you want.*

I wasn't asking for permission.

No, I—can you just wait? You visit him whenever. I support that. But I do NOT support your decision to take our DAUGHTER to a PRISON.

She's quiet for a while. I lean in closer, but still, she says nothing.

I don't want her going there again, my dad says.

She won't. The words fall like heavy stones. *He hated knowing she saw him like that anyway. The next time she sees him, it won't be in there.*

She's partially right. I will never go to the prison again.

But there will be no next time I see him.

Addiction runs in my family. Before my uncle, there was my grandfather, then all the parents and siblings who came before them. It's why my mother has always refused to take a sip of alcohol or a pull from a cigarette. Why I don't even know what a joint looks like.

That summer, just as it begins to warm up, my uncle is moved to a rehab facility, then sent home, where he overdoses, falls asleep, and never wakes up.

CHAPTER SEVEN
Biggest Liar on a Fitness Test

BY THE TIME I jolt awake, I'm already crying.

Sitting up, I wipe my tears with the back of my hand. I don't think of my uncle that often anymore. I was only seven when he passed away, and by then, we weren't all that close anyway. My parents and I always acknowledge his birthday, and my mom will occasionally buy something he likes and place it beside his framed picture, but I can't pretend I knew him well.

It was still hard to see him again.

I pull myself to my feet and take a look around. About ten feet behind me, the silver hook of the phone glints in the dimness.

"What *is* this place?" I mutter. Then, figuring I have nothing to lose, I repeat it, louder. "What *IS* this place? What is your goal here? What does any of this"—I make a vague gesture to the silver hook—"have to do with resurrection?"

No response.

"Shiori?" I call out. "Are you there?"

Again, nothing. I can only hope her experience has been better than mine. Though she cried after the first set of memories, and if the visions are only expected to get worse, I'm thinking she's not in for a good time.

"Okay," I say. "Well, thanks for the chat."

I turn back around. I wonder what happens if I decide I

don't want to do this after all. Would it be as easy as throwing my arms in the air and saying *I GIVE UP*? Would I have to walk all the way back? How far have we gone?

I didn't think to research how long the tunnel actually is, but I'm not sure it would've made a difference. This place can recreate people's memories. I don't think it can really be accurately defined by its length.

That's what she said, I can practically hear the other Japanese Club people saying.

God, I hope college students have better jokes.

I shouldn't expect a huge change between high school and college. I'm not moving across the country like most of my classmates. Like Thea. I'm going to the state university. I'm not even moving out of the house.

Most days, though, I can't imagine myself in college at all.

I press forward, still trying to figure out what the tunnel is trying to do. Maybe it only showed me my uncle to test me. To see how personal it can get, how far it can push me, before I break. This is not a game, as Shiori was so quick to tell me.

I stop.

Where *is* Shiori?

I turn to look for her, but my foot catches on something, a stone skittering out from under my boot.

And just like that, I'm falling again.

When I hit the ground, I'm holding my breath, my palms sweaty.

One, a familiar voice says.

I turn my head to the right. Thea sits beside me, her legs crossed. A piece of cardstock rests on her kneecap, a golf pencil clutched in her hand. Her hair has been swept up in a sloppy ponytail. Over her shoulder, rows of girls are grabbing metal bars and pulling themselves up, their backs straight and their teeth gritted.

Oh, God. It's the fitness test.

Thea and I haven't had many classes together, but back in the sixth grade, we were in the same PE class. I noticed Thea right away, one of the few other girls who hid in the locker room the way I did. The girls in sports were used to changing in front of others, stripping jerseys off their bodies as casually as they peeled their post-workout bananas and oranges. Some girls were unshakably self-confident, walking around without a towel and even checking themselves out in the mirrors mounted to the sides of the lockers.

Thea and I, meanwhile, found secluded places and changed as quickly as possible so no one could look at our bodies.

The first time we had to do the fitness test—a mile run, stretches, push-ups, and modified pull-ups—Thea and I gravitated toward each other. Maybe she knew that even if one of us was far better than the other, we would be too shy to say anything mean. As it turned out, though, we were right at the same level of athleticism.

By which I mean we both sucked.

Did that even count as one? I gasp to Thea, my voice raspy.

I don't know, she admits, glancing at the girl beside me, *but let's just go with it.*

Okay. My body trembles, silently objecting to this cruel and inhumane punishment. *Okay, okay, okay. I can do this.*

Twenty-seven, the girl beside me counts. *Twenty-eight.*

Oh my God, I say, panting. *I suck at this.*

Thea giggles, her ponytail bouncing as she tips her head back. *Me too.*

You haven't even—I struggle to pull myself back up, but my chest doesn't reach the bar—*done it yet.*

Thea glances at the PE teacher, then turns back to me. *Let's count that as two.*

I hang from the bar like a sloth and angle my head to get a look at the girl beside me. *I can't do this.*

Okay, Thea says as I ease myself back onto the ground and fling my arms over my face. *Let's call that three.*

I pull my arms back to my sides and sit up. *Do you think we can really do that?*

Thea shrugs and spins the golf pencil between her fingers. *Why not? It's just a fitness test. We can say we're EXERCISING our right to STRETCH the truth.*

I make a face. *That was terrible.*

I know. She holds up my fitness test card, where my mile time and other stats have already been filled in. We may end up lying about the pull-ups, but for the entire span of our PE class, we're honest about all the other numbers. *So? Three?*

Three. It's a pathetic number, and I didn't even earn *that*.

Thirty-four, the girl beside me counts for her partner, who's currently chest-bumping the metal bar with no signs of slowing. *Thirty-five.*

Three, I repeat to Thea. *That's fine. That's good. Thank you.*

Great, Thea says, penciling in my three modified pull-ups. *Okay, now I guess it's my turn. Wish me luck.*

Good luck, I say, and though I mean it, I'm also a little afraid she's going to blow me out of the water.

Spoiler alert: She does not.

Oh my GOD, she mutters, her hands slipping on the metal bar. *How did you even do this? The bar is—it's slipping.*

Here, I say, grabbing one end. The metal squeaks beneath my fingertips. I have to cling to it to keep it from spinning as Thea struggles to pull herself more than a few inches off the ground. *You can do it.*

I-I don't know, she says. *I might actually die.*

No, don't, I say. Which is very helpful and will definitely save a girl from death. *You can't. We've just formed an alliance.*

An alliance? she parrots. Her teeth are clenched so tightly, I can feel it in my own jaw.

I nod. *The alliance between people who suck at modified pull-ups.*

She laughs a little, then says, *Stop, stop, stop. I'm going to fall off the bar.*

I miss Thea. Even now, as I'm trapped inside my sixth-grade body—truly the fear of all fears—I miss her. It's strange to think if we hadn't partnered up for this fitness test, we may never have become friends. I can't imagine how empty my life would have been without her.

I need to make it back to Thea and tell her how much she means to me.

You got this, I hear myself say to Thea. *Come on. You're stronger than you know.*

I don't think I know anything, she hisses, still struggling to pull herself up.

Thea bares her teeth and pulls herself up, her body just barely brushing the bar, then immediately collapses, her chest heaving. The teacher gives her a concerned look but turns away without commenting, a Twinkie wrapper sticking out of the pocket of her athletic shorts.

Great job, I say to Thea, writing a neat *3* on her card. *You did it.*

Uh-huh, she pants, her arms crossed over her face. She sits up, her eyes flicking to the teacher, then gets to her feet. *I need water.*

Together, we leave the modified pull-up station and make our way to the water fountain. It's one of the best in the school, relatively clean and ant-free. As Thea takes a drink, I say, *Thank you.*

She lifts her head, her lips dark from moisture. *For what? Helping me.*

I mean, you did the same for me. She leans over to take another drink. *I just hope you know now that we share a secret, we're bonded for life.*

I smile.

Thea and I head back to the gym to turn in our fitness test cards. We try to maintain poker faces as we set our pieces of cardstock face-down on the pile. As I flip mine over, I catch the eye of the girl who had completed over forty-five modified pull-ups by the time Thea and I had finished our combined total of six modified pull-ups. I wonder why she looks the slightest bit angry.

Oh. Now I remember what happens next.

Thea and I make awkward, shy-girl small talk as we head down the ramp to the locker rooms. It's an enclosed area, everything made of cold, hard, marble-like material that takes our voices and tosses them from wall to wall like rag dolls.

My sixth-grade self is paying attention, overthinking every word in the conversation and wondering if Thea could really be a friend, but my present-day self isn't listening. I'm hyperaware of our surroundings, of the other girls' amplified voices and the rust-colored gummy bear stuck to the ceiling, as if I think I might be able to change the past if I focus hard enough.

Thea and I split to head to our lockers. Hers is in a completely different row, farther from the showers. As my younger self grabs my soap and towel, I try to take control of my old body, willing my hand to spin the dial of my lock. But I leave my locker unlocked, the way I always do when I head to the showers. All I can do is sit in my old self and wait for the rest of this memory to unfold.

When I reach my row of lockers, the girl from earlier is waiting for me, accompanied by two other girls. Their glares stop me in my tracks.

Um.

That's all they ever let me say.

It's really crappy of you to lie on your fitness test, the main girl says. *The rest of us actually have to WORK for our grades.*

In retrospect, I realize this is a stupid thing to say. It's like Thea said: The tests don't matter. Our PE class isn't graded based on how many modified pull-ups we complete.

In the moment, though, all I can do is pull my towel closer to my body. *I don't—*

You might want to lock your door next time, the way your friend did, the girl says. *It would make doing that—*she points upward—*a lot harder.*

My stomach clenches as I follow her finger to the ceiling beam.

My clothes are at least twenty feet up. Based on the way they're slung over the wooden support, I'm guessing the girls stood on the benches and threw them.

Snickering and elbowing each other like the one-dimensional, cardboard-cutout bullies they are, they leave me shivering where I stand.

Oh my God, Thea says. I don't know when she arrived, but she's already staring up at my clothes, her eyes wide. *What do we do? I don't think we can reach them even if we jump.*

My heart warms at her repeated use of the word *we*.

Shaking my head, I say, *You should go, before you're late to class.*

Nope. I heard what they said. They would've done it to me too.

But they didn't, I point out, *because you're smart enough to lock your locker.*

Yeah, well, I'm paranoid. She squints at my clothes. *Do you have anything else to wear? I have a spare PE uniform.*

I do too, but I'm not about to wear that out in public.

It's fine. I've gone entirely numb, my tone flat. *I'm going to get the PE teacher and ask her to help.*

You're in a towel, Thea points out. *I'll get her. Don't worry. Stay here.*

I try to object, but Thea sets her stuff down on the bench and takes off.

I sit beside her bag, still looking up at the ceiling beam, and decide I hate this middle school and everyone in it, aside from Thea.

Thea returns with the PE teacher, who has disposed of her Twinkie wrapper and is now armed with a grabby claw. We step aside as she gets up onto the bench, shifts her weight onto the balls of her feet, and pinches my clothes down with the plastic claw.

As I retrieve my shirt and jeans from the floor, thanking her, the teacher says, *What happened? Why were your clothes up there?*

I hesitate. I can feel Thea's eyes on me.

It was my fault, I say. *I was tossing them up there for fun, and they got stuck.*

Thea lowers her head and scuffs the sole of her shoe against the floor. In the moment, I'm afraid she's judging me for refusing to come forward. Later, she'll tell me she would've done the same thing. Then we'll never speak of it again.

Well, the PE teacher says, *don't do that anymore.*

I won't, I say. *I'm sorry. Thank you for your help.*

I turn to close my locker, but before I can touch the dial, it fades away, leaving me grasping at nothing.

CHAPTER EIGHT
Most Likely to Bring Snacks

THE FIRST THING I do when I open my eyes is check that I'm wearing clothes. Now *this* feels like a proper reaction to waking up from a nightmare.

I stay on the ground for a few seconds. That was a lot easier to swallow than the memory of my uncle. I'm surprised it even came up. I could never forget how Thea and I became friends, but I had nearly erased the memory of what happened after the fitness test.

If I wanted to be kind to myself, I could consider it a repressed memory; I barely remember it because my brain is trying to protect my heart. But I don't think it's that deep. I just don't like remembering it because I hate how easily I gave in. I never even considered telling the PE teacher what had actually happened.

It wasn't just because if I had snitched on those girls, they probably would've told the teacher Thea and I had lied on our fitness tests. It was because I had assumed, immediately, it really *had* been my fault. I deserved to have my clothes thrown onto that beam.

I've been so passive. Instead of saying something to Shun when he laughed at my spill on the stairs, I absorbed it and hated myself for being so clumsy. Instead of telling my dad I had wanted to see my uncle, I let my mom take the blame and never once asked if I could visit again.

Of course, even when I take action, I never seem to do anything good. I just trip on the stairs and visit my uncle and don't know what to say. I lie on fitness tests and leave my locker unlocked and make my new best friend late for class.

I go into a mythical tunnel and expect to emerge a hero, dragging a lost soul out of the darkness like I think he can go back to life as normal, even though, no matter what happens, nothing will ever be the same.

If I *do* succeed, how can I possibly explain it? Will he know what happened? Will he remember he died? Is his mother going to scoop him back up in her arms? Or will she scream, call him a demon, and doom him to a life in the corner of my room, where I'll keep him like a large, unruly pet?

What if I *don't* succeed? How could I ever face anyone again, knowing I failed them all over again? Even if they never know, I always will.

I sit up and dust off my hands, shivering from the cold seeping out of the tunnel ground. Wrapping my arms around myself, I get to my feet. A thin streak of light shines from somewhere above. I glance up, hoping to catch even the tiniest glimpse of the sky, but all I find is a dark, rocky ceiling.

"Hello?" someone calls out.

I blink and take a small step forward. It takes me a moment to remember her name, my mind still fuzzy. "Shiori?"

The footsteps stop. "Monika?"

She sounds close. I turn and start heading in the direction of her voice. "Yeah, it's me. Hold on. I'm on my way."

My heart pounds with the need to see someone else. Someone real.

"I'm here," she says. "Can you hear me?"

"Yeah," I say, edging forward. "I can."

When I round the corner, my footsteps weaving between

the strips of dim light, I find Shiori standing in the tunnel, her arms crossed. Her grip on her elbows loosens as our eyes meet. Her eyes are red again.

"Hey," I say. "Funny running into you here."

"Yeah. What a crazy coincidence." She clears her throat. "So listen. I think I woke up before you. I had been calling your name for a while, but you never responded."

"Sorry," I say, the apology almost automatic.

She gives me a look, irritation and amusement skittering across her face. "For what? Being knocked unconscious to relive some of your worst memories?"

"Yeah," I say, playing along. "I'm so sorry about that. It must have been terribly inconvenient for you."

"Terribly." A smile sneaks along her face, then disappears as she runs a hand through her lavender hair. "I don't know how it happened, but after a while, I started wandering around. And then I ran into this."

She kicks something into the light.

I narrow my eyes. "A backpack?"

"*My* backpack." She crouches and slaps a hand over the front pocket like she's pinning it down in a wrestling match. "I had it when I got here, but somewhere along the way, maybe when we got split up the first time, it disappeared."

"Oh." I think for a moment. "So our phones probably *aren't* lost."

She shoots me an annoyed look. "Well, yeah, but that's not really the point." Tugging the zipper with one hand, she peels one of the pouches open and holds something up.

"A granola bar?"

"I don't know about you," she says, pinching the ridged edge of the bar's wrapper between her fingertips, "but I'm starving."

I'm not. If I tried to eat now, I think I would throw up.

"Here," Shiori says, taking a second bar out of her bag and checking the label. "Chocolate and peanut butter or cinnamon and brown sugar?"

"Thank you, but I don't want one."

"Yes, you do. If we have to keep doing this, you need to make sure you keep your energy levels up."

My eyes flick to hers. "We're not fighting a war."

"We kind of are. A mental one." She wiggles the two bars. "Choose. I'm trying to be nice here."

She is, isn't she?

I take the cinnamon one and peel the wrapper apart. "Thank you."

"No problem." She opens her own bar and takes a bite. "So what have you been seeing? Is it getting worse for you too?"

I break off a piece of the bar. I'm still not all that hungry, but the smell of the brown sugar is intoxicating. "The memories are sadder. More personal."

She nods, chewing her bar. I can smell the chocolate.

"How bad are they?" I ask.

"I'm not having *fun*, if that's what you're asking. But I don't know. I guess what makes it hard is just . . . how everything connects back to my mom."

I take a small bite of the bar and cover my mouth with one hand. "All of them?"

I shouldn't be surprised. The person she lost was a central part of her life.

"Well, no," Shiori says. "Not *all* of them. Most of them, though."

We nibble on our granola bars in silence for a while.

"Is it getting harder for you to tell what's real?" Shiori asks.

I hesitate. "What do you mean? Like you're falling deeper into your memories and forgetting what you're really doing? Or you're not sure if your memories are accurate?"

She pushes the end of her granola bar out of the wrapper. "Both. Even now, a tiny part of me is screaming, 'YOU'RE STILL DREAMING, AND THE GIRL NEXT TO YOU IS JUST AN ILLUSION,' and no matter how many times I tell myself this is real, no matter how many details I make myself concentrate on because I know I wouldn't notice so many things if I were dreaming, I'm not totally sure."

I keep chewing the granola bar.

So it's not my imagination. She's really opening up to me.

Is it because of what she's seeing? Because the horrors of having to relive fragments of her life is getting to her? Or is it the tunnel itself?

What if it's changing us? What if it really *does* contain some kind of hallucinogen, and when we get out, if we ever do, we'll never quite be the same? I've read so many stories of people trying drugs once and being forever changed.

I glance over my shoulder, half expecting to find that chipped phone on the metal hook hanging somewhere behind me.

It isn't even that I've read those drug stories. I've seen them. Up close and personal.

My breath catches in my throat.

Swallowing hard, I swivel back to Shiori. "Oh, yeah? Would an illusion do *this*?"

I have no plans. No forethought. No shame, really. I just start wiggling my arms like a cartoon octopus, keeping my feet rooted just in case taking a step accidentally sends us tumbling back into the abyss.

Shiori stares, her mouth slightly open, as I continue to dance. The only sound, aside from the occasional crack of my wrist, is the crinkling of my granola bar wrapper.

After a painful few seconds, I slow to a stop, inhaling little by little so she can't tell I'm already out of breath. Once I'm sure I'm not going to sound like I'm dying, I say, "Well?"

She opens her mouth, closes it, then opens it again. "What the hell was that?"

"Dancing," I say. Then, because I don't want her to think I'm completely untalented, I add, "*Intentionally bad* dancing."

"Oh, thank God," she says, putting a hand to her chest. "Though if your goal was to make this *less* uncanny, I'm not sure you succeeded."

Great. Now I'm going to have a *new* painfully embarrassing memory that can be used against me.

Shiori's eyes run along my face. "Were you just trying to cheer me up?"

I wish I could be that selfless. If anything, I was trying to cheer *myself* up.

I fold the granola bar wrapper into a tiny square. "Depends. Did it work?"

"It made me less freaked out about the tunnel." She tips her head. "But also a little more freaked out about you. Are you slowly spiraling into madness?"

"Because of the tunnel? Or in general?"

She rolls her eyes, half smiling. "I'm serious. That guy from the Cultural Center said other people have come here, right? They must not have gotten very far into it if they thought they just had a bad trip or something."

"Do you think they started the journey but backed out?" I ask.

"I have no idea." She gnaws on her thumbnail. "How would that even work? If we wanted to stop, could we?"

"I don't know."

"Maybe they didn't see everything we've seen because they didn't go in to resurrect someone."

I think this over for a minute. "You mean because they weren't trying to save someone and were probably just looking for a place to hang out, they didn't get pulled into the visions? The tunnel just scared them off with initial tests? Or booby traps?"

Shiori snickers. "*Booby* traps."

I roll my eyes. "Oh my God. Are *you* going to start making 'That's what she said' jokes now?"

She sobers. "I would never."

"Good." I study the ground. I think I dropped an oat. I just hope it doesn't come back to haunt me like everything else here. "I think that's a solid theory, though. That would explain why they were freaked out but not, like, questioning their sanity."

"I wonder what would happen if you brought someone completely unrelated to your loss with you." She snatches the empty wrapper from my fingertips and tucks our trash into the side pocket of her bag. "Do you think they would see the same things you do? Or do you think anyone who comes with you sees their own memories?"

"I have no idea." I gesture to her bag. "Thank you, by the way. For letting me have the bar and for taking my trash."

"Yeah. Whatever."

We're quiet for a few minutes. I don't think either of us really wants to leap back into memories, especially if they're only going to get harder.

"Do you want to talk about anything?" I ask Shiori. "The memories you saw, maybe? I'll share one if you do."

She frowns. "What is with you and talking about your feelings?"

"I'm just *offering*. It's hard to keep it all inside."

"No." She lifts her head and straightens up. "We should

probably get back to it. We're not accomplishing anything just standing around here."

I hesitate. I don't really feel ready to plunge back into memories, but I guess there's no point in delaying the inevitable.

"Okay," I say. "Good luck."

"You too," she says.

We give each other one last look, then turn away and start walking, waiting for our worlds to fall apart again.

CHAPTER NINE
Most Awkward

THE FIRST THING I sense is the breath of an air conditioner on my back, coldness trickling through my cotton blouse and pressing into my skin. I instinctively try to move away, only to remember I have no control.

Hey, a voice says. It's familiar, but I can't quite place it. I can't even see anything yet, my vision still foggy. *How are you?*

The last thing I spotted before falling into the memory was a wooden chair. Not much of a clue. I blink hard, but everything remains hazy. I can barely even hear myself as I say, *I'm okay. I'm good. I'm fine. How are you?*

I'm good, the voice says as I listen to the *shiff-shiff* of papers being rearranged.

The realization slams into me just before my vision clears.

My name is Eli, he says.

His dark hair is neat, curving along his ear and feathering out in the back, à la Michael Moscovitz from the first *Princess Diaries* movie. He holds himself in such a strange way, his shoulders hunched like he's afraid to take up too much space. It's actually kind of a valid fear here, since this is a middle school library and he's an abnormally tall senior, but even when I see him later, he'll still be crumpled up, his arms close to his sides.

His eyes crinkle as he extends a hand over the wooden table

between us. His lips are parted, but I can't quite say he's smiling. When I nervously take his hand and shake it, I'm acutely aware of how tiny I seem in comparison.

He scratches his cheek. *So, uh, what did you want to start with?*

My eyelashes flutter. Not because I'm flirting. Just because I'm dying. *I was thinking I could just learn, um, how to write better? In general?*

Oh, cool. Do you want to be a writer? Or do you have trouble in English? I just want to kind of get a feel for what you need.

No, no. I'm definitely not a writer. I never write unless I have to. And I'm not good at it. Which is why I'm here.

He nods like he understands, even though he doesn't. He was born to write. *Well, what kinds of stories do you like?*

I can't stop looking at him. The sweetness and slight nervousness in his eyes. The curve of his smile. The way he holds himself, his thumbs twiddling even as he focuses on me.

Should I try to impress him? Mention *A Tale of Two Cities* or *War and Peace* or, God, maybe something by Shakespeare?

Honestly, I blurt out, *I really like stories in video games.*

He tilts his head. His bangs fall to one side. *Video games?*

Not, like, shooter games. I'm sweating. Oh, man. I'm sweating. Thank God the air conditioner is blowing on my back. *More like, um, narrative games? The ones that focus more on the story. You know?*

I hold my breath, afraid he's going to give me a blank look and say he has no idea what I'm rambling on about, and maybe someone else would be better equipped to help me. But after a moment, he says, *I actually went to this seminar recently, and it touched on narrative video games. It's really interesting, how stories can be told through a different medium . . .*

That's what I think too, I say, getting overly excited.

He smiles. *What are some of your favorite video games?*

I freeze, the way I do every time someone asks me about video games. I can read a thousand forum posts and watch hours of analysis videos, but when it comes to talking about them in person, I go mute. Even now.

Especially now.

Over the next hour, we struggle through a conversation about some of my favorite games, identifying themes and character strengths. I can't help but notice the other pairs in the writing center aren't spending nearly as much time together. I ask him if I'm taking up too much of his time, and when he promises me I'm not, I decide he is the best person I have ever met.

By the time we wrap up our appointment, my social battery is depleted, and I have the feeling his is too. When he invites me to return to the writing center sometime, he gives me a smile that, while genuine, reminds me of smudged steam on a mirror. I have to keep myself from reaching out to wipe it away like the last wisps of a dream.

Every time I'm dropped back into a memory, it's a little harder to remember I'm eventually going to be taken out of it. At this point, a part of me wonders why I should even bother going back. Middle school may have been torturous in a lot of ways, but at least I was excited about something, even if it was just a crush on a boy I would never have.

At thirteen, I've already lost my uncle. But he's the only one. My memories of him, of his incarceration, of his funeral are distant and ill-defined. Death is still a stranger to me. Five years later, it will be everywhere. So why can't I go back? What's the point in pushing forward?

I stare at Eli, that gentle smile so different from the wide, unabashed grin of yet another boy I would never have.

Until I heard about the tunnel, I thought Shun would forever be a ghost in the back of my mind.

I don't want more ghosts. I want him back. The real him. Not the one I only ever see in my nightmares.

When the memory resumes, I'm sitting beside Thea, staring up at the lizard perched in the overhead light.

I have something to tell you, I say to her.

She keeps her eyes on the lizard. *What is it?*

I don't speak for a moment.

After our bonding experience in the sixth grade, Thea was happy to rattle off a list of every single crush she'd ever had, starting with her babysitter's son and ending with a guy in my class. I, on the other hand, am pretty sure I've never had a crush on anyone before.

Thea is the only person who has never found my lack of romantic interests strange. Even my mom used to constantly ask if there was anyone interesting in my class.

One boy pulled a fire alarm during our spelling test, I would say, *and one girl can recite the alphabet backward.*

That's not really what I meant, she would tell me.

Then I don't get it, I would reply.

Well, I get it now.

I think I have a crush on someone, I say to Thea.

Her jaw drops. She whips around so quickly, her hair smacks my shoulder. *WHAT? WHO?*

His name is Eli. I pause. *He's a senior.*

A SENIOR? she repeats.

I flap my hands, trying to shush her without actually slapping a hand over her mouth. *Shh. Oh my God. Don't say it so loudly.*

Like a HIGH SCHOOL senior? she whispers.

I roll my eyes. *No. An old-person senior. He uses a walker.*

You're joking, right? She assesses my expression. *You're joking. Okay. Good. But still. A senior? How did you even meet him?*

The writing center. My cheeks are warm. I set the back of my hand against my face like I'm absorbing the heat. *He's really nice. He let me talk to him about video games.*

Thea and I may both suck at modified pull-ups, and we share a love of stories, but she has never been as interested in video games as I am. She didn't grow up playing platformers on a console, didn't spend more time farming in a game than she ever has in real life, and didn't waste hours of time dressing characters up in fancy outfits and decorating virtual cakes. Whenever I tell her about a new game I've been playing, I can practically see her eyes glazing over.

Wow, Thea says. *Is he into them too, then?*

Not really, I admit, *but he was telling me about this seminar he went to where he learned about writing for video games, and he's really awkward and tall.*

She blinks. *Is there supposed to be a connection there?*

That's why I like him. I clear my throat. *Because he's awkward.*

She lifts her eyebrows. *Wow. You're blushing. You REALLY like him.* She pokes me. *Tell me more about him.*

My eighth-grade self starts recounting the entire experience at the writing center, words tumbling over each other like water over stones.

Well, Thea says once I've told her everything in excruciating detail, *I think he sounds—*

I gasp so loudly, I startle both Thea and myself. Grabbing Thea's hand, I hiss, *That's him. Over there.*

What? She jerks her head from side to side, as twitchy as a chickadee. *WHAT? WHERE?*

SHHHH, I hiss. *THERE. See? Right next to the tree.*

She squints at him, then declares, *He IS tall.*

I frown, but before I can ask if that's really all she has to say about him, I spot my mom's car in the pickup line and gasp again.

What? Thea asks.

My mom's here. I tighten my grip on her hand. *And her car's RIGHT NEXT TO HIM.*

No way. She cranes her neck. *Oh my God.*

What do I do? I ask, shaking her hand up and down. *Can I say hello? Or is that weird? Can seniors even say hi to eighth graders?*

I mean, it's not illegal. She salutes me as I haul my backpack onto my shoulder. *Good luck out there, soldier.*

I give her a solemn nod, turn on my heel, and start marching.

When I reach him, he's scribbling in a notebook. I tell myself to toss a casual hello over my shoulder. That way, even if he doesn't remember me, I won't have to awkwardly stand there and die inside.

But because this is my first crush and I don't know how to do anything remotely normal in even the best situations, I come to a screeching halt and say, in an unbroken run-on sentence, *Hi Eli it's me Monika I saw you from over there and thought I would say hello so this is me saying hello thank you for helping me at the writing center earlier it was fun to talk to you my mom is here I have to go but anyway okay thanks again.*

A tiny crease appears between his brows like a valley fold in origami. *Oh, yeah. Uh, hi, Monika. It's nice to see you.*

Yeah, I say.

Then I turn and run to my mom's car.

My phone buzzes. In a few seconds, I'll see it's a message from Thea, telling me that was the most painful thing she's ever had to witness. For now, though, I'm just focused on getting into my mom's car.

I remember what happens next. I'm going to fall into the backseat and shout, *DRIVE* to my mom. She, not at all appreciative of my raised voice, will then tell me to stop shouting. I will repeat it, quieter, refusing to look out the window to see if Eli's still there. As the car peels away from the curb, I will allow myself a quick glance over my shoulder and discover Eli is still scrawling something in his notebook. I'll have the feeling it isn't a love poem for me.

Mentally preparing to relive the memory, I set my hand on the door handle. I usually ride in the passenger's seat, but when my mom's picking me up by the curb, it's easier to just tuck and roll into the back. As I reach for the seat belt, I wait to hear myself yell, *DRIVE*.

But I don't say anything.

I keep my head low and pinch my fingers hard, the skin of the pads going white. When I wrench them apart, I smash them together again, harder. It's eerily quiet. Usually, when my mom picked me up from school, the radio was playing.

Is your seat belt on?

I tense. That wasn't my mom.

Yes, Mommy, I say.

But this isn't me. This isn't my voice. And these hands, the ones grasping the seat belt to ensure I really did secure it— these aren't mine either.

I raise my head. The woman in the driver's seat has dark hair, just like my mom, but everything else, from the shape of her face to the curve of her neck, is wrong.

How was your day? the woman asks.

I glance out the window, then lift my eyes to the woman.

It was good, I watch Shiori say.

Our mouth barely moves in the reflection of the rearview mirror.

CHAPTER TEN
Prettiest Kimono

MY BREATH FLUTTERS through my chest, stirring in my rib cage like a tiny autumn windstorm. I keep staring at my reflection, willing it to morph me back into my old self, but the only girl there, trapped in the rectangular mirror, is Shiori. She's younger, smaller, and her hair is long, straight, and black.

Did you get your science test back yet? the woman asks, glancing at me in the mirror.

Shiori shakes her head. *He said maybe tomorrow.*

Tomorrow? She clicks her tongue. *How much work can it be, grading a bunch of middle schoolers' science tests?*

Shiori forces a smile. I can feel the strain in our mouth, the pull in our cheeks, as if we're about to split apart. Then she tugs at her seat belt and looks out the window.

I'm sure you did fine, though, the woman says. *You studied hard, didn't you?*

I try to search her mind, hoping to reach her inner thoughts, but they're sealed away. The only voice in this head is my own.

I studied really hard, Shiori responds.

I know you did. You're my good girl. The woman flips on her blinker. *Your kimono is waiting at home. You remember how to put it on, don't you?*

Shiori swallows. *Yes, Mommy.*

I would frown if I could. There's nothing immediately

insidious about this conversation, but something feels off, like they're waiting for the other shoe to drop.

For a while, the car is silent. I wish we could turn on the radio.

How was your day? Shiori asks her mother. In her lap, Shiori turns her phone over and over, the case slapping against her skin with every rotation. *Was work okay?*

It was work, Shiori's mother says with a shrug. *Maggie's driving me nuts again.*

Ugh, Shiori says. *Maggie.*

Shiori's mother laughs. It's so different from my mom's half wheeze, half guffaw, much more reserved and almost practiced. I would wonder if it was fake if not for the gleam in the woman's eyes.

Maybe I shouldn't say that, Shiori says. *Isn't Maggie the one who gave me those gummies for Girls' Day?*

No, Shiori's mother says. *That was Christie.*

Oh. Shiori drums her fingertips on the car door. *Then UGH. Maggie.*

The woman laughs again as they pull into a clean white driveway. It's a nice area, the houses lining the streets all neatly spaced apart and painted white or ivory or, for the *truly* daring, a placid eggshell blue. This is the kind of place I've really only seen in movies or when my parents take me to visit their rich friends.

Once the car has been parked, I instinctively try to reach for the door handle—only to remember I can't move. I wait for Shiori to do it, but she doesn't either, simply unbuckling her seat belt and facing forward, her eyes running along the outline of the driver's seat. She licks her lips. They're dry. The top one is cracking in the middle.

The door opens. When Shiori turns to look, her eyes meet

her mother's. As Shiori clambers out of the backseat, I get the feeling this is their usual routine. She doesn't even close the car door. Her mother pushes it closed with one hand, then locks the doors, takes Shiori's hand, and leads us up the driveway.

I'm not judging. Really. I held my mom's hand way past elementary school too. If I didn't have Thea, I'm pretty sure my mom would be my best friend.

I just can't shake the disquieting feeling in my stomach.

Shiori's mother unlocks the front door, inserting one key into the top lock, then a second into the doorknob. Both locks are a polished gold so beautiful, they don't look real.

When we step inside, I can't help but notice the strange colors of the door. From the outside, it's a pristine white, matching the rest of the house. On the other side, though, it's a slightly different color, closer to a dirtied cream.

Hurry, Shiori's mother says. *We don't want to be late.*

Okay, Shiori says.

She sounds different. Her voice is higher and just a little raspy, but that's not the main difference. The Shiori I know says everything harshly, expelling each syllable from deep within her body. This Shiori speaks in a softer, almost apologetic tone, each word bubble-wrapped.

After washing up at the kitchen sink, Shiori heads straight for her bedroom, giving me hardly any time to examine the house. It's definitely nicer than mine, the walls and ceiling smooth instead of popcorned. The wooden floors are cool beneath our heels. I catch a glimpse of a giant TV in the living room.

I don't have time to guess what Shiori's room will look like, but somehow, when we step inside, I'm taken aback. The walls are painted a light pink, sakura-tree decals affixed to each side of the room. A blossom-shaped rug leads to a twin bed covered in pink sheets and a mocha-colored pillowcase. Above her bed, a calendar hangs from a hook, each day filled with what I suppose must be Shiori's neat print. After all the X-ed-out days is a two-inch square, the words JAPANESE FESTIVAL written in the center.

Shiori glances at the kimono draped across her bed. Dyed a deep red, it comes with an ivory obi matching the white five-petaled flowers printed along the fabric. After a deep breath, she starts stripping off her school clothes.

I wish I could look at literally anything else, but I can only see what she sees, and Shiori is spending a lot of time scrutinizing her body in the full-length mirror mounted to the back of her door. She runs a hand along the stretch marks on her upper thighs and lifts an arm to study the stubby black hairs sprouting from her armpits.

Pivoting away, she pulls on some tabi, then a light slip. She skips over some of the other garments, picks up the kimono, and slips it over her shoulders. I instantly feel the weight of it, the whisper of cotton against her skin. It's comforting, in a way. Like we're being hugged.

Crossing the left side over the right, she adjusts the kimono a few times before setting the obi below her bust.

Tap, tap, tap.

She looks up just as her mother enters.

Oh, her mother says. While one hand grasps the doorknob, the other lies flat against her chest. *You look absolutely beautiful.*

Shiori's face flushes. *Thank you. So do you.*

It's not an empty compliment. Shiori's mother is dressed in a white kimono decorated with scarlet koi and fan-like clouds. An ornament dangles from her dark hair, brushing her exposed ear. She looks like a dream.

In a handful of years, she will be dead.

Here, Shiori's mother says, taking us by the shoulders and spinning us around. Dizzy, we fix our gaze on the wall calendar. *Let me fix your obi.*

Once we've both checked ourselves in the mirror and taken quick drinks of water, we head back to the car. Again, Shiori's mother opens the door for us. We slide into the back.

I'm probably reading too much into this. People get the door for each other all the time. It's just a nice thing to do. But even Shiori seems uncomfortable, mumbling a thank-you as she avoids the eyes of a neighbor across the street.

As her mother starts the car, Shiori takes out her phone and sends a message to her father: On our way to festival.

Can you tell your dad we're headed over? Shiori's mother asks.

I wince, waiting for Shiori to snap *I DID already* in that disgruntled tone all young teens use with people who get on their bad sides—the same tone she uses with me.

But she doesn't say it that way. She doesn't say it at all. She just looks up from her phone, her father's thumbs-up response sitting at the bottom of her screen, and says, *Yes, Mommy.*

The car ride is silent, aside from the occasional buzz of Shiori's phone on her knee. I stare at the interior of the car, trying to pull myself out of the memory, but it doesn't work. Shiori runs the kimono between her fingertips, her lips pursing and unpursing, completely oblivious to the stranger occupying her mind.

Shiori's mother pulls into the lot of one of the Japantown areas. There's a sizable Asian population around here, so we have multiple Japan-, China-, and Koreatowns. In elementary school, we visited at least one each year. It was one of the most anticipated field trips of our lives, all of us saving up money or begging our parents for twenty bucks, only to bring back an overwhelmingly aromatic sandalwood fan or a clunky Chinese lion-dance marionette puppet, soon to be stuffed in a closet to collect dust.

A white banner hangs from the pillars of the torii. JAPANESE FESTIVAL: FOOD, GAMES, FUN has been printed in large black letters. Shiori mouths the Japanese characters running beneath the English lettering to herself.

The car door opens. Shiori's mother helps us out of the vehicle. We look back to ensure our kimono hasn't snagged in the car door.

It smells amazing, hearty teriyaki mingling with the powdery scents of sugar and flour. Shiori's mother keeps our hand in hers, her grip firm but not tight enough to hurt. As we pass beneath the torii and follow the cobblestone path, Shiori studies almost everything, from the goldfish-scooping booth to the cart of wagashi. She's so enamored, she almost walks right into an elderly woman stopped in the middle of the path.

My, the woman says, a hand to her cheek as she studies us. *Niatteru ne?*

I try to pull back, still startled from her sudden appearance, but Shiori dips into a bow, already shaking her head. *Not at all. Thank you. You flatter me.*

The woman's hand drops to her heart. To Shiori's mother, she says, *What a well-behaved girl. You have raised her well.*

She's a good child, Shiori's mother responds. *She makes it very easy.*

A rush of pride surges through Shiori's body, warming her fingertips. She looks over at her mother and lightly squeezes her hand.

My heart aches, knowing this is the woman Shiori is fighting so hard to bring back. Is this the tunnel's way of telling me only one person can be revived? A scheme to make me empathize with Shiori? Maybe once I understand why she wants her mother back so badly, I'll feel pressured to drop out and let her make it to the end alone.

What if, at this moment, the tunnel is showing her *my* memories? What is it letting her see? What is she thinking? She judged me for wanting to save Shun. If all she's seeing is that time I tripped on the stairs, my mission will seem pointless to her.

Oblivious to my panic, Shiori accompanies her mother to a gourmet mochi shop.

And that's where Shiori spots him.

Natsuki, the Stanford-bound former president of my school's Japanese Club, stands in the aisle with his friends, dressed in a blue happi with the words JAPANESE FESTIVAL painted across the back in white-outlined lettering.

Heat floods Shiori's face as she watches him. I'm not sure what's on her mind, but I'm thinking I've just witnessed a miracle: It *is* possible to find nerdier-looking glasses than the ones he was wearing the other day at the Cultural Center.

Shiori gawks at him, her fingers twisting around each other as she half-heartedly attempts to hide behind a bag of chestnuts. The moment their eyes meet, he starts heading over. Her body fills with prickly manic energy, as if she's been lit on fire.

Hey, Natsuki says. By now, she's broken out in a cold sweat. *Funny running into you here.*

Funny, she says. Then, to our horror, she lets out a nervous laugh. *HA, HA.*

Shiori's mother turns to us. One of her hands is still grasping Shiori's. The other is curled around a four-pack of chocolate-peanut-butter mochi.

Shiori? her mother says. *Who is this?*

She stiffens, her insides knotting.

Oh, I'm sorry, Natsuki says. *Shiori and I know each other from school. My name is Natsuki.*

Her heart softens, his name blossoming in her chest: *Natsuki, Natsuki, Natsuki.*

Oh, and you're one of Shiori's—her mother pauses—*friends?*

Shiori holds her breath. She doesn't feel like *friends* adequately captures what he is to her.

Yes, he says. *She's a very good friend.*

She turns her head. He makes everyone feel like a friend. That's part of why she likes him so much. Part of why it hurts to know he will never think of her as anything else.

He glances over his shoulder, where his friends are openly rubbernecking, and rotates back to us. *Sorry, I should get back. We're supposed to be picking up some food for the miko. I hope you enjoy the festival.*

Thank you, Shiori says. Then, as he turns, she adds, *It was really nice to see you.*

He looks over at her, his expression as pleasant as ever. *It was nice to see you too.*

Shiori whips back around, picking up a pack of mochi and crinkling the clamshell packaging between her fingertips. Beside her, her mother is quiet. Once the boys have purchased their mochi, they head out, the president calling out a goodbye. Shiori's face flames, the exact same way mine did with Eli.

Shiori, her mother says.

She jumps. Behind her back, she crosses her fingers. *Yes, Mommy?*

That boy is your friend?

She shifts her feet. *Sort of. He goes to some of my Japanese Club things.*

Mmm. Shiori's mother picks up a pack of mochi. *He seems nice.*

Shiori swallows. *He is.*

You like him.

Her face erupts in a belch of mortification. *I mean, he's a nice person, but I—but it's not like that. We just kind of know each other.*

So you don't "hang out" outside of that?

She shakes her head.

Shiori's mother's fingers curl around the edge of the package. Tugging Shiori toward the cash register, she says, *Don't. Stay away from boys.*

Shiori lowers her head, studying the wooden floor of the shop. *Yes, Mommy.*

CHAPTER ELEVEN
Most Likely to Shout at Inanimate Objects

I STRUGGLE TO untangle myself from the threads of the vision, pushing myself upright before I even know what's going on. Lifting one hand to my face, I study my fingers, then the tunnel floor. The air smells stale, so unlike the sweet smell of mochiko. It whispers along my bare skin, making me wish I could have stolen the kimono from Shiori's memories and brought it back with me.

When I get to my feet, I stumble. Placing a hand on the tunnel wall, I wait for the world to stop spinning. I can't tell if it's just the comedown from a memory or if it's specifically because I was in someone else's body.

I take a deep breath. Glancing over my shoulder, I start searching the area. Every few steps, I pause and listen for rustling, crying, or the faintest hint of Shiori's voice. But there's only the sound of my own lonely footfalls.

"Shiori?" I call out. "Are you awake? Hello?"

I slow. Maybe it isn't time to meet up again yet. Maybe it's going to drop me into another memory. Maybe I'll have to slip back into Shiori's skin. I don't know if I'm ready for that. But then again, I wasn't really ready for any of this.

Letting out a breath, I lean against the wall and close my eyes for a moment.

How much longer is this going to take? How many more times will the tunnel change things up on us?

I could leave. I could open my eyes, straighten up, and walk right out of here. I'm sure it wouldn't be as easy as I want it to be, but I bet I could do it.

Could I, though? Would I be able to live with myself if I ran away? Now? Before seeing Shun, or even Shiori?

"Now's not really the time for naps."

I startle at the sound of Shiori's voice. When I turn to find her standing right behind me, her arms crossed, I almost do a double take. I'd forgotten her hair is lavender now.

"Before you ask," she says, one hand raised, "yeah, it was more memories of my mother. There. I opened up to you. And you didn't even have to guilt me into it."

I blink, struggling to keep up with her. Every time we speak, she seems just a little less hostile.

And I *feel* a little *more* hostile.

"I didn't guilt you into anything," I say a little too harshly.

Her eyes zip over to my face, then back to the wall. "Jeez. I guess I don't have to ask how bad *your* tunnel memories were."

She should. She *should* ask. I just don't know how I would even begin to answer. Why would I see her memories, especially if she's not seeing mine?

Unless she really did see my memories. She's proven relatively trustworthy so far, and in a twisted way, I'm more inclined to trust skeptics like her, the ones who don't open up easily. Would she even tell me if she saw something from my life?

"Maybe you're just thirsty or something. You're not you when you're hungry, thirsty, or tired. That's what my mom used to say."

I flinch, but she's too busy unzipping her bag to notice.

After pulling out two water bottles, she hands one to me. "It's not cold anymore, but it's better than nothing."

I run my tongue along the roof of my mouth. "Are you sure I can have this?"

"Well, these are the only two I have, so don't drink it all in one go." She wiggles the bottle in my face. "Take a few sips, then tear the label so we know which one is yours. I'll keep it in my bag."

I eye her warily. "Why are you being so nice to me?"

She gives me a look. "What is that supposed to mean?"

"Nothing," I say. "You just seem different. Did something happen?"

"We're in a magical tunnel. A lot of things happened."

My focus wavers as I study the water bottle in my hand. "Why did you have two?"

I look up just in time to catch the anger flashing across her face. "What kind of question is that? The whole reason I came down here was to bring my mom back. I'm not going to haul her back into town hungry and dehydrated, now am I?"

I stare down at the water bottle. "But if I drink one and you drink one—"

"It's fine. My mom and I can share. I'd much rather do that than have you collapse somewhere and make me go through the rest of this alone. Even though all you've done is eat my food."

I breathe a small sigh of relief. That's more like the Shiori I know.

"I'm sorry." I try to return the bottle. "I'm okay. Really."

"No, you're not. You're down here for some guy you barely even knew."

My stomach clenches. "You don't get it."

"And I don't have to. Once you revive him and I revive my

mom, we can have a nice little chat, okay? But until then, you need to drink. Dehydration won't do much to help your questionable mental state."

Biting back a grin, I twist the cap and take a small sip. The water is cool, even after its time in her bag. I greedily steal one more sip before capping the bottle. "Thank you."

We're quiet for a while. She opens her own bottle and wets her lips. I keep trying to catch her eye, but she seems intent on looking at everything but me.

What if it's because she really *did* see something from my past? What if she's not telling me because I didn't tell her first? Am I being smart here? Or is the tunnel making me paranoid?

I take another sip of water, hoping all the fogginess in my head will dissipate, but all it does is pool in my stomach, lapping around the giant tangle of unease that just keeps growing.

"Shiori," I say. "Something odd happened this time."

"Something odd." She licks her lips. "What does that mean?"

"I think"—I hesitate—"I saw one memory that wasn't mine."

Her expression remains unchanged. If she *had* seen something from my past, she would have reacted, right?

Right?

"Okay?" She pulls her brows together like she's waiting for the punch line. "And?"

"It was yours," I whisper. "Your memory."

Her eyes jump to my face, then narrow. "What?"

"You were younger. Middle school. You and your mom went to a festival. You wore a kimono."

She presses her lips together. "If this is some kind of joke—"

"Your room was sakura-themed. You went to a mochi shop."

I hesitate. "You saw one of my classmates. Natsuki. The president of the Japanese Club."

She pulls back, her eyes burning with rage. "How the hell do you know that?"

"I *saw* it. I was in the middle of my own memory when it morphed, and the next thing I knew, I was you."

She either shivers or shakes her head. Her grip on her water bottle is tight enough to make the plastic crinkle and whine beneath her fingertips. "Why?"

"I don't *know*. I kept trying to leave, but there was no way out."

She inhales. I'm afraid she's going to start yelling at me, but instead, she raises her head to the ceiling and shouts, "WHAT KIND OF SICK PLOT TWIST IS THIS? WHAT IS YOUR PLAN HERE, HUH? WHAT ARE YOU TRYING TO DO?"

Her voice echoes through the tunnel, ricocheting off the walls. I'm tempted to cover my ears, but a small part of me is fascinated by the way her words carry themselves, flinging sound as far as they can in the hopes of making some kind of difference.

Bringing her hands to her face, she lets out a long sigh. "God, I'm losing it. I'm *losing* it in here. I can't do this anymore."

My eyes flick to her face. Is she going to leave?

I can't lie; I want to know what happens if we try to get out before reaching the end. But I don't want her to go. Don't want to be the only one in this tunnel. Don't want to be the only one struggling under the weight of my own memories.

My memories . . . and hers.

Uncovering her face, she rests her chin on her knee. "So what did you think?"

I pause. "Of what?"

"Of being me for a few minutes." She brushes her hair out of her face, lavender strands sticking to her fingers. "Disgusting, isn't it?"

I bite the edge of my tongue. "I wouldn't say that."

"I would. I *did*." She closes her eyes. "This is stupid. It's stupid, right? And we were stupid for coming in here."

Every time I blink, I swear I see a flash of that white cross. "Don't you want to see her, though?" I ask. "Your mother?"

She maintains a poker face, but her fingers keep pulling her hair tighter and tighter until I can almost feel the pain in my own scalp. "I don't know. Why don't *you* answer that, since you can apparently see my memories now?"

"Not all of them. Just that one."

"Yeah? And what about next time, huh? What are you going to see then?" She bites her lip. It's begun to bleed. "I have no clue why you got to see into my memories, but whatever you think you saw? It wasn't the full picture. So don't act like you know all about my mother. Or me."

"Okay. I'm sorry. I just didn't want to hide anything from you."

"Why? Because being open will fix everything?" Her expression hardens. "How do I know your poking and prying isn't the reason why you saw my memories?"

I blink. "What?"

"Maybe making me open up is what got the tunnel to let you into my mind." She starts tearing the label on her water bottle, the paper dangling from the sticky adhesive. "Did you ever think about that? Or were you too busy being *open* and *vulnerable*?"

Trying to keep my voice level, I say, "I'm really sorry. I don't understand why this happened, and I'm not criticizing you or your mother. I just wanted to tell you because I trust you, and I'm worried about you."

"I never asked for any of that."

"Well, I'm giving it to you anyway."

She opens her mouth, closes it, then turns away. After a long pause, she says, "This is a lot, you know. For someone you claim is just a classmate."

I glance over at her. I consider saying nothing, since it's not like that requires a response anyway. But then I say, "He was more than that. Even if I'm the only one who ever knew it."

She nods. Then, still turned away, she says, "I hate when people ask how it happened, but . . ."

The question has been lingering in the back of my mind too, edging its way along my tongue ever since she first mentioned her mother. I didn't feel comfortable asking, though, especially since it's been just about impossible to ask her anything without having her tear me open like a dog left alone with a rotisserie chicken.

"It was an overdose," I say quietly.

Her eyes narrow. "Huh."

Annoyance blows through my stomach like a tumbleweed. I told her exactly what I didn't want to talk about, and all I get is *Huh*? As if I just rattled off a fun fact I saw on the internet?

I open my mouth, but she speaks before I can.

"It was a car crash for me." Shiori narrows her eyes even further, her fingertips digging into the fabric of her jacket. "For her."

I think of Thea by the curb. Of Shun in his driveway. Of all the times I've heard cars screeching outside the apartment, as if the vehicles are screaming, desperate for salvation.

"I'm sorry," I tell her, because I don't have anything else to say.

"Yeah," she replies, because she doesn't have anything else to say either.

Then, before I can even begin to think of something else to add, she turns and starts walking, her arms crossed so tightly, her jacket sleeves seem to be collapsing in on themselves. I want to say something else, to bring her some comfort, but in the end, all I can do is watch her go.

I wait for a moment, then start following her, still hoping I'll find something to say.

But when I round the corner, there's nothing but darkened walls.

Pivoting on my heel, I glance around the tunnel. Is she already in a memory? Am *I*?

I give it a few more seconds. Then, when neither Shiori nor my next worst nightmare appears, I start retracing my steps.

My head has begun to spin. Is it possible to die in this tunnel? What if someone comes down here to revive *me*? Would it become a fatal train of resurrection attempts?

I wonder what's going on outside. My parents probably haven't noticed my absence yet. If they have, did they contact Thea? Did she manage to squeak out a lie? Did she already blow my cover? Lying has never been her strong suit.

Still. If someone gave me an out right now, with a one hundred-percent guarantee Shiori would be fine and everything in my life would go back to normal, as if I had never entered this tunnel at all, I wouldn't take it. I couldn't. Because if there's even the slightest chance for me to bring Shun back, I'm going to do it.

It wasn't supposed to end like that. *He* wasn't supposed to end like that. I may not be able to get into Columbia or Stanford, but I can do this. I can save him. Then it will all be worth it.

I've just taken another step when my boot slips on something. I let out a tiny scream as my feet slide out from under me. As I fall, I get a glimpse of my undoing: a ballpoint pen, the barrel gray and the tip a glistening black.

I close my eyes and wait for the impact.

But it doesn't come.

When I finally manage to open my eyes, I find myself looking into the eyes of an unfamiliar boy, his face so close, I would scream if I could.

I love you, he says. *I love you so much.*

My first instinct, aside from shrieking and running away, is to say, *Well, this is awkward. I have no idea who you are.*

But, of course, this a memory.

And, I realize a second later, it isn't even mine.

I love you too, Shiori says. She presses a hand to his chest, some strands of her still-black hair sticking to her palm before slowly falling away. *But we can't do this here. We've already gotten caught today.*

The guy's voice rumbles in his chest as he says, *Oh, come on. The dean doesn't care.*

Shiori glances around and, upon seeing the ballpoint pen just an inch from her heel, kicks it away. The guy turns, his eyes hooded as he watches the pen skitter along the concrete like a leaf on a rickety old road.

She shifts on her ledge, a row of lockers just behind her heel. Raising her head, she whispers, *What if they tell my—our parents?*

He scoffs. *What are they going to say? "A couple was caught making out in the halls again"? Oh, man.* He puts a hand to his cheek, scandalized. *Call the police at once.*

She giggles against his neck. *You're so naughty.*

My skin crawls. I wanted to get closer to Shiori, but I didn't really mean it like *this*.

But, Shiori continues, pulling back and placing her fingertip to his lips, *I have to get to class. And you do too. You can't give up so close to graduation. They still might fail you.*

Wow. What a vote of confidence.

She shoves him. My fingers tingle at the contact. *Shut up. You know what I mean. Senioritis is a real thing.*

How would you know, junior pip-squeak? He kisses the apple of her cheek, leaving a trail of heat along her face. *You haven't even taken the SATs.*

I will, though, she points out, *and I'll do a lot better than you.*

His eyebrows skyrocket. *Oh, really?*

Yeah. What did you get? A ten?

I would laugh if I could, not only because of her quip but because of the look on his face. Frowning, he says, *I don't think you can even GET a ten. Isn't the lowest score, like, a four hundred or something?*

Well, you would know, wouldn't you? She slides a leg around him, trying to get off the ledge, but he just blocks her way again. Rolling her eyes up to his face, she sets her hands on her hips. *I'm serious. I have to go.*

Yes. Let's go. Before he drools on us.

Later, then, he says. *Meet me after school.*

She lowers her arms and clenches her hands at her sides. *I can't.*

He waits for her explanation, then sighs. *What? Is it your mom again?*

I startle at the mention of her mother. Of course it all comes back to her. The tunnel seems hell-bent on telling me more about the person Shiori has lost—without her input, permission, or knowledge. Maybe that lack of consent is part of her torture. She has to continue on this convoluted journey with me, knowing I have, for some reason, been granted access to her memories.

If that's the case, though, why isn't she seeing my memories too? I'm getting an unfair advantage, and I doubt it's because the tunnel likes me better or thinks I'm a worthier candidate. Aside from that first memory, none of this has even had anything to do with Shun.

You're sixteen, Shiori's boyfriend says, pulling me out of my own thoughts. *When is she going to loosen up?*

Shiori bites the inside of her cheek, then presses her tongue into the tiny wound. *Since when do sixteen-year-olds get parental permission to do whatever they want?*

Since never, he admits, *but when has that ever stopped us? It's pretty hard to have a teenage rebellion phase if you never rebel.*

I would roll my eyes if I could. This guy is clearly the type to call himself a freethinker and sketch the anarchy symbol on all his stuff, but really, deep down, he doesn't know what it means to break away from the crowd.

Shiori does, though. She's the one who took a rumor and ran with it in the hopes of bringing her mother back.

She loves me, Shiori says, doing her best to keep her tone light. *That's all.*

Yeah, right. He moves closer, pushing her legs apart and standing between them, and leans forward. *She loves you so much, she wants to keep you under her thumb forever.*

He runs a hand along her jawline, and while there's a tug in her belly, an urgent desire to have him, I instinctively try to recoil.

You shouldn't say that about her, Shiori says. *She's good to me.*

Yeah, right. She won't let you get your license.

Maybe that's not such a bad thing. Driving is terrifying, actually, especially since I know Shiori's mother died in a car crash.

She won't let you practice driving, the guy continues. *Not even in empty parking lots.*

Hey. She tries to keep her tone light, but frustration has begun to burn her throat like acid. *She won't let me practice driving because without a permit, that would be illegal.*

Yeah, well, she won't let you get that either.

I wonder if he knows Shiori's mother opens the car door for her. I wonder if she still does. If she's a junior now, more than a few years have passed since the previous memory.

And your curfews, he continues.

Annoyance pricks the bottoms of her ribs. *Wow. You want me to ditch class so we can hook up, and THIS is where you take the conversation?*

I obviously don't have much of a say here, but I'm glad the aforementioned hookup has been delayed.

Okay, okay, he says. *I'm just saying—*

What? She raises an arm and pushes him away. Slowly, not unkindly, but with no uncertainty. *What are you "just saying"?*

Nothing. God, you get so weird about her.

Her eyes narrow. *She's my mom.*

Yeah, and? He shakes his head. *You know, you keep talking about how you're going to go off to an Ivy League or a UC or something and become a doctor or a lawyer or whatever.*

A little flame of curiosity flickers in my mind. I didn't know Shiori wanted those things. It's not like she's been an open book with me.

What does that have to do with anything? Shiori says, her voice dangerously sharp.

Nothing, her boyfriend says again. *It's just, you know, if you really ARE going to go—*

Nice. Now you're doubting me.

Even as the words leave her mouth, cold and scathing, I can feel the anxiety gnawing at her insides. She turns her face, afraid if he looks at her too closely, he'll see the uncertainty she feels so strongly in her blood, whispering through her veins, telling her she's not good enough. No matter how hard she studies, no matter how many times she writes and rewrites her personal narratives, she will never please her—

That's not what I'm saying, he says, *and you know it.*

She does. She knows a lot of things. Things she wishes she didn't have to know.

I just hope your mom realizes she's pushing and pushing and PUSHING you to get into all these good colleges, but really, when it comes time for you to go, she won't know what to do with herself. And you probably won't have a clue what you should do either.

She's stunned for a moment. Breathless. I can feel the air catching in her lungs, hooking on every one of her sharp edges like she's nothing but broken pieces.

Yes, Mommy, I can almost hear her saying now. *I understand, Mommy.*

Shiori thrusts one hand out and shoves it against her boyfriend's shoulder. *What the HELL is your problem?*

He staggers back a step, his eyes wide. Bringing a hand to where she pushed him, as if he's more hurt than he's letting on, he says, *I don't have a problem.*

He looks at us. For a split second, I honestly think he knows I'm here. He can see me too.

But I think you do.

CHAPTER TWELVE
Most Clueless

HIS EYES ARE burned into my vision, two dark pupils boring into my soul. Even when I put a hand over my face, I see them.

I know I shouldn't take that guy's words at face value. I've never spoken to him. I'm not even sure how well he knows Shiori—but then again, how well do *I*? Besides, if something about her relationship with her mother really *was* off, she obviously wouldn't be going through all this trouble to bring her back now.

I just can't stop thinking about the conviction in his eyes. Like he knew everything Shiori didn't want him to say. With just a breath and a few words strung together, he could have taken her down. Dismantled everything she had been working so hard to build up in her mind.

Suppressing a shiver, I make my way through the tunnel. This time, I don't call for Shiori. We'll end up running into each other eventually, and honestly, I'm not excited for our reunion. It wouldn't feel right to lie about what I saw, even by omission, but she didn't react so well the first time. I doubt bringing up her boyfriend's issues with her mother would do much to placate her. And that's not even considering what would happen if I admitted I kind of technically made out with him.

I press my tongue to the roof of my mouth. I may not be thirsty now, but I will be soon. When the water runs out, or if

Shiori decides she doesn't want to share with me anymore, it's all over. I could actually die down here. We both could.

My footsteps stutter to a stop. I listen for a moment, half-convinced I'm hearing things.

Nope. That most definitely *is* someone zipping and unzipping a bag to the rhythm of "We Wish You a Merry Christmas."

When I round the corner, Shiori's sitting on the ground, her legs stretched out and her backpack placed over her lap. I almost manage to close the gap between us, my soles crunching against the darkened ground, before she lifts her head.

"I saw your memories," she blurts out. "*As you*. It was like . . . like I *was* you."

I nod. "That's how it was for me too."

She keeps playing with the zipper. Her pale-lavender hair is sickly in the dimness.

I crouch beside her, my lower lip trapped between my teeth. "What did you see?"

She chews her own lip, her eyes skimming the shadows. "I'm not really sure. You were at this, like, piano, I think." She pauses. "I didn't know you could play."

"I can't," I say. When she gives me the same look I wish I could give every humble-bragger I've met in school, I add, "Not well. I mean, I know some chords, but even those don't sound good when I'm playing them."

She side-eyes me. "They sounded fine to me."

I'm not really a musically talented person. I quit piano in the fifth grade after struggling through a few years of lessons and can count, on one hand, the number of times I've touched the piano since then. Each time I have, it's been for the same reason.

"You were singing," Shiori says. "Quietly, like you didn't want anyone to hear."

"I didn't," I say softly.

She studies my expression, even as I do my best to turn my face away. "I've never heard that song. What is it from?"

"A video game."

I kept that song on my phone for the longest time. Once, I played it on a loop for days. I haven't heard it for a year now, but it's stranded in my top ten most frequently played songs, hovering near the top of the list like a ghost.

"What game?" Shiori asks.

You probably haven't heard of it, I almost say. Not because I think I'm some hipster interested in only the most obscure indie titles. Just because if she had known anything about the game, she wouldn't be looking at me with such innocent curiosity.

"*Bitter Mouse*," I hear myself say.

Her eyelashes flutter. "That's the name of the game? *Bitter Mouse*?"

I try to make myself meet her gaze, but the lump in my throat makes it hard to breathe. I manage to nod, but even that small motion is enough to drop the veil of sadness over my shoulders, coating me in that all-too-familiar shame.

"What is it about?" she asks.

I remember exactly how it's stated online. "It's a single-player adventure game with a focus on narrative and character exploration."

She tilts her head. "Interesting. So it's not one of those, like, esports games or anything? With all the"—she makes *pew-pew* sounds with her mouth—"kind of stuff?"

I suck in my cheeks. "No. No *pew-pew*s for me. It's an indie game by this small company called Sour Mouth."

Her eyebrows lift. "*Bitter Mouse*. Sour Mouth. What is with these names?"

I almost smile. I wondered the same thing when I first heard of the game and its developer. I put off playing it for a few months. I told myself I was waiting for the price to drop, and that admittedly was a big part of it. Like most gamers, I'm a sucker for sales.

But it was primarily because I was afraid.

In my junior year, three years after rambling to Eli about video games, I decided to replay one of my old favorites, a highly artistic game exploring mental health. Once I finished, sinking into my usual post-game hangover, I decided to scour the web for similar works. *Bitter Mouse* kept popping up, sneaking its way onto almost every list and forum I found.

Oh my God, I thought to myself as I prepared to close the tab. *I don't want to play a game with a name that stupid.*

But then I saw the editor's note nestled below the suggestion: *Content warning for addiction, dissociation, and grief.*

I didn't know how a game would tackle topics like those. What if they were nothing but throwaway jokes? *Ha, ha, drugs. Ha, ha, death. Ha, ha, anthropomorphic animals turned into roadkill.* It was better, I thought, for me to stay away.

Then, sometime in the fall, I received an email notifying me of a special sale. *Bitter Mouse* was 15 percent off.

Shiori lets me soak in the silence for a minute. Then, scooting closer, she asks, "What happened? What is it about this thing?"

I close my eyes. I shouldn't be making a big deal of this. It's just a game.

"It was special to me," I say. "There's not really anything else to say about it."

She takes a breath. I can feel the questions bubbling up in her throat, but she swallows them and nods. "How about you, then? What did you see?"

"Yours," I say quietly. "I saw more of yours."

She cracks a wry smile. But I catch the slight twitch of her eye, discomfort wriggling along her mouth like a worm on the rain-soaked pavement. "Right. Of course. I finally see one of your memories, thinking the playing field's evening out. But no." She shakes her head. "I don't get this."

"I don't either. Maybe the tunnel is trying to get you to resent me." I give her a tight smile. "Though I don't think you need any help with that."

She rolls her eyes. "Oh, yeah. I provide food and water to all my mortal enemies."

A pang of guilt pricks my side. I pull my arms closer to my sides, finding a sick sort of pleasure in the pain curling along my rib cage. Or maybe it's not pleasure. Maybe it's just the satisfaction of feeling something I knew would come for me sooner or later. I was so blinded by the hopes of resurrecting Shun, I showed up here with next to no plan.

"Oh, come on." Shiori nudges me. "Don't make that face. It's not that serious. Just tell me what you saw. Then I'll know how embarrassed I should be."

I raise my eyes to the ceiling, trying to find the best way to put this. "Well, you were at school. With someone. A boyfriend, I think."

Her expression goes flat, a soda left on the counter overnight. "You made out with my boyfriend."

I swallow. "I never said that."

"But you *did* make out with him, right?" She crosses her arms, her eyes on something over my shoulder. "God, no wonder you were being so weird."

"It's not like I *wanted* to," I say. "Besides, it wasn't, like, making out. It was just"—*weirdly intimate. Extremely uncomfortable. Seared into my brain. Inappropriate for a school environment; think of the children. And by "children," I mean me*—"some touching."

She makes a face. "I think that's worse."

Yeah, okay. I could've phrased that better.

"So what else happened?" she asks. "Or was the tunnel just, like, a total perv, wanting to make you do 'some touching' with my ex?"

"Ex," I repeat.

She keeps her arms crossed. "Yeah. We didn't last that long."

I shouldn't be surprised. It would be hard to stay with someone who said such negative things about a parent.

It's hard, though. Letting go of people you thought you would have forever.

"I'm sorry," I say.

She shrugs. "It's not like it was all that serious. We were just fooling around."

I'm not so sure about that. I could *feel* how much she liked him. I'm not sure she loved him, but their relationship seemed like more than a casual fling.

"Why did you break up?" I ask.

She must have known the question was coming, almost as inevitable as *How did they die, though?* but her eye twitches anyway.

"We just weren't compatible."

I nod slowly. "It doesn't have anything to do with what he said about your mom?"

Her bottom lids twitch again. "No. Why? What did he say?"

"I don't know." I bite my tongue. "He seemed to think she was too overprotective."

"Yeah, well, that's just because he never got along with his own parents. He wouldn't know what a healthy family dynamic looked like if it slapped him across the face."

I don't think a healthy family dynamic should involve any slaps across faces, but I have the feeling I shouldn't point that out.

"I don't know what you saw," she says, "but whatever it was, it was just some stupid thing some stupid boy said some stupidly long time ago. It doesn't matter."

"Okay," I say. "I believe you."

"I mean, yeah. You should."

She lifts her chin and opens her mouth. I wait for her to say something scathing, but when she speaks, her voice is shaky and laced with something dangerously close to fear.

"What is that?" she asks.

"What is what?"

"*That*." She points at something behind me.

Clenching all the muscles in my stomach, I slowly turn and follow her gaze.

The tunnel is still dim, highlighting only bits and pieces of the ground, as if to remind us we will only see what it wants us to see. About a foot away, in the center of a small, apple-sized beam of light, is a tiny figurine.

"Do I even want to know?" I ask under my breath.

I glance at Shiori, hoping she's willing to take the lead here, but she's frozen. I'm not sure she's even breathed since I turned my head.

Pivoting back to the spotlighted object, I crabwalk my way over to it. My eyes flick around the tunnel, but no matter where I look, all I see is darkness. Darkness, Shiori, and that lone figurine.

When I reach it, my stomach drops.

"What?" Shiori asks, catching the look on my face. "What *is* it?"

I swallow.

I don't remember exactly when it was. Recently, and a lifetime ago. I was still struggling to understand what had happened to Art Harris and what it meant for Sour Mouth and *Bitter Mouse*, but the rest of the world had already finished processing it. Had already accepted it. Had already moved on from the tragedy of what had happened, focusing instead on what was to come.

The game's official social media accounts announced a limited-time run of *Bitter Mouse*: Collector's Edition. With a beautifully packaged physical copy of the game's soundtrack and an exclusive figurine of the titular anthropomorphic mouse, it revived the community in a way no one could have expected. I had to leave the game's subreddit because all anyone ever talked about was how excited they were for the bonuses.

I didn't buy it. I couldn't. I loved that game, but the thought of keeping physical representations of it in my room, like a miniature shrine, made me sick.

Here it is, though, right in the palm of my hand. That little figurine. But instead of wearing her usual dress, complete with a bold, dark semicolon on the front, she's been dressed in a T-shirt reading F•R•I•E•N•D•S.

"Monika?" Shiori gets to her feet and takes a few steps forward. "What is it?"

Instead of answering, I hold the figurine out to her. I know she won't understand, having never played *Bitter Mouse*, but if I open my mouth, I might start screaming.

My eyes rivet themselves to Shiori as I wait for her to toss me a confused look.

But she inhales sharply, her dry lips parting. "How did you—where did—how—"

She staggers back. Her heel slips on a loose piece of rock, and though I reach for her, my arm shooting out before I even know what's happening, she manages to catch herself on the wall, her fingers scrabbling for something solid.

The pad of my pinkie runs along the back of the figurine, tracing the mouse's tiny shoulder blade. "You know what this is?"

Shiori's eyes flick to me. "Of *course* I do. That's—those are—they're my mom's keys. Her car key is—it's right—"

I pull my chin back. "What?"

She doesn't answer. She just stumbles back, adjusts her bag strap, and takes off running. I'm not even sure she knows which direction she's heading until she's already halfway around the corner.

"Shiori," I call out.

No response.

I chase after her, but when I round the corner, she's gone. My fingers tighten around the figurine, tracing the edges like they're trying to memorize every last curve.

This isn't her mother's car key. It's the *Bitter Mouse* figurine. Isn't it?

I tighten my grip on the figurine. As soon as I do, it crumbles in my hand. Then I crumble too, until there's not a single piece of me left.

CHAPTER THIRTEEN
Best Friend

THEA IS SITTING close enough for me to smell her shampoo, fruity with just the faintest hint of chemicals. Her head is propped up on her hand, her chin resting on her knuckles as she studies my screen.

And that's the mouse? She squints, struggling to make out the blurry figure. *Why does it have two dots on its shirt?*

It's a dress, I tell her, as if it matters, *and that's a semicolon. It's symbolic.*

Sure it is.

I remember this day. I was deep in my *Bitter Mouse* obsession, but I never let her see me play it. It was such a solitary, individualized experience, it would have felt like stripping myself naked right in front of her, the way our body-positive classmates did in the PE locker rooms.

I was happy to show her art from the game, though. She was probably bored out of her mind, staring at a bunch of characters to whom she felt no connection, but she pretended to be interested anyway.

Lucky for her, my mother's about to knock on the door just to say hello to Thea.

Tap, tap, tap.

Right on cue.

I don't have to get up. My mother will open the door on her own in a matter of seconds.

Only when the door opens, it's not my mother in the doorway—it's Thea.

I instinctively turn to take another look at Thea, remembering too late that I can't move in memories.

But I *am* moving. My head rotates, giving me a perfect view of my open laptop. Except instead of a picture of *Bitter Mouse*, the screen has only two words, white text on a black background.

TURN AROUND

I whip back around, my heart hammering in my chest.

Thea is still standing in the doorway, one hand on the silver handle. For a moment, her image flickers. She appears beside me again, inches away, then teleports back to the doorway.

Weird, right? Thea says, her eyes bright but her mouth pulled into a slight frown.

What's happening? I ask.

She shrugs. *You're asking me? I'm not the one who took some stranger's ghost story to heart and made it my life's mission to bring a classmate back from the dead.*

I pull back. A chill runs up my spine. *Who are you?*

Wow. Six years of friendship, and this is how you treat me? She lets go of the door handle, steps into the room, and closes the door behind her. As it clicks, she flickers, an electric ripple running along her hand.

I scrabble back, my knee knocking against my laptop. Its screen has returned to the image of the anthropomorphic mouse—but she's wearing that F•R•I•E•N•D•S shirt again. *What's going on?*

Funny, isn't it? Thea reaches out and walks her fingertips along the keys of my laptop. *Just when you get used to being dropped into memories—which, by the way, is NOT what most of our classmates are doing with their summers—the rules change.*

What rules? I ask. *Why can I move?*

Don't worry about it. Thea takes my hand and pulls me up. *Come on.*

She feels inhumanly cold. *Where are we going?*

You'll see. She tugs me toward the door. *By the way, what's with you and Shiori?*

I blink. *What do you mean?*

Is she, like, your new best friend? Thea pauses, then laughs humorlessly. *I feel like we're in elementary school again. Next thing you know, I'll be buying friendship necklaces and begging you to wear one with me. Remember those? Our classmates would always fight over which girl would get "best" and which would get stuck with "friends."*

What's wrong with "friends"? I ask, my eyes roaming around the room. We're heading for the door, but time is warping around us. We seem to be fighting against friction, our feet moving but our bodies staying in almost the exact same place.

Well, you know how it is, Thea says. *Everyone wants to be the best at something.*

I glance over my shoulder at the window, my blinds left open, but the usual scenery—palm trees, slowly dying grass, a rickety path leading from the front of a nearby building to a giant dumpster—has vanished. Now there's nothing on the other side of the glass at all. Nothing but pitch-black darkness.

I don't know, I say to Thea. *I think I would rather have the "friends" half.*

She tilts her head. *Why's that?*

I hesitate. I know this isn't the real Thea. There's no point in talking to her.

But if I don't talk to her, what do I do? Stare at her? Fight her? Try to pull away, even though she's the only person I have? Isn't pulling away the last thing I would ever want to do, especially now?

Well, I say, struggling to keep my voice level, *I would much rather be known for being a friend. Having to be the best at much of anything sounds like a lot of pressure.*

Very true. She extends a hand, but we're still at least half a foot from the door. *I actually think I would rather have the "friends" side too. It would be my reminder to myself to be a good friend to you. Plus, without the other half, it could be referring to the TV show.*

They WERE on a break, we say at the exact same time.

But, I add, *that doesn't make it right for him to have immediately run off and hooked up with someone else.*

Thea laughs, but I have to push down my discomfort. We've had this conversation in real life before. But not here. Not like this.

So, Thea says. *You and Shiori?*

She's nice, I say. *Way nicer than I thought she would be when we first met. But you're still my best friend. That's not going to change.*

Isn't it?

I frown. *What does that mean?*

Giving me an unnerving, almost sadistic grin, she slams a hand down on the handle and flings the door open. *Come on. They're waiting for you.*

Who? I ask.

I receive no answer. I should have known better than to expect one. And maybe I *didn't* expect one. But I want one. I want all of them. I don't understand why Thea's here or how I can move or what's going on now or when all of this will end. Sometimes, I'm not even sure I remember why I'm doing this.

Then I step through the door.

As soon as my shoe hits the ground, I'm back in the graduation hall, standing on the third row of the bleachers. Every time someone moves, the benches whisper and shiver and creak beneath our feet.

I slowly raise my head. The pews and plastic chairs have been set up across the marble pavilion floor, but though all the seats are filled, both here and in the audience, every body is shapeless and every face is blank. Even my parents' chairs have been taken over by blobs.

Thea, the only discernible figure, has dropped my hand. As I study her, she lifts her chin, her eyes on the audience.

What are we doing here? I ask.

Do you remember what happened in this place?

I concentrate on her, my eyes locking onto the twin beauty marks beside her right ear. A part of me had been hoping the tunnel wouldn't have been able to recreate those spots. But of course it got this right. It knows everything.

She turns to me. *Do you?*

We graduated, I say flatly.

Well, you're not wrong. She bumps me with her hip. She feels frighteningly real. *Besides that, though. What did you—you specifically—do here?*

I squint. *I graduated?*

She sighs. *You can play dumb as much as you want. I'll just keep asking. It's not like I have anywhere else to be.* She cocks her head to the side, her hair tickling my arm. *Or do I?*

I swallow.

When we first got here, I thought this was going to be about Shun. The framed picture in his place. His mother's acceptance of his diploma. His cross, where his mother stood, her head bowed, her fingers crushing a tissue into her palm.

No, Thea says. *It's about me.*

Did you just read my mind? I ask.

Haven't we kind of been reading it this whole time? Isn't that kind of how all of this—she gestures vaguely to the entire auditorium—*is even possible?*

I shift my weight from one foot to the other. The bleachers creak. *I don't know. I have no clue how the tunnel knows any of this.*

Her laugh is like little white puffs flying out from the center of a dandelion. *Is that how you conceptualize it? "The tunnel." It sounds like an eldritch entity. An ancient god. A monster.*

I have no idea what it is. I pause. *Can you tell me?*

Oh, no. Definitely not. Her eyes narrow as she smirks. *I'm just a figment of your imagination, after all.*

Are you? Or are you a part of the tunnel's illusion?

There you go again. She waves a hand. *Look, I'm not here to talk to you about the tunnel and what it is or isn't. And you still haven't answered my question.* She tilts her head. *Do you remember what happened here?*

I look her in the eye. *I cried.*

She nods. *That's right. But why? Why did you cry?*

I hesitate. *It was an emotional time.* I cross my arms tightly over my chest. I realize, for the first time, I no longer have a heartbeat. *You cried too. Everyone did. Because of Shun.*

Thea purses her lips. *Okay, true. That's not what I mean, though.*

I know.

Do you need a reminder? She brushes her hair behind her ear and twists the strands around her index finger. *Something to jog your memory?*

Before I can speak, she blinks out of existence.

My stomach drops. Whirling around, I search the graduation hall for Thea. I leave my place and start pacing along the bleachers, my eyes running across the featureless faces of my classmates. Blank. Blank. Blank. Panic pushes at my lower ribs as I step out of my row and nearly stumble off the stage. If I had a heart, it would be hammering in my chest.

Here we are.

I spin around. Thea stands in the aisle, right in the middle of the audience. Leaning over, she plucks something from the lap of one of the faceless blobs. I take a step, but in the literal blink of an eye, she's back at my side, sitting on the edge of the low wooden stage. Swinging her legs, she looks up at me.

Do you know what this is? she asks.

I slowly ease myself down. *A very prolonged nightmare?*

Ha. She conks my knee with hers. *No. Take a look.*

Why? I've already seen it, I say.

She sets the commencement program on my thigh. I can feel the chill of her fingers even through my graduation dress. I focus on the faint sting of her touch as she says softly, *Read it.*

I reluctantly take a peek at the ivory cardstock. Unlike the real thing, which listed all four hundred of our names, along with a brief, two-to-six-word explanation of what we would be doing with our lives (*mission trip, University of Pennsylvania, employed at dead-end job*), this program shows only one name: *Cynthia Maddison – Columbia University.*

I swallow. *Is this supposed to be news? You've only been rambling about Columbia for the past, oh, ten million years or so?* I glance at her. *Congratulations, by the way.*

She laughs. *You're the worst.*

Hey, I say, shooting her a playful glare. *I'm not the one who's ditching this place for some stuffy New York school.*

We stare at each other for a moment.

So you do know what this is about, Thea says.

I look over my shoulder. There. I can still see the framed photo, right where Shun should be. Keeping my eyes on the photo, I say, *This isn't supposed to be about us.*

Why? Because I don't matter?

You do. You obviously do. I press my thumbnail into the program, leaving a crescent mark on the edge. *But you didn't—*

Die? she suggests, and though she doesn't even blink, I can't help but wince. *That's true, but our friendship could. And that scares you, doesn't it? The possibility of losing me.*

I don't say anything.

Here. She points to the program. *Look.*

I follow her finger, where a new line has appeared. On the real thing, my name is accompanied by the name of the state university. In this falsified memory, this living hallucination, there is only a curly question mark, typed out in the same fancy font as the rest of the program.

That's a little melodramatic, isn't it? I say.

Hey, I didn't make it. She studies my face, then nods. *Okay, let's go. I'm supposed to take you somewhere, but I'm making the executive decision to, uh, not do that. This way.*

What? I let her pull me to my feet. The program falls from my lap, then dissipates. I peer down at the naked floor. *Where are we going?*

She tugs me down the stairs. *If you come with me, you'll find out.*

I let her pull me along.

As soon as my sole hits the bottom step, the floor ripples, a shock wave pulsing out from beneath me. As the wave drains the graduation hall away, a familiar floor pushes its way to the surface. I watch as the auditorium morphs into my bedroom.

Thea releases my hand and plops down on the floor. She reaches for what looks like nothing, but as she pulls empty air into her lap, one of the pillows my parents keep in the closet materializes in her hands. She looks up, and just like that, she's back to her sixth-grade self, her face round and the edges of her jaw less defined.

What are you waiting for? she asks.

I don't know, I say. *I have no idea what we're doing.*

I sit beside her, my knee hitting the floor. She stretches out her fingers, and though I initially think she's trying to hold my hand, when she pulls away, she's holding my old game console, a familiar mark running along the side. I had always prided myself on the near-perfect condition of my electronics, so when I ended up scratching it somehow, I agonized over it for months. I still don't like looking at it.

It's funny, isn't it? Thea says, sliding my metallic stylus across the screen. *You were always way more into games than I was.*

I try to take a peek over her shoulder, but she angles the screen away. Frowning, I ask, *How is that funny?*

I guess it's not. She keeps rolling the ball of the stylus along the console, the motion lazy and slow. *Maybe it's more sad than anything.*

Sad, I repeat. *You think I'm sad?*

She gives me a look. *Is that a real question?*

I bite back some choice words. She may be nothing but an illusion, but I still don't want to fight with her. *What does any of this have to do with games?*

She rolls over onto her back and holds up the console. *So Shiori saw that memory of that game.*

I look away. *I guess.*

You're not sure how much she saw, though. Thea flips back over. *How much she knows.*

If she knew something about the game, she would've mentioned it.

Thea's eyes sparkle with bittersweet amusement. *You were always strangely proprietary of that game. You loved it so much, you didn't want anyone else to experience it the way you had. I mean, even when I asked about it, you were so tight-lipped. It was like you were afraid talking about it would ruin it.*

That's not true, I say. When her eyes flick to me, I add, *Okay, I was weird about it. But I didn't think telling you would "ruin it." It was special to me. I had never felt so seen by a game before.*

Uh-huh. She shakes her head. *At least you can admit you didn't want to share it. Not in any way that mattered.*

We don't speak for a moment. I scoot closer, hoping to catch a glimpse of the screen, but she spins around.

Are you mad at me? I ask her.

What, for not wanting to talk about the game? She shrugs. *It was special to you. That made it special to me too, even if I didn't understand it. And I thought about playing it without telling you, you know, but I didn't. Because somehow, that would've felt disrespectful to you.*

I hesitate. *How real are you? If you're just from my imagination, how can you know what the real Thea did or didn't do?*

She powers off the console—without saving, God help her—and flicks the lid closed. *Really? You're in a magical tunnel, on a mission to revive our classmate, and THIS is your question?*

I have a lot of questions. You haven't exactly answered any. I crawl over to her and lie beside her. *So can you at least tell me if you're real?*

She raises her eyebrows. *I'm as real as anything else here.*

That doesn't tell me anything. I breathe in. *Why are we here?*

In a while, I'm going to have to take you somewhere else. Thea hesitates. *It's not going to be easy. So I just wanted to bring you here for a while. Spend a little more time together. Even if you're not sure what's real or if either of us will remember this by the time you wake up.*

She reaches for my hand. It's cold and ghostly, but I take it and hold on anyway.

CHAPTER FOURTEEN
Most Likely to Jump into a Casket

WHEN THEA AND I first met, I didn't spend much time examining her face. We were usually in PE, after all, and as a general rule, it's rude and borderline creepy to watch people when you're both sweating and suffering under the tyrannical rule of a teacher equipped with a silver whistle and a half-eaten Twinkie.

Then, once Thea and I started seeking each other out before and after school, I started to memorize her. Some things I remembered intentionally: the color of her hair, cool tones lying beneath the flat, inky blackness; the flexibility of her limbs, which came in handy whenever something was just out of our reach and neither of us wanted to actually get up; the sound of her footsteps so I would know when to turn around and accuse her of attempting to sneak up on me. Others, like the way her hair curls when it rains, pressed themselves into my memory without my explicit acknowledgment. I know everyone has look-alikes, but there's something about Thea that no one could ever reproduce.

Aside from this figment of my imagination.

At some point over the course of our time together, she has aged, transforming from the soft sixth grader still clinging to her baby fat into the Thea I've come to know. Her hair is sleek and just a little curly, and her arms are long and sinewy. As she holds my gaze, her focus unwavering, I realize I haven't really *looked* at her in years.

Why are you staring at me like that? Thea asks now.

I feel like I haven't seen you much recently, I say, and though I expect her to tell me that's stupid, considering how much time we spent moaning about how we had to practice our standing and sitting in the weeks leading up to graduation, or even how many texts we've sent since commencement, that's not what she says at all.

Whose fault is that?

I pull back. *What do you mean?*

Do you really think I didn't notice? she asks. *You've been trying to extricate yourself from this friendship since I told you I got into Columbia.*

That's—I swallow. *I didn't*—

She waves a hand, forming a loose, lazy circle. *We can argue over semantics. Maybe you started withdrawing as soon as I told you I didn't want to stay here for college. Maybe you managed to hold out until graduation week. But we both know you've been doing everything you can to make this as painless as possible.*

I lie flat on my back and press my lips together, saying nothing. Partly because she isn't real. Mostly because, real or not, she's right.

I've let you get away with it, she says, *because I'm kind of scared too. I'm the only person in our class actually going to Columbia. Do you know how terrifying that is? When I visited, it was like I was in an entirely different universe.*

I know, I say. *You sent me pictures.*

Over winter break, while I sat at home and pretended to work on scholarship essays, Thea flew to Columbia University to explore the campus. It was hard to believe she was actually there. Our town may not be a total dump, but it's no New York

City. Every photo she sent me looked like it could have come straight out of a brochure.

I almost wanted to think she was faking. She wasn't really all the way in New York. The pictures she was texting me were all ripped from the internet, a way to throw me off the trail. She was actually checking out the local university and deciding it wasn't so bad after all. Once she got back, she would admit she was staying here with me. Of course she was. How could I have ever thought she would leave me?

Can you imagine going there alone? Thea asks.

I can't imagine going there at all, I say.

See, I never understood that. She sits up. *You've always been a good student. Sometimes, you got better grades than I did. Why didn't you ever try? For all you know, you could've come to Columbia with me.*

I stay on the floor. *I don't really want to get into this again.*

Well, I do. We both know we'll never bring it up in real life.

Then what's the point? I close my eyes, only to immediately open them again, afraid she'll disappear. *You're nothing more than a trick of the light. Duking it out with you now isn't going to change anything.*

Not for me, maybe. Her eyes dart to me, her mouth a thin, flat line. *But you won't even have this conversation with yourself.*

What conversation am I having? You're going. I'm staying. What else is there to say?

That's essentially what I told the guidance counselor. He kept encouraging me to at least consider applying to other schools, but I wasn't interested. I'm going to end up with a degree no matter where I go.

That's not what you really thought, Thea says.

I don't look at her. *What do you mean?*

You weren't just being cynical about your degree. She crosses her legs and leans against my bed, which, in a perfect re-creation of my sixth-grade room, has been left unmade, the blanket haphazardly tossed across the mattress. *You think no matter what happens next, you're still going to end up sad and directionless. You've felt that way ever since the* Bitter Mouse *incident.*

My stomach twists. *I don't want to talk about that.*

She gives me a small smile. *You don't want to talk about ANYTHING.*

Who said we even had to talk? I thought this was supposed to be our moment of rest and relaxation before you take me to God-knows-where to see God-knows-what.

She smiles again, pity lining the edges of her mouth. *We should go.*

I don't even bother asking questions. I just follow her lead, pulling myself up and crossing my arms over my chest. As we head for the door, she does a double take. A poster for one of the games I liked back then, a social simulation game where you served drinks and desserts to cute anthropomorphic animals to earn a living wage, has been stuck onto the closet door with blue painter's tape.

I remember that game, she says, her voice barely above a whisper. *I always liked the characters more than the actual gameplay. So whenever I came over, I would make you serve the customers and do the work. Then I would run around your town and talk to them until they started repeating the same lines.* She nudges me with her elbow. *Do you remember that?*

I laugh a little. *Obviously. I even drew the characters—*

On my birthday card that year. She tucks her hair behind her ear. *I still have it. I'm going to keep it for the rest of my life. Maybe I'll even bring it with me to Columbia and tape it to my wall or something.*

Please don't. It was a terrible drawing. I keep my eyes on the poster. *Besides, you don't need reminders of the past. You're supposed to be starting over, not dragging me behind you.*

I'm not dragging you anywhere. I'm carrying you. She pauses. *Now come on. Get out of here.*

I turn as she good-naturedly pushes me toward the door. Shivering at the chill of her fingertips, I ask, *You aren't coming with me?*

Her smile is pained. *I am. In a way.*

I take a breath, preparing to respond, but her hand comes down on my shoulder with a surprising amount of force. Her expression unchanged, Thea pushes me through the doorway and slams the door. I can actually feel the air spitting on my face.

I remain still for a few seconds, waiting for something to happen. I glance over my shoulder, but all I see is a wall. I turn and press a hand against it.

The door flies open to reveal a middle school Thea, her eyes watery.

What happened? I say.

Or, well, I try to. But no words come out.

Thea, I hear myself say. *I'm—I'm so sorry.*

Thea tightens her grip on the doorjamb. Her parents appear behind her, their figures blurry and indistinct. Despite our years of friendship, I never got all that close to her parents.

It's not like anything's wrong with them. I just couldn't let my guard down somehow. Thea's parents once told her they thought I was shy, which made her laugh so hard, she choked, then immediately texted me about it, which made *me* laugh so hard, I choked.

My mother steps out of the car and gives her condolences to Thea and her parents, then kisses me on the cheek and drives off. As Thea brings me inside to set my stuff down, I realize I remember all of this.

This is just another memory. One from the seventh grade. Thea's aunt has passed away. I'll be attending the funeral with Thea. Afterward, we'll have a sleepover, and while she'll return to her usual self by the time night falls, she'll spend the entirety of the funeral fidgeting and squirming and alternating between laughing nervously and crying hysterically.

When we arrive at the funeral home, we're greeted by a giant collage of photos glued onto a white posterboard and placed on a black easel. Thea points to one of the many identical faces on the collage and says, *That's my aunt*, as if maybe I couldn't have guessed. She holds her finger there, just under her aunt's pixelated jaw. Her hand begins to shake.

Thea, I say softly.

She shakes her head. *I'm fine. I just, you know.* Now her entire body is trembling.

I take a step closer and give her a hug. She wraps her arms around me and buries her face in my shoulder, her tears dripping down my hair.

We stay there for a little longer, then follow Thea's parents inside. The deeper into the funeral home we go, the more jittery I feel. Thea's parents warned me, on our way here, some people may jump into the open casket. I've never seen a dead person before. All my relatives who passed have been cremated.

The casket is beautiful dark mahogany with polished gold edges. As we stand in line to give our condolences, Thea bounces on her heels, her arms crossed. Goose bumps have risen on her skin. She pulls her shawl over her shoulders, but if anything, that only seems to agitate her more, her fingers tugging at the fabric.

I'm scared I'm going to throw up, she says suddenly. *Or faint.*

She raises her eyes to the stained glass. Blue and violet panels are set along the edges of a transparent cross. The evening light filters through the window, color whispering across the floor.

One of the women in line reaches the casket, takes one look at Thea's aunt, and bursts into soul-crushing sobs. The man with her has to hold her up as she sinks to her knees. I glance at Thea, but she and her parents are entirely unruffled. Not wanting to stare, I grit my teeth and lift my eyes to the stained glass.

When my uncle passed away, we had a small funeral. My mother cried, and that made me cry too. Everyone thought it was because I missed my uncle, but I barely knew anything about him, and the guilt of realizing I was at the funeral of a man I was supposed to be grieving but couldn't even really remember only made me cry harder.

The man drags the woman back to the pews. Thea's hand darts out from beneath her shawl and wraps around my wrist, fast as an eel. I jump a little.

We step forward. I take a deep breath, the heavy scent of incense already giving me a headache. I slowly lower my head and take a look at the body in the casket.

It's me.

Me on our graduation day, still in my dress. My skin has been leached of all color, my hair disturbingly dark in comparison. Only my upper half is visible, but my arms have been crossed over my chest, as if to guard my heart.

My eyes are wide open.

I reel back, suddenly regaining control of my body. I hit the first pew, but though I can feel the impact, there's no pain. I look up, expecting Thea to be right beside me, asking if I'm okay, but she's still standing beside the casket.

Thea, I say. *Thea. Oh my God, Thea. Thea.*

She looks over at me, her expression blank. *Come back here. You're being rude.*

That—that's ME, I say, raising a quivering hand and pointing at the casket.

What are you talking about? She frowns, and in the blink of an eye, I'm beside her again, standing over the casket. *That's not you.*

Yes, it is. I edge closer, intending to gesture to what is unmistakably my face.

But when I look down, my body is gone. The only thing remaining in the casket is a pair of cheap, rusty necklaces, the pendants hidden under the pillow.

I lean in and trace the loops of the chains with my fingertips until I reach the ends. When I pull out the necklaces, I find two matching pendants, each one half a broken heart. One says BEST. The other says FRIENDS.

You're terrified, Thea says.

I turn to her. Everyone else in the funeral home has disappeared, leaving us alone with the stained-glass cross.

You think you're going to lose me, Thea says. *Every day, you mentally prepare yourself for what's coming next. You keep telling people you're proud of me. And you are. But you also hate me for leaving.*

This isn't a secret, I say. *I've known that all along.*

Yeah, but you would never admit it. She shrugs. *I can't blame you. It's hard to acknowledge your own shortcomings.*

I narrow my eyes. *How is that a shortcoming? You're going to Columbia. I'm a little sad about it. That's not a flaw; it's a fact.*

A fact you don't want to accept. She takes my hand, her fingers icy, and leads me back to the entrance. I glance at the posterboard on the easel. Her aunt's collage has been replaced with photos of Thea and me. Just when I'm about to reach out and touch it, it rips itself in half and falls to the floor.

I shoot Thea an irritated look. *Could you be a little more tactful with the metaphors? At this point, you may as well be beating me over the head with that collage.*

I'm not doing anything, she says. *This is your mind, not mine.*

So what, then? I say. *You're trying to tell me Thea is completely fine with this? She's never sad about going away? You said it yourself, didn't you? It's scary.*

Of course it's scary. She tilts her head. *I don't remember ever saying I would be sad about it, and I certainly never promised I would miss you.*

You didn't. I try to pull out of her grasp, but her hold is tight. *The real Thea did, though.*

Because you always said something first.

I blink. Is that true? Is Thea only ever responding to what I say? Have I pressured her into telling me she'll miss me?

I shake my head to clear it. *That's not true. Thea and I have been best friends for years. She loves me. I know she does.*

Do I? Thea turns back, stopping right in the doorway. *Remember when you were telling me about the tunnel and you said you really loved me? I never said it back, did I? I never told you I loved you too.*

I close my eyes.

I was hoping she wouldn't mention that.

And what about when I get to Columbia? she continues. *Even if I DO love you now, while we're here, what happens afterward? Once I'm gone, who knows what will happen? I could have the time of my life at orientation and get an amazing roommate and make a ton of new friends. Friends who don't obsess over video games. Friends who don't hide the games they obsess over. Friends who don't break down over stupid pixels on a stupid screen made by stupid people who made stupid mistakes. Friends who actually know what they're doing with their lives.*

Wrong, I say. *College kids never know what they're doing with their lives.*

She rolls her eyes. *Do you seriously believe that? Or is that just something you read somewhere and decided to cling to because it made you feel better?*

I yank my arm back and run my fingers over the places her hand has touched. *You're not the real Thea. You can't hurt me.*

Maybe not. But you've already been hurting yourself. If you weren't so insecure, you wouldn't be here at this very moment.

I swallow. Hard.

She takes one step back, over the threshold. Then, with a small, malicious smile, she slams the door.

Holding back a sigh, I open the door. *That wasn't very nice.*

Thea turns around, her eyes wide. Innocence lines her face, softening her mouth. As she looks at me, her eyebrows pull together.

I'm sorry, she says. *Who are you, again?*

CHAPTER FIFTEEN
Most Damaged

I WAKE UP with a headache and a dried tear in the corner of my eye. I rub at it, ignoring the slight sting as the crust peels off my skin. When I glance over my shoulder, I catch a glimpse of something sparkling in the distance. The friendship necklaces, maybe, or the stained-glass window. I don't want to retrace my steps just to find out.

I get to my feet and cross my arms. It's colder than I remember. Not as cold as that imaginary Thea, maybe, but still chilly enough to make me wish I could have stolen her shawl.

It takes me a couple of minutes to find Shiori. It doesn't seem like she's moved since escaping her memories, splayed out on her back with her eyes on the ceiling. As I crouch beside her, I say, "The ground is probably pretty unsanitary."

She drops her arms over her eyes. "I don't care."

"Do you want to talk about it?"

She keeps her arms over her face. "How did I know you were going to say that?"

I don't respond. Every time a silence falls, it feels like a mourning. Like I'll turn my head and find my own casket waiting for me again.

"Did you see anything from my life?"

Her voice is startling in the darkness.

"No." I pause. "Did you see anything from mine?"

She shakes her head, dislodging one of her arms. Inch by inch, she pulls herself up and lets out a long breath. "What did you see?"

I study her face for a second. She has made no effort to wipe away the tear tracks, as if she's daring me to say something about them. Lowering my head, I say, "They weren't just memories. Some of them were, but sometimes, they were . . . something else."

Shiori's expression is grim. "I think mine were like that too. They were my memories, but at some point, they diverged from what I remember and started going rogue."

"Did you have control over yourself?" I ask. When she nods, I do too. "So the tunnel is changing things up on us. That must mean we're getting close."

"God, let's hope." She chews her lip. "What kinds of things did you see?"

I hesitate, but only for a second. "My best friend, mostly. She's going away for college. I think the tunnel knows I'm nervous about it. So it exploited that fear in every way it could." I set my elbows on my knees and lean my chin on my hand. "What about you?"

I expect her to say it's none of my business, but this time, she breathes in, her chest rising like dough, and says, "My boyfriend." Her eyes flick to me. "You know. The one you made out with."

My cheeks burn. "That wasn't my choice."

"But you're not complaining," she says. "Not that it matters. Like I said, we broke up not long afterward."

"What happened between you two?" I ask.

She glares at me. "Has anyone ever told you you're, like, insufferably nosy?"

I decide that's better left as a rhetorical question. I mean, the answer's yes, and I'm sure she knows it, but I'm not about to give her the satisfaction of a confirmation.

She sighs. "Fine. He was older. A senior when I was a junior. And even though it's not like we were the first ones to ever date outside our grade, he sometimes acted like we were. Like that one-year gap was as wide as the Grand Canyon."

"What would he do to make you feel that way?"

She takes another peek at me, as if to check if this is a trick question. "I don't know. He seemed to think I was immature."

I hesitate. I have the feeling that's true, but not for the reason she's implying.

"When I was in your memory," I say, because that's a normal way to start a sentence, "he was kind of pressuring you about certain things."

Her eyes widen. "Whoa. What kind of memories were *you* seeing?"

I blink, then wave my hands, my face hot. "No, no, no. I mean, like, driving and obeying your parents."

"Oh." She purses her lips. "Well, this is awkward."

Then she laughs. The sound hops around the tunnel, hitting the walls and bouncing back to us. I give her an unamused look, but that only makes her laugh harder.

"I'm glad you find this so funny," I mutter.

"You either find it funny or lose your mind." Crossing her arms, she pulls her backpack onto her lap. "But fine. Yeah. He thought I was immature because I couldn't drive then. And he thought I cared too much about what my parents thought. Or, well, what my mom thought. It was always about my mom."

I catch the conflicted look on her face. "I'm sorry."

"What?" She laughs again, but it's hollow. "Why are you apologizing? He just didn't get it. He never could. He cared about me and everything, but he could never understand."

I think of the first memory of hers I saw. The way her mother did everything for her. Softening my tone, I ask, "Did you ever agree with him, even a little?"

"About what?" She picks up the zipper of her bag and fiddles with the metal edges. "How come we're focusing on me? What about you?"

I had the feeling she was going to pull back. "What *about* me?"

"You saw your friend or something?" She speeds up, her hand blurring as she zips and unzips her backpack. The movements grow erratic, then manic. "What's going on there? What kind of nightmarish stuff did the tunnel show you?"

I drop my hand over hers, forcing her to go still. She tenses at first, then gradually relaxes. Taking my hand back, I say, "It really wasn't anything special. She's going to Columbia in the fall, and I'm sad about it."

Shiori crosses her arms, unimpressed. "Okay, but what *happened*? When you broke out of the memory and entered that weird dreamlike state, what did you do?"

"Well, at one point, I was in a casket."

Her jaw drops. "*What?*"

I give her a quick recap of what I saw, ending with the way Thea opened the door and no longer recognized me.

"Wow," Shiori says. "So the tunnel got, like, super psychoanalytical on you."

I turn my head. It didn't tell me anything I don't already know, deep down. But that doesn't make me feel any better about it. "I think we have to be careful. The tunnel suddenly switched things up on us, right when we were starting to get used to the memories. We need to be prepared for anything."

"How helpful." She resumes torturing her poor backpack zipper. "Too bad we have no idea what 'anything' could mean."

I get to my feet. She obviously isn't interested in speculating or debriefing with me. "Well, good luck."

"Hey," she says, and when I don't respond, she repeats it. "HEY. Where are you going? What, are you chickening out now? Ditching me? After everything?"

"What do you mean, 'after everything'?" I ask, whirling around to face her. "All you've done is *fight* me. Every time I try to talk things through with you, you shut me down. It's like I'm nothing but an annoying pop-up ad to you."

She opens her mouth, then closes it, her arms pulled tightly to her sides.

"I'm not leaving," I tell her. "I don't know if you care, but that's not even remotely a possibility for me now. It never was. I came here for a reason, and I'm not leaving until I know it's all over."

I pause, giving her a chance to speak, but she just stands there, silent.

Breathing out, I say, "I'm just trying to help, okay? And I know you've helped me too, with the granola bar and the water, but that's not enough anymore. I kept telling myself maybe you just needed time to adjust and learn to trust me, but at this point, it's like everything I say elicits some sassy, unhelpful response. So why don't we stop pretending we're friends and just finish this already?"

The dimness of the tunnel does nothing to disguise the hurt splashed across her face. I hold my breath, waiting for her to cuss me out and storm away, but she just keeps staring at me, her eyes dark and wide.

Then, in a tiny voice, she asks, "Do you want to know something?"

I don't respond immediately. I even consider simply walking away before we get ourselves into more trouble. But then I ask, in a voice almost as tiny as hers, "What?"

"After he broke up with me, I kind of . . . lost it. Just a little. I didn't, like, bust the windows of his car or sneak into his house and replace his shampoo with Nair or anything, but I started questioning things. Mostly my mom. My relationship with her."

I study her face. "What about it?"

She chews her lip, reopening old wounds. "You know how it is down here? How, when you take a step, you never know if you're safe or if everything will come crashing down around you?" A breath skitters out from between her lips, as if she's not quite sure she's really telling me this. "That's what it was like with her."

I slowly ease myself back down beside her. "She had a temper?"

"We all have tempers." Her fingers find the zipper again, but this time, she just sets her thumb over the pull tab. "She had a scary one. But she wasn't a bad person. She was the best mother ever."

Wouldn't we all think that if we only had one mother as our reference?

"Everything she ever did was for me," Shiori says. "For my protection. She had been through so much as a kid. She told me some things. I heard about some others. And there were, I'm sure, a million things she never said. So when she had me, she decided she would do everything her parents didn't."

I get that. I've always had the feeling my mother was afraid of doing the same thing, of being the parent she wished she could have had, only to overcompensate and fail me in some other life-ruining way. It would have been so easy to let me do whatever I wanted, even if it meant allowing me to become a voracious, capricious, recalcitrant monster. Yet at the same time, she had to be careful not to smother me or push her aspirations and expectations onto me, turning me into the human embodiment of all her broken dreams.

I sometimes think that's why she was so upset with my father when he scolded her for taking me to see my uncle. She had been trying so hard for so long. The thought of having ruined it, of having ruined *me*, must have devastated her.

"For a while," Shiori says softly, "I lost sight of that. I forgot why my mom would act the way she did. Why she treated me like a baby, even when I was almost done with high school. So I pushed her away and convinced my dad to take me to get my permit. My mom nearly lost her mind when she found out what we had done."

I tilt my head. "Was she upset because you had gotten your permit? Or because she wasn't the one to take you?"

"I don't know. Both? But that's not the point. I got my permit and started trying to be more self-sufficient, and I—"

I wait for a minute, but she doesn't continue.

"You don't have to tell me," I say.

"I want to," she says—but even those three words are strangled, squeezed out by tired hands.

Without really thinking, I press my knee to hers. She startles at the movement but doesn't pull away.

"I thought getting my permit would fix everything," she says. "And it did, at first. When I got my permit, we had this long talk about boundaries and I told her I wanted a little more independence."

She falls silent again.

"Did it work?" I ask.

She nods. "Before, my mom would drop me off right before school and would be there, idling in the parking lot, by the time it ended. But then she started letting me stay later if I wanted, and just like that, I made friends."

I try not to frown.

"Don't look at me like that," she says. "It's not like I didn't have *any* friends before. It was just hard. She didn't like when I slept over at other people's houses, and my friends didn't like being at my house because they thought my mom was too strict.

"If I just stayed at school, though," she continues, "my friends didn't have to know anything about my mom. Most of them didn't even realize my mom was still picking me up. I had to come up with a lot of reasons why I couldn't give people rides home, and I would have to time everything perfectly so I could run to my mom's car without being seen, but that was okay with me."

"That seems like a lot of work, though."

She shakes her head. "It was freeing. I had never been in extracurricular activities, aside from ones my mom and I could do together, and even then, I think she only did them because she thought volunteering at shelters would look good on my college applications, not because she genuinely wanted to help."

She puts a hand over her mouth.

"Oh my God," she whispers. "I can't believe I said that."

I wave a hand. "It's—"

"It's *not* okay." She grabs her zipper and tugs it so hard, I'm afraid she's going to break it. "My mom was a good person. A *great* person. I know how I'm making it sound, but it wasn't so bad. When I was a good daughter."

"A good daughter?" I echo.

She nods too hard, her lavender hair bouncing along her shoulders. "When I listened to her. Life was fine, before I got my permit. It should've stayed that way."

I look away. I feel so sad for her. I'm sure she would slap me if she knew, but I can't help it. There's something very off about this, and the more we discuss it, the more obvious it is.

She's still yanking at the zipper with reckless abandon.

"When did you join your school's Japanese Club?" I ask.

Her hand slows. "Right around then."

"Junior year," I say, and she nods. "So what did you think, then, when you met up with the club president from my school?"

She gives me a blank look.

"I saw him in the first memory of yours, when you went to a festival with your mom. You were both younger then, but it was obviously Natsuki."

She sets her teeth on her lip. "What do you want me to tell you?"

"I don't know. The truth?"

"The truth," she repeats. "Okay, well, I thought, 'Oh, hey, it's that boy I knew a long time ago. He looks so grown-up now. Much more grown-up than I feel. And he knows what he's doing. No surprise there.'"

"Did you still have feelings for him?"

She narrows her eyes. "What?"

I narrow my eyes right back. "Oh, come on. I was in your body, remember? I know how you felt back then."

"Oh? Do you?" She leans forward, the ends of her hair swaying and sweeping along her kneecaps. "Tell me, then. How did I feel about him?"

"You liked him."

She gives me a tight smile. "I liked what he represented. And you can call me pretentious if you want, but that won't make it any less true."

"I wasn't going to say anything," I tell her, though frankly, I did kind of think she was spouting English-class,

I-didn't-read-the-chapter-so-I'm-going-to-drop-the-word-*represented*-and-hope-that's-good-enough BS.

"He always seemed so strong," Shiori says, "and so self-assured, and it made me realize how—how helpless I am. How much I've had to depend on my mom. And even if—*if*—I ever had any feelings for him, I never could have done anything about it."

I hesitate. "Why not?"

"Because." She lets go of the zipper. It shivers, then goes still. "No one would ever want someone as needy and damaged as I am."

A pang of sympathy strikes me in the chest.

"You're not needy or damaged," I tell her. "You were sheltered. That's all."

"Oh, yeah?" Her nostrils flare with her sharp intake of breath. "You wanna bet?"

I take a breath too, as if to prepare myself for a long-winded ramble or, God forbid, a motivational speech. But all I manage to say is: "What?"

She gives me a small smile. "You want to know how my mom died?"

I blink. "You told me. A car crash."

"Right." Her smile widens. "You want to know how my mom *really* died?"

No. I don't think I do.

She leans in. A strand of her lavender hair springs out from over her shoulder. I watch it as it plays with the feeble light of the tunnel. I'm so busy staring at it, I almost miss the three words she says next.

"I killed her."

CHAPTER SIXTEEN
Most Self-Sacrificing

FOR THE FIRST few seconds after she's said it, I can't do anything. I'm not sure I even breathe.

I killed her, she said, and in the dimness of the tunnel, her eyes seemed to glow.

My eyes rise to her face. She's transfixed, her gaze hungry as she waits for me to respond. It's like she *wants* me to react in the most overblown way possible.

So maybe that's why I just look at her and say, "I don't think that's true."

She pulls her mouth to one side, disappointment gleaming in her eyes. "More like you don't want to believe it is."

"The real question," I say, still working to maintain my poker face, "is why you want *me* to believe it is."

She rolls her eyes. "Enough with the psychoanalysis already."

"Why are you so intent on making yourself out to be a monster?"

She pushes her lips into a moue. She's beginning to remind me of the tunnel's version of Thea. "The real question—as you would say—is why you won't just believe I'm a monster. I mean, are you *that* convinced I'm a good person?"

"Frankly? No. But," I say, raising an index finger to silence her, "there's no way you would've held it in for this long."

"Why not? Maybe I just didn't want to face it, and now,

after all of this"—she flings her arms out—"I have no choice but to accept it."

She starts tugging at her backpack zipper again. It takes all my willpower not to confiscate her bag and throw it as far as I can.

"Go on," she says. "Tell me what you're thinking."

My mind circles back to the house I saw in her first memory, the locks pure and untouched.

No one has ever gotten close enough to see all the things she's been keeping locked up.

"You want me to say you're bad," I say. "Yet you also want me to say you're good. You want me to tell you I don't believe you murdered your mother in cold blood. Which I don't."

Her eyes narrow. The *zerk-zerk-zerk* of her zipper keeps time like a metronome.

"But," I continue, "you feel responsible for your mother's death. You blame yourself but can't handle the burden of it, and that's why you're so convinced everything is your fault. More than that, that's why you're down here, trying to save your mother."

With every passing second, Shiori's mouth has gotten smaller and smaller, a dry, pale bud holding in all the words she can't bring herself to say. Even once I've finished speaking, she doesn't say anything for a good five seconds, forcing us to stare at each other in a tense, crackling silence.

Then she says, "You're so self-righteous."

I blink. A draft breathes its way through the tunnel, leaving a trail of goose bumps in its wake. "What?"

"Just because you saw, what, two of my memories, you're convinced you know everything about me?"

"I never said that. You asked me what I was thinking, so I told you."

As she grabs the zipper of her backpack, I wonder if the tunnel is influencing her somehow. When we first started seeing our memories, she seemed a little shaken but managed to keep her emotions in check. Now I can practically feel the turbulence stirring in her stomach.

"I don't know what happened to your mother," I say. "I'm not asking you to tell me, and I'm not claiming to understand any of it. But I don't think you deserve to carry this guilt, especially considering everything you're putting yourself through now."

Shiori plays with the zipper for two more seconds, then stands. Her bag falls to her feet. I start to reach for it, but she snatches it up and clasps it to her chest.

"This has been a waste of time," she says. "I'm leaving. You should too."

I stay on the ground.

A couple of years ago, I would have wanted to accuse her of being difficult. She's cruel. She's irrational. She's manipulative.

But I've learned what grief can do to people. *Grief* is cruel. *Grief* is irrational. *Grief* is manipulative. It can change the most levelheaded person into a screaming, weeping, lifeless mess. Add in the pressure of the memories and the fear of doing this all for nothing, and you've got a total disaster on your hands.

"Shiori," I call out. She's already at least twenty feet away, not even slowing at the sound of my voice, but I know she hears me. "I'll see you soon. Don't give up."

She stops. Slowly, without moving her feet, she looks over her shoulder. Her eyes glisten. Then she turns back around and disappears.

AFTER THIS LAST round of twisted memories and warped visions of the future, I don't know what to expect. For all I know, Eli's going to appear in the form of Edgar Allan Poe and ask me the difference between a raven and a writing desk, then lead me on a search to find rabbit-sized versions of those girls who threw my clothes over the locker room beams.

But when the tunnel finally drags me down and drops me into the middle of nothingness, it's not Eli I see; it's my grandfather.

He looks exactly as he does in the single picture I've seen of him, down to the faded colors, his face unnaturally pale and his shoulder crinkled from that time my mom accidentally smashed the edge of the photo with the album cover. When he tries to smile, it looks the slightest bit off, like an AI program is struggling to rearrange his features in its database.

Monika, he says. *Do you remember me?*

Not really. He passed away when I was young. I have the faintest memory of sitting in his old chair and watching cartoons on a square TV, but I was still a shy little kid, and he had long forgotten how to talk to children. Even when my mom would encourage him to spend more time with me, warning him I would be the only grandchild he would get, he would just nod and stare at me for a minute, his eyes dark.

We didn't get much time together, I say to him.

No. We didn't. He studies me. *Do you wish we had?*

I don't know. I pause. *I mean, yes. Of course I do. My mom misses you all the time. Whenever your birthday comes around, she tells a story about you. It's usually the same one, but I listen to it anyway.*

He nods. *I know.*

So there's consciousness after death, I say.

He doesn't answer, instead taking a look around. At first, there's only darkness. Slowly, though, every place his eyes touch comes alive. There's the chair. The TV. The low table, which he insisted on sitting at long after he should have. My mom would always tell him to just give up and use a regular table so he wouldn't hurt his knees, but he would wave her off, his mouth set in a determined grimace.

You're eighteen now, my grandfather says. *Aren't you?*

I nod. *I just graduated.*

Ah. He lets out a breath. *I remember my graduation.*

My eyes flick around the room and latch onto the door to the right. An exit, maybe, or a portal to something even worse.

I grew up in a small town, he says, *so the ceremony was rather underwhelming. My parents were, I believe, quite disappointed. They had come from the metropolitan area of Japan, so they were used to more formal graduations.*

I can't stop myself from frowning. I don't know how much of this is scrounged up from my memories and how much is from the tunnel. Maybe my grandfather's spirit really *is* here. How am I supposed to know for sure?

Are you in on this? I ask him.

He blinks. His skin is leathery and spotted, and every time he moves, the marks seem to leap across his face. *In on what?*

This tunnel thing. I sit on the carpet. As if I've given him his cue, he crosses the room and eases himself onto his chair. *Do you know what's happening?*

Ah. He reaches into the pocket of his shirt and pulls out a pack of cigarettes. Sliding out a thin tube, he sits up and scans the room, then gestures to the coffee table, his palm facing up. *Hand me that lighter, would you?*

I glance over at the plastic lighter. *I don't think you should smoke in here.*

He grunts and sticks the cigarette between his teeth. *And why not?*

Because smoking is bad for you.

His laugh is harsh. *I'm already dead. What is it gonna do to me? This is all in your mind anyway. You're not gonna get lung cancer from a hallucination.*

I cross my arms. *You can smoke when this is over.*

He shakes his head. *You're just like your mother.*

I turn back to the lighter. It's a translucent blue, giving me a good look into its inner mechanisms.

She hated cigarettes, you know, my grandfather says. *Always frowned when I lit one.*

I think I remember. Sometimes, when we came over, my mom would start cleaning the living room, her brow furrowing every time she came across a pack or a lighter.

Even brought me some posters about it, my grandfather continues. *It was annoying as hell, for sure, but kind of endearing too.* He coughs out a laugh and takes the cigarette from his lips. *Guess you could say the same about me.*

I don't smile. *Why are we here?*

He leans back in his chair. *We're here because you went into the tunnel.*

What does that have to do with you?

He laughs again. The sound is jarring, almost frightening, like the bark of a seal or the clap of thunder. *According to you, this tunnel can bring people back from the dead.*

That's the rumor, I say.

One you believe in, he shoots back. *So if you're gonna revive someone, why didn't you ever even consider choosing me?*

I open my mouth, then close it. *You?*

I expect him to laugh again, but he remains entirely serious, his heavy-lidded eyes glued to me. *Why not? We hardly got any time together. You can barely remember my face. And you just told me, didn't you? Your mother misses me.*

I fidget, pulling my sleeve. *Well, yes, but—*

My life wasn't even really mine.

I raise my head. *What do you mean?*

He pulls the cardboard box back out of his shirt pocket and drops the cigarette back in. *When I was young, I lived for my parents. They'd gone through the trouble of uprooting their lives in Japan and moving to America, all in the hopes of giving me something they thought we couldn't get there.*

What did they want to give you? I ask.

He shrugs. *Hell if I know. Maybe they, like so many others, were caught up in the idea of that old lie. "The American Dream."*

Is that what I'm living? The American Dream? Nowadays, it feels more like the American Nightmare.

We lived on a farm, my grandfather continues, *and I would have to help out every single day. Sometimes, I would recite words and formulas while digging up weeds. All so I could make my parents proud. I mean, I didn't care about school. I never thought about my own future. It was for them. Always for them.*

I think back to my conversation with Shiori. Families can become so dysfunctional, even when all the people involved think they're making sacrifices for someone else.

That must have been hard, I say.

It was. He shakes his head. *But it was nothing compared to what I fought for next.*

I don't have to ask. *The country.*

I don't even know which war he fought in, really. Whenever anyone referenced it, it was just *the War*, and I was too young to know there had ever been more than one. I was, however, old enough to be told I was not allowed to ask about it. I could listen if he brought it up, but if he didn't, I was not to broach the subject.

I'm not gonna bore you with the details, he says. *If you ask me—and I say this knowing no one ever DID ask—all war stories are the same. They're all ugly. They're all bloody. They're all gonna end with broken homes. Broken leaders. Broken families. Broken bodies. Broken minds. That's why there's no point in talking about it.*

I don't think that's the reason he refused to discuss it, but I let it go. I can't pretend to be an expert in war. I definitely can't tell him how to feel about it.

That's how I found out "The American Dream" is nothing but an illusion, he says.

I lower my head. *I'm sorry you had to go through that.*

He waves a hand. *That's what everyone says.*

Maybe that's how everyone *feels*. We're all sorry something was built up, was promised, was fabricated. We're sorry it was disappointing. We're sorry we're benefitting from it when others have suffered.

Regardless, he says, *once that was over, I dedicated my everything to my wife, then my family. They were all I had to live for.*

My mom has said something similar. She told me he never seemed happy unless the whole family was together. Yet even then, there would be an unshakable sense of melancholia, as if he felt something was missing.

I never got to know true happiness, my grandfather says. *I thought I had it when I married your grandmother. When I held your mother for the first time. When my son fell asleep on my shoulder.*

I stiffen at the mention of my uncle. It's difficult to remember he was ever a child. To me, he has always been as he was when he was on other side of the glass, never older, never younger, forever frozen in time.

Why not? my grandfather asks.

I look up. *Why not what?*

Why not me? He places a hand over his heart. The cigarettes rustle in his shirt pocket. *If you get to the end of this, why not bring me back to life?*

My stomach drops. *Well, you were—*

Old? His smile is pained. *Past my prime?*

And there are no guarantees, I add. *Of the rumor being true, obviously, but also of the logistics. What if I brought you back, but you were still as sick as you were, in the end? Besides, bringing you back wouldn't do anything to change your past. It wouldn't erase the bad memories or help you live for yourself instead of others. Whatever life you would have left would be marred by all the things I COULDN'T fix, even with the tunnel.*

He rests his head against the back of his chair, raising his eyes to the ceiling. *If you're gonna turn me down, the least you can do is be honest about it.*

His words sting my chest. I bring a hand to my heart like I think I can actually feel the barb. *What do you mean?*

He kicks his feet up onto the table. I wait for a *clank*, but his heels land soundlessly on the edge. *You're not gonna choose me? Fine. But don't pretend you're doing it for me.*

I recoil. *But I—*

You know what you're doing when you say things like that? He takes out his pack of cigarettes and shakes it. *Trying to live for me. Trying to live to please me. Or maybe those two are the same thing.*

I shake my head. *I'm not—*

Look me in the eye, he says, *and tell me why you really can't choose me.*

I keep my head turned. *Why? It seems like you already know.*

Maybe. His voice softens just a bit. *But I'm old and tired and dead. So humor me, won't you?*

Slowly, I pivot until I'm facing him. If I could have a heartbeat here, it would be pounding in my ears. In a quiet but firm voice, I say, *I still wish you could have had a better life. I miss you every time my mom brings you up, and I feel guilty for not knowing you better. This is the deepest conversation we've ever had, and I'm not even sure you'll really remember it.*

But I can't, I say. *I can't choose you, because if I make it to the end, and if the myth is true, you're not the one. Before this, I wouldn't have even thought of you. I'm sorry.*

He shrugs. *At least you're telling the truth now.*

I keep holding his gaze. *For whatever it's worth, though? I'm really glad I was able to see you again. I love you.*

He blinks. His thick silver eyebrows pull together, then edge back into place. *I—I love you too.* He clears his throat. *Now get out of here. You've still got a ways to go.*

Where am I going? I ask.

I never get an answer. The ground falls out from beneath me, plunging me into nothingness.

His face lingers in my mind like the scent of cigarettes.

CHAPTER SEVENTEEN
Most Regretful

WHEN I OPEN my eyes, I'm flat on my back, staring up at something blurry hanging above me, just out of reach. I squint, trying to get myself to focus. It looks like a white spider, plastic arms spread wide. Pastel-colored plush toys dangle from each piece.

Is that a mobile? Am I a baby?

We are all babies.

I bolt upright at the sound of an unfamiliar voice, just barely avoiding a head-on collision with the mobile. Wincing, I scoot away. When I turn to survey my surroundings, I find myself on a regular twin mattress. The only strange thing, aside from the mobile attached to nothing, is the white gate running around the rim of the bed.

I'm in a crib.

You are a baby, the voice says. *The child of your parents, each of whom was a baby. I was a baby too. Just because we grow up doesn't mean we stop being someone's baby.*

I scan the area, but aside from my makeshift crib, there's nothing but shadow. *Where are you?*

Never far, she says, and though I'm sure this is meant to be reassuring, it feels more like a threat.

Don't be afraid, the voice says. *You're safe here.*

A chill sweeps along my spine. *I would feel a lot safer if I knew who you were.*

Monika, she breathes. Then she laughs a little. *I was the one to suggest writing it that way. With a "K," so it could be easily translated into katakana. Of course, it doesn't sound quite the same if you pronounce it using Japanese syllables, but still. Your grandpa kept worrying you would be too "American," so I made the suggestion.*

I watch as the shadows melt away, leaving my maternal grandmother in its wake. She sits in an old-fashioned rocking chair, her elbows placed on the armrests.

I don't have many memories of my grandmother. She was usually out when my mom and I visited my grandfather, either spending the day with friends or volunteering. I could tell, even then, my mother hated it. When she thought I wasn't listening, she would tell her father, *I wish she could have at least had the decency to tell me she wasn't going to be around.*

You know how she is, my grandfather would say. *She's gonna do what she wants, when she wants, and nothing you do will stop her.*

After he passed away, my mom worked to coordinate visits with her mother. Most of the time, something went awry: My grandmother had a church luncheon, or one of her friends was stopping by for only that one afternoon, or she had agreed to watch a friend's grandchild.

What about YOUR grandchild? my mom shouted once. *Your own child's child. When are you going to watch HER?*

Lowering her voice, my grandmother says, *I remember how, after my husband passed away, your mother would bring you over to the house. You were young then, barely able to write. You learned to read early, but writing was much harder for you.*

That sounds about right. I struggled to grip the pencil and form anything besides scribbles. Even now, I hold my writing utensils wrong. I've spent years trying to correct myself, buying rubber grips and watching actual videos on how to use a pen, but it's too late. There's no fixing it.

I gave you a few sheets of paper and a pencil, my grandmother says, *and you went to town. I thought maybe you were making up a story, but as it turns out, you were just writing your name over and over again.*

I stay silent. Behind me, the mobile spins in a small, lazy circle.

Do you remember this? my grandmother asks. When I shake my head, she gives me a sad smile. *That's probably for the best.*

Why? I ask. *What happened?*

Your name, she says. *You were spelling it wrong. With a "C" instead of a "K."*

Most people assume it's with a *C*. Even Thea would get it wrong sometimes, when we first became friends. I did the same thing, though. When she told me her real name is Cynthia, I assumed I was supposed to spell her nickname with an *I*.

I got so frustrated with you, my grandmother says.

Frowning, I turn back to her. *Because I spelled my name wrong? Wasn't I, like, four?*

She sighs. *It was soon after my husband died. I was a wreck. I didn't even want to see your mother anymore because all she did was remind me of him. And oh, I hated seeing your name written like that. It felt like one of the few things I had left of your grandfather, one of the last marks he had made on the world, and even though I knew it was irrational to be upset with a child—my own granddaughter—I couldn't help it.*

What did you do? I ask, my voice hushed.

I started yelling. She bows her head, her shoulders hunched. *You instantly burst into tears. You must have been so scared. Until then, I had barely even spoken to you.*

I still don't quite remember this. I could almost believe she's mistaken. She must have been thinking of someone else. She isn't my grandmother at all.

But the chagrin smeared across her face like chalk on a board tells me this has to be real.

A weak smile sneaks onto her face. *Your mother shouted right back at me. I don't even know what she had been doing—cleaning, if I had to guess; that woman was convinced I was living in a constant state of filth—but she ran right into the room, got in my face, and gave me a real talking-to.*

I close my eyes for a moment. I remember that part. My mom came flying out of the bedroom, a duster still in her hand. In my child mind, she was a superhero, swooping in to rescue me from the ashen woman grabbing my pencil and correcting my writing with a slash through each *C. moniKa. moniKa. moniKa.*

I don't think I had ever seen her like that, even when she was a teenager, my grandmother says. *And she was quite the nightmare then, let me tell you.*

My mom has always been headstrong. It must be genetic. I did, after all, dive right into an abandoned, potentially haunted, definitely paranormal tunnel with barely any hesitation.

Your mother swept you off your feet, stuck her finger in my face, and said, "You're never seeing your granddaughter again. Not until you get your act together."

My grandmother chuckles, the sound low in her throat. *I was so surprised. I had never seen her like that before. But then again, I suppose she had never seen ME like that before either. Not with you.*

My mom wept on the way home. I kept asking her what was wrong, how I could help, but that only seemed to further upset her. When we stepped into the apartment, my dad shouted from another room, *How was it?*

She cried for hours.

She didn't talk to me for a long time, my grandmother says, her fingers interlaced in her lap. *I don't blame her, of course. I didn't even then. I kept telling her I was sorry, but she no longer wanted me around you.*

I already felt like a failure as a grandmother, she continues, *and God knows I had failed as a mother long ago. But I tried anyway. I really did.*

My grandmother's exhalation is long and fatigued. *You remember your uncle, don't you?*

For a split second, I'm back in the visiting room, my hand on the pane, my breath fogging up the glass. *Of course I do.*

I turned all my attention to him. My grandmother pauses. *Well, perhaps that isn't true. I'm afraid I was always more devoted to him than I was to your mother.*

I don't say anything, but I'm glad she acknowledged it. My mom spent a lot of time struggling with that fact. I think a part of her still does. Even her memorials to her mother seem just a little off. They aren't half-hearted or insincere; they're tainted, as if there's a bitterness she can't swallow, even after all these years.

He needed me, my grandmother says. *He was the baby of the family, and almost from the very beginning, he struggled. Not just with addiction. With everything. The world, I thought, wasn't built for a boy like him.*

Was it built for any of us? I ask.

She starts to speak, then changes her mind, her fingers worrying the edge of her collar. She's wearing a long-sleeved nightgown, pale pink with tiny flowers dancing across the fabric. It is, I realize, what she's wearing in an old photograph from when she brought my uncle home from the hospital, days after his birth. My mom is in the picture too, but she's already been pushed off to the side, barely more than a blur in the corner.

Your mother didn't seem to need me, my grandmother says. *Not the way my son did.*

Yeah, and look where all that help got him.

My grandmother sighs. *When the judge handed down that prison sentence, I wanted to march up to her, sitting so high and mighty in that black robe of hers, and scream at her, the way your mother had screamed at me.*

I know that would have been wrong, though. You hadn't done anything bad. But my son . . . my son had. And that killed me. She pauses. *For a while, after he was incarcerated, I couldn't see him.*

You mean you didn't, I say, because I know she could have.

She closes her eyes and turns her cheek, as if I've spit in her face. *I tried. I made it all the way to the car. But I just couldn't. I couldn't see him like that.*

So you abandoned him, I say through my teeth. *Your son. The one you said you loved so much. You just left him there.*

I wrote him letters, she says, her voice weak. *And when he was released to the rehabilitation facility, I reconnected with him. I was there all the time. I promised him I would be the mother he had always deserved.*

She hadn't been the one my own mom had deserved, though. As far as I know, even after my uncle's release, my mom and her mother barely spoke. My mom said when they talked on the phone, it was like her mother was timing their conversations, always begging off after twenty minutes.

I promised him, my grandmother whispers. *So why did it have to happen?*

The overdose, like so much else about my uncle, was kept from me. The day it happened, my grandmother called my mom, who left work and called my dad from the parking lot of my uncle's apartment. My dad offered to meet her there, but she refused. She just wanted him to pick me up after my summer classes finished.

After my uncle's death, my grandmother distanced herself again. All my mom could say was: *Typical. This is so typical of her. I shouldn't even be disappointed anymore. In fact, I'm not. I expected this. I really did. Because of course she couldn't be the type of person who realizes what she lost and what she still has and goes, "Oh, maybe I SHOULDN'T alienate the family members I have left. Maybe I should be a good mother, a good grandmother, a good mother-in-law for once." Of course she couldn't do that. Why am I surprised?*

Just give her time, my dad said. *She might still come around.*

She didn't.

Because before my uncle's funeral, my grandmother passed away.

Do you ever think, my grandmother says softly, *you would give everything you had just to be able to take back all your mistakes?*

I don't respond. I don't think she's actually expecting an answer. Even if I gave her one, I'm not sure she would hear it.

I wish I could start over, she says. *I wished it for so many years. The very first time I made your mother cry, when I bumped her head on that stupid mobile, I thought, "I wish I could do this all over again. I wish I could erase all the pain and protect her better this time."*

But you didn't, I say, and she winces. *You may not have been able to unhit her head, but you could have apologized afterward. You could have asked for her forgiveness. You could have been there to heal the hurt the next time something happened.*

The white barrier of the crib lowers, then disappears. I run my hand along the naked edge of the mattress. When I look up, my grandmother is right beside me, her eyes wide.

That's why you're here, she says. *You can bring me back to life, can't you?*

My shoulders tense. *Well, I—*

If you save me, I can fix things. With your mother. With you. I can be everything you want me to be. How couldn't I? I would literally owe you my life.

But I—

Please. I made a mistake. I made many. But it doesn't have to end here. Let me try again.

I watch her, sadness pooling in my ribs. *I'm sorry.*

No, no, no. Don't apologize. She clasps her hands together and kneels in front of the bed like she's about to say a prayer. *Just help me. Please.*

I'm sorry, I say again. *If there's any merit to the rumors, I already know the person I'm choosing. I can't change my mind.*

You can, she says. *You can. You won't regret it. I promise.*

I can't, I say. *I'm sorry.*

Then can you tell her? she asks, her voice breaking. *Tell her I wish I could have done things differently.*

I search her face. She searches mine. She looks just the way she did the last time I saw her, aside from the nightgown. But I am an entirely different person to her.

Okay, I say. *I'll tell her.*

She closes her eyes. I can see the tiny pale veins branching out along her lids.

And I'm sorry, I say. *I'm sorry I couldn't choose you.*

She gives me a sad smile. *I'm sorry too, Monika. For what comes next.*

I open my mouth, but before I can speak, the mattress gives out beneath me.

And I fall.

CHAPTER EIGHTEEN
Most Improved

I FALL. AND fall. And fall. I fall for such a long time, I begin to think I've soft-locked myself, the way I did before the final boss of a game I played back in elementary school and never managed to beat.

Maybe this is the end. Maybe I was supposed to have chosen my grandmother, and because I didn't, I've failed the test. I've doomed myself to fall for the rest of eternity. Maybe if I close my eyes, it'll all be over.

You're not giving up now, are you, kiddo?

I lift my head.

My uncle sits behind the glass, his orange uniform bright against the faded walls. Almost everything is exactly as it was in my memory. Even the guard is here, his spine straight and his expression passive. I am the only thing that's different.

I can't believe you're here, I say to him.

He smiles faintly. *Me neither. I just wish it were under better circumstances.*

He keeps grinning, as if he expects me to laugh, but I can't. I just stare at him, trying to commit him to memory. Before entering the tunnel, I hadn't thought about him for so long. Now I feel like I'll never be able to get him off my mind.

It's funny, he says. *There were lots of times when I thought I was going to die.*

I flinch at the word.

When I was like this, he says, gesturing to his uniform, *I was always afraid something was going to happen to me. Whenever I was pulled over or got busted or spiraled out of control, I thought, "This is it."*

I look away. I don't really want to hear this.

But it happened when I least expected it. He closes his eyes, his lids almost translucent. *It happened when I was finally getting better.*

I can't recall exactly how my mom reacted when she learned her brother was being transported to a rehab facility. If she was excited or relieved or skeptical. If, when she learned he had completed treatment, she fought for him to stay there for just a little longer, or if she, like the caseworker and my grandmother and even the rehab facility people, thought he was ready to return to the outside world.

It happens more often than you'd think. I sound distant. Clinical. *After remaining sober for a while, people—*

Addicts.

—people, I repeat, louder this time, *will go back to their usual dose, only to learn their body's tolerance has dropped.*

His mouth twists, pain warping the edges of his lips. *You've done your research.*

I don't say anything. I've spent my whole life attracted to anything related to addiction, grief, and, later, dissociation, the whispers of generational trauma leading me to ask, over and over, what happened to my family. Why we fell apart.

Do you think, he says softly, *if not for me, you wouldn't have played that game?*

My stomach clenches. *What game?*

*You know. The one with the—*he places his hands on either side of his face and wiggles his fingers—*that thing.*

I can't help but laugh. *Mouse?*

That's it. He grins. *The old brain ain't what it used to be.*

I let my smile cling to my face for a moment longer. Then it drops away. *I don't know. Maybe. Maybe I never would've thought to play it.*

What was it called? He scratches his chin, his fingernails making a *scritch-scritch* sound against his stubble. *Was it* Sour Mouse*?*

It was Bitter Mouse, *actually*, I say. *Sour Mouth was the name of the company.*

Right, he says. *Of course.*

I press my shoulder blades into the back of the chair. *Why are we talking about that?*

His mouth twitches again. *You've been trying really hard not to think about it.*

I cross my arms and stare at the metal panel on the wall. I only now realize we can hear each other perfectly, even without the phone. *Then don't you think maybe you shouldn't make me?*

My uncle blinks. Then he laughs, his eyes sparkling. *You're so different.*

I try not to bristle. *From what? The little girl who sat here and breathed on the glass and asked a million stupid questions?*

He sobers. *You didn't ask a single stupid question.*

Yeah, well, I didn't ask a single smart question either.

You were a kid. And sheltered, he says, and if he notices the way I wince, hearing the word I used to describe Shiori, he doesn't acknowledge it. *Your parents tried to shield you from the ugly things in this world.*

Is that why my mom brought me to visit you in prison? I ask.

My voice seems too loud here, like these walls can't contain it. My own ears ring from the anger pushing at the boundaries of my clipped words.

He drops his gaze to his hands, his palms pressing into the counter. *Does that mean you wish you hadn't seen me?*

No, I say. *Because that was the last time I ever did.*

He blinks. *But you just said—*

I know what I said. I tighten my grip on my elbows. *My thoughts about it are complicated. Just like everything else involving you.*

He rubs his chin again, his nails scraping his skin. *You resent me.*

I don't, I say, and I'm pretty sure I mean it. *I just don't want to talk about this with you.*

"This." He studies me for a moment. *And what, exactly, is "this"?*

I fling out an arm. *Any of this. I don't want you to tell me how sorry you are or how you wish you could have gotten the support you needed. I don't want you to list all the things you would do differently, if only you could be brought back to life. I don't want to have to sit here and cry and say "I can't choose you, and I'm sorry. I'm sorry. I'm so, so sorry."*

He regards me with a cool gaze. *I'm not going to ask you to do that.*

Maybe. But he'll still keep hoping I'll pick him.

I made a lot of excuses in life, he says. *I'm not going to make more now.*

You wouldn't be the first to ask.

I don't think I have any right, he says. *I loved you, for sure, but we weren't close. I was too busy getting into my own trouble to ever help you out of yours.*

I was a kid, I say. *I didn't get into much trouble.*

He scoffs and waves a hand. *Being a kid has nothing to do with it. I got into trouble all the time when I was young.*

I lean forward, resting my forearms on the edge of the counter. *What kind of trouble?*

It's not hard to guess. He shrugs. *Your mom and I grew up in a rough area at a rough time. It was either buck up or fu—fudge up.*

I lean back. *Nice save.*

His smile is sheepish. *I once swore around you, you know. You were really little. It was an accident, of course. I had stubbed my toe or hit my shoulder on something, and it just slipped out. But your mom got so mad. I thought she was going to ban me from seeing you ever again.*

I laugh a little. *How old was I?*

Young. You couldn't even talk yet. I remember thinking, "Jeez, it's not like she's going to start parroting me." Because you know, at some point, most kids do that. Echo whatever other people say, even if they have no idea what the words mean.

I nod. I don't know where he's going with this, but I'm willing to sit and listen. I just can't believe I'm seeing him again, even if it's only in my mind.

But, he continues, *I guess that doesn't just go for words. Kids are so easily influenced. I know I was. Because, kiddo, you have to understand: No one ever sits down one day and goes, "Hey, I think I want to get addicted to drugs."*

The way he says it makes me want to laugh. That's something I had nearly forgotten about him: He was so wickedly funny, it drove my mom crazy. Whenever they fought, all he had to do was make a funny face or pitch his voice up to mimic their mother or crack a groan-worthy joke, and just like that, she would be laughing, furious with herself for breaking so easily.

I only did it because I wanted to fit in. Same old story, I know. He pauses. *A lot of my life was just another part of that same old story.*

I find myself thinking of *Bitter Mouse* again. I had loved games before. Had identified with characters and storylines and even little moments, like when NPCs admitted they were just standing there and staring off into space with no real purpose. But I had never felt like a story was mine as much as I had with *Bitter Mouse*.

You don't do them, my uncle says. *Do you?*

What, drugs?

The word comes out too harshly. Hurt flickers across his face.

I don't, I tell him. *I wouldn't.*

Good, he says. *I'm proud of you.*

I stare at the metal panel, trying not to think of Shun, not just because we're talking about addiction but because he was wickedly funny too. Laughing felt so wrong once he was gone.

I still remember when you were born, my uncle says. *I kept thinking your mom wasn't going to let me meet you. She sure hadn't said I could. But then again, I guess I didn't ever say anything to her. I didn't even call to congratulate her. When I finally reached out, I kept waiting for her to tell me I wasn't allowed to visit. For all I knew, she was going to tell you she was an only child.*

She wouldn't have done that, I say. *She loved you.*

I know she did. He picks at his fingernails. *Too much, maybe.*

I purse my lips. I've been examining the metal panel for so long, my eyes are starting to cross. I force myself to focus on the edge of the counter instead. There's a nick in the corner. I concentrate on it, even as my uncle lifts his eyes to me.

When she told me she wanted me to meet you, I drove over to her apartment. I got all the way there, then realized maybe I was supposed to bring something, like a rattle or a blanket or something.

I keep scrutinizing the countertop. *What did you do?*

Turned around, drove to the store, picked something up, and went back. As soon as your dad opened the door, I practically threw the bag in his face and said, "DIAPERS."

I look up. *You brought DIAPERS?*

I know. I panicked. He shrugs. *Your mom said they were actually very helpful. You apparently went through a lot of them.*

I make a face. *Moving on.*

He laughs. I love the sound of it, rich with just a little bit of a wheeze.

We're quiet for a while. I can still hear the hum of the overhead lights. I look over my shoulder. The guard hasn't moved from his post. I don't think he's even blinked.

When I saw you, my uncle says, *I thought you were fake.*

I turn back around. *What?*

I saw you in your mom's arms, this tiny, fragile little thing with perfect lips and these teeny-weeny little hands, and I thought, "There's no way that's real." He shakes his head. *But then I got closer, and you blinked—blink, blink, blink, blink—and yawned and looked at me, and there was no denying it.* His eyes meet mine. *I loved you.*

My eyes start to burn. I close them, but that only makes it worse.

You know how your mom is, he says. *Even though she must have been tired, she raised an arm and reached for me and said, "Get over here and hold her already."*

I smile. That sounds like her.

I didn't want to, he says. Then his head snaps up. *I mean, I DID. I really did. But I was scared. I didn't know what I was supposed to do with a baby. I had heard you're supposed to support the head because babies' necks are weak, but I kept thinking I was going to drop you, and then your mom would DEFINITELY never forgive me.*

I kept telling her, "No, no, no. That's okay. I'll just look." But she got so mad. She was like, "You're gonna get over here and hold your niece if it kills me." Inside, I was thinking, "What if I kill HER?"

but I couldn't say that. So I shuffled over there and opened my arms, and then you were there, blinking up at me.

That, he says, his voice softer now, *was when I promised I would quit. I would. I would get clean. Just for you. Then you would have the uncle you deserved.*

There's a lot of talk of *deserving*. Deserving second chances. Deserving people. Mothers and fathers and grandmothers and uncles. Over time, the idea of deserving something loses all meaning.

Or it should.

But it doesn't. Not with him.

I was okay for a while, he says. *I really was sober. I was doing better. I managed to hold down a job and pay rent without issue. Then life just got hard, and*—he sighs. *I promised myself I wasn't going to tell you my sob story.*

You can, I say. *I'm here.*

Yeah, but you shouldn't be. You didn't come down here for me.

My toes curl in my boots. *I'm sorry.*

I didn't say it to make you feel bad. He locks eyes with me again. His gaze is so intense, I can feel my insides boiling. *I don't want you to choose me. I want you to keep going and do whatever you need to do. I'm just sorry I let you down.*

You didn't, I say. *I mean—we let you down too.*

He shakes his head. *You didn't. I may not have chosen to get addicted, but I chose not to get help for years. I chose to hinge my sobriety on you, this little baby who couldn't even understand my existence. I chose to keep using until I got to jail. After rehab, I chose to do it again instead of calling someone. Anyone. My mom or yours. I was scared of letting them down again.*

They would have helped, I say quietly. *Your mom—I met her. She loved you so much.*

I know that now. He runs his tongue along his bottom lip. *I loved her too. Her and your mom and you and your dad and everyone I left behind. So—so when you get back up there, tell your mom I'm sorry, okay? Tell her I miss her. Tell her she was the best big sister I never even knew I wanted until it was too late.*

I swallow. *Okay. I will.*

There's a creak from behind me. I glance back to find the door has opened. When I face my uncle, he says, *That's for you, kiddo. Get out of here. Go on.*

I slowly get to my feet. *I love you. You know that, don't you?*

He smiles. *I love you too.*

I swallow again, my throat tight. *I wish . . .*

He waits for me to finish. When I don't, he says softly, *Me too.*

I force myself to leave the chair, my steps heavy. Every so often, I look back at him. But he just watches, resolute acceptance on his face.

I'm just about to reach the door when he says, *Hey, kiddo.*

I turn. *Yeah?*

When I said you were different, I meant different from what I'd imagined you'd become. In all the best ways. He takes a breath. *I'm proud of you.*

I close my eyes for a moment. They sting from the effort of holding back tears. When I open them, everything is blurry. Everything except him.

Thank you, I say.

Then I turn and take the final step.

CHAPTER NINETEEN
Most Innocent

I just want to fly / back home to you
I wish I could fly / back home to you
So take my hand; we'll fly / back home (ooh, ooh)
Wish I flew / home to you (ooh)

THE MOMENT I hear the music, I know exactly what I'm going to see. So as the world forms around me, bright light slipping away, I close my eyes. I don't think I'll be able to face what's coming next.

Maybe this is where it ends. If I refuse to open my eyes, I won't progress. I won't fail either. I'll just stay here forever. I'm okay with that. I don't want to do this anymore.

Yet the little voice in my head keeps whispering, *Are you really going to give up now? It isn't your own family that breaks you; it's this near-stranger who probably didn't even remember your name by the time he—*

My eyelids lift.

He looks exactly the same. Not the way he looked in pictures online, most of which had been taken before the development of *Bitter Mouse*, when he was still dyeing his hair a darker shade of brown. The way he looked when I met him.

His full name is Arturo Harris, but he always went by Art. It was kind of a joke; he was an artist named Art. But he also thought his full name was, in his words, *unbearably pretentious.* There was an entire interview about it, back when *Bitter Mouse* first released.

I knew everything about him, just as I knew everything about the rest of the members of Sour Mouth, the game development team, and *Bitter Mouse*, the only game it ever produced. I think most of us thought Sour Mouth would come out with another game eventually, maybe even a sequel, but I now know, as the rest of the community does, that was never going to happen. Sour Mouth had disbanded behind the scenes. The other team members vowed never to work with Art again.

When we met, though, I didn't know that. I'm not even sure *he* did.

Um. Art reaches up and tugs at the collar of his light button-down. *Hi.*

I don't say anything. I don't know how to talk to him.

Bitter Mouse tells the story of a disillusioned anthropomorphic mouse coming to terms with the death of her best friend, who has just died in a drunk-driving accident. The player controls the character as she goes through the grieving process, each step its own separate game level.

As the story unfolds, the player uncovers the secrets behind her best friend's death: The protagonist and her best friend, both high school seniors, go to a party and get wildly drunk. The best friend wants to go home, but the protagonist says she wants to stick around and sober up. The other creatures at the party, also all anthropomorphic animals, say maybe the best friend shouldn't be driving. He insists he's fine and asks the protagonist to back him up. She does, saying he's more responsible than he looks, and the next thing she knows, he's dead.

In the aftermath of the accident, she starts drinking every day. The combination of alcohol and grief causes her to dissociate. In her mind, she is literally working her way through the stages of grief, overcoming obstacles and, more often than not, falling short and having to start all over again.

Yet even when the game is at its most frustrating, when the levels seem unbeatable, it's impossible to hate it. Its animation is flawless, the motions smooth and fluid. The soundtrack is top-tier, with synth keyboards, theremin samples, drums, and strings. The game is rarely ever silent, and when it is, it's for a devastatingly good reason. It is, in short, beautiful.

And so much of that beauty came from Art.

I know you probably don't want to see me, he says now, his voice shaky.

I close my eyes, but that doesn't stop them from stinging. Tears gather in the corners of my eyes.

He's wrong. I've wanted to see him so badly.

As soon as I finished the game, crying through the entire last half hour, I followed *Bitter Mouse*, Sour Mouth, and all the developers on every social media platform I had. I joined all the fan communities but rarely commented. I just wanted to be a part of it, even if I never made my presence known.

Then Art announced he would be visiting my city in late December and asked if any followers living in the area would want to grab a cup of coffee sometime.

It was for research, he said. He had been seeking out small towns, hoping for a spark of inspiration, and had found my particular neck of the woods interesting. A part of me now wonders if he had heard something about the tunnel. If there had been a book or a blog or a post somewhere on social media about it.

I would ask him now if I could say even a single word.

As soon as I saw his post, I messaged him, introduced myself, told him how much I loved the game, and said I would be around if he wanted to meet up. No pressure. None whatsoever.

In the gap of time between when I sent the message and when he responded, I felt like I was in a dream. I wasn't even sure I had actually done it. If I had, the message probably hadn't reached him, forever lost in cyberspace.

When a notification popped up on my phone, I nearly fainted.

Cool! his message said. Sure, meeting up sounds great. Do you have any recommendations for fun cafés?

Fun cafés. Fun cafés. Oh my God. What qualified as a "fun café"? What was fun? What were cafés? How was I supposed to know when almost all the food I consumed was either from the supermarket's frozen section or the school cafeteria?

Then, just as I was about to go into full-on research mode to find the best fun cafés, I realized there was a tiny problem.

I hadn't told my parents anything. I had never even talked to them about *Bitter Mouse*. The only person I had told was Thea, and even then, I had been stingy with the details. *Bitter Mouse* was mine and mine alone.

My parents generally let me do what I wanted. They never told me what classes to take or what clubs I had to join so I could include them in my college applications. The only times they ever got upset with me was when I put myself in danger.

Meeting Art didn't feel like putting myself in danger. It felt like it just might save me.

Maybe that's a little overdramatic. Back then, not much had gone wrong in my life. I was still struggling with the abstract concepts of grief and addiction, but I didn't really need saving. I just wanted to meet someone who had been involved in the game I held so closely to my heart.

I was pretty sure my parents wouldn't see it that way, though.

When I finally brought it up to them, I tried to strike the perfect balance between *this is a casual thing, so don't freak out about it* and *I have put a lot of thought into this meeting and have decided it is a safe course of action*, telling them I had the opportunity to talk to a creator of one of my most favorite games ever and would very much like to meet him at a fun café.

Absolutely not, my mom said.

My jaw dropped. *What? But—*

This is a game developer? An adult male game developer? She picked up her phone and showed me the picture on his Wikipedia article, in which his hair was still that jarringly dark brown. Though that, in all honesty, was how I saw him in my own head. He rarely posted pictures of himself. *This—this Arturo Harris?*

Art. I pointed to her phone. *It says it right there. "He goes by Art."*

I don't really care, she said.

Okay, I said.

Why do you want to meet this guy? my dad asked, squinting at his own phone, reading about either Art or the game. *What is this even about?*

It's a good game, I said. *It's important. I've never, in my life, cried at a game like that before. Please. Please let me go.*

You don't even know him, my mom said. *And now he knows where you live.*

He knows the town I live in, I pointed out. *It's not like he's going to march up here and knock on the door of our apartment.*

As far as you know.

I suppressed the urge to roll my eyes. *Please. I'm begging you.*

My parents glanced at each other. When my dad shrugged, I turned my eyes to my mom and held my breath.

She grabbed her phone and read silently for a minute. I was

about to ask whether she was looking at the Wikipedia article for Art or for *Bitter Mouse*, but the expression on her face told me it was the game. She was reading the synopsis, her eyes lingering on certain words. *Addiction. Death. Dissociation.*

It's a good game, I said again. *A really good game. It means a lot to me. Please let me go.*

She pursed her lips and lifted her head. *What do you know about this guy?*

He's talented, I said. Then, because that clearly wasn't what she was looking for, I added, *He's nice, I think. I mean, I don't know what you want me to say. He's never done anything to make me believe otherwise.*

I force myself to look at Art. We're seated at a table in the back of a café. All the other tables are empty. There's not even a barista at the front, though pastries have been arranged to form neat lines in the glass display case. The windows are decorated for the winter, gel stickers in the shapes of snowflakes and snowmen stuck on the insides. A round Santa statue about one foot tall stands in the corner, a mug in his mittened hands.

My eyes snag on the blackboard hanging above the ordering counter. There's only one word, written in blood-red chalk: GOODBYE.

Maybe I should go, Art says.

The sound of his voice makes my stomach hurt.

No, I say. *Don't. I just—I need a minute. I'm sorry.*

He nods and takes a breath like he's going to say something, only to seemingly change his mind, concentrating on the mason jar of water on the table. Every time he extends a hand, the jar scoots away. The same thing goes for his chocolate croissant, its plate edging closer and closer to my side of the table.

I frown and pick up the plate. It feels solid in my hand. Weighty. But when I try to push it toward Art, it vanishes, then reappears beside my elbow.

He gives me a tight smile. *It's okay. I'm not really hungry anyway.*

If you really want to go, my mom had said then, *you can. But I'm going with you.*

I was stunned into silence. Then, shaking my head to clear it, I said, *What? WHAT? You—you WHAT?*

There's no way I'm letting you meet a stranger from the internet all by yourself.

It's not like he's not some random guy I started chatting with online. He's a GAME DEVELOPER. Of my favorite game.

You've never even talked about this game, my dad said.

If I did, would you let me go alone instead of tagging along like I'm five years old?

My mom's eyes narrowed. *I don't like your tone.*

I clenched my teeth, already imagining what I was going to have to say: *Oh, hey, Art, grown-up game developer of the most life-changing thing I have ever experienced. Thanks again for not running away screaming when I said I would be interested in meeting you. Quick update: My MOTHER wants to tag along because she thinks you might be a total creep and stalked all your online profiles. Hope that's cool. If not, I guess NOW you can run away screaming.*

Oh my God, I said, holding my head in my hands. *This is embarrassing. YOU are embarrassing.*

Better to be embarrassing than dead, she said.

Oh my GOD, I said again. *You're not really going to make me bring you along, are you?*

She crossed her arms, then her legs, turning herself into the most intimidating human pretzel I had ever seen. *I hardly think it would be YOU bringing ME along, considering we would be the ones driving you wherever you want to go.*

I sucked in my cheeks. I had my permit but couldn't drive on my own. I had planned on taking the bus, but as I thought about it, I realized I didn't want to show up all sweaty and gross. Maybe it would be better to let her take me. And she clearly wasn't going to allow me to go alone.

I'm almost an adult, I said, my pathetic last-ditch effort to change her mind.

You're still my baby, she said.

So it was settled.

I can't remember whether I warned Art ahead of time or not. Maybe I didn't. Maybe I was afraid that telling him my *mother* would be there would scare him off for good. At least my dad had agreed to come along. That way, we could almost pretend they were on a date, watching me from a distance.

When the day of our meeting arrived, I spent the entire morning vibrating with anticipation. I couldn't believe I was actually going to see him and talk to him and tell him how much *Bitter Mouse* meant to me. Even as we got into the car, with me relegated to the backseat, I had to take deep breaths to keep myself from freaking out.

It was a shock, seeing him in person. His hair was lighter than in his photos, and he had lost weight, which somehow made him seem even more innocent, the kind of boy other kids pick on at school because he's so gangly. I could tell, as my mom extended a hand and welcomed him to town, she was thinking the same thing.

Good. Maybe she finally realized how stupid it was to worry about me.

I could tell Art was thrown by my entourage, but he handled it well, and frankly, so did my parents. Once they deemed him a non-threat, they picked out some pastries and sat in the corner, far from us.

I can't recall exactly what I said. I know at one point, I launched into an entire rambling monologue about how *Bitter Mouse* was so special to me, and its soundtrack, which he had created, as if maybe he didn't know, was what had gotten me back into music. I had forgotten how just a few notes, just a couple of perfect lines, could capture a human heart in such excruciating detail.

He nodded the entire time and blushed at a few of my compliments. He was awkward, I realized, in a way that reminded me a little of Eli from the writing center. When I asked what he was working on next, he said he had gathered a new team. He wasn't allowed to say much at the moment, but his eyes gleamed as he gave me the few details he could. He even showed me a few samples of songs he had been working on, and I got so excited, I nearly spilled water on his laptop.

What happened to them? I ask Art now.

He looks up. *What?*

The songs you played for me that day. I swallow. *What happened to them?*

He pauses, his eyes dark behind his glasses. *Nothing. They're still on my laptop somewhere, but I'll never—*

He cuts himself off, leaving his sentence unfinished too.

On the way home, my mom had asked, *Did you have a good time?*

Yeah, I said. *I did.*

We were quiet for a while.

Thank you for looking out for me, I said. I could still hear his songs in my head. *But I hope you know he really was nice.*

He was, my mom said. *I'll give you that much.*

When we got home, I messaged him to thank him again for everything. I told him I would be a fan of his forever, and I was so excited to see what he would do next. It took him a while to respond, but when he did, he thanked me too, and, as I did with Eli, I let him go.

Then, that summer, everything fell apart.

CHAPTER TWENTY
Most Impactful Soundtrack

I'M SURE A lot of things happened over the summer between my junior and senior year: Thea and I started working on college applications. While Thea took a math class, I snuck in some history credits to free up my schedule for the upcoming semester. My mom almost rage-quit her job because her coworkers were driving her crazy.

To me, though, only one thing defines that entire summer. I look at Art. He's still sitting quietly, his hands in his lap.

Content warning for addiction, dissociation, and grief. That was what had been typed out, white font on a black background, at the beginning of *Bitter Mouse*. I had always figured Art and the other developers had some experience with at least some of the topics. I just didn't realize how closely the events had mirrored real life.

Arturo "Art" Harris of Bitter Mouse *fame has been accused of emotional and psychological abuse by an ex-partner.*

While Bitter Mouse's *Art Harris has not yet spoken up about allegations of abuse, former development team members have come forward with their own recollections of Harris's angry, drunken, unprofessional tirades.*

New (now former) game development partner of Bitter Mouse's *Art Harris opens up about Harris's substance abuse problems.*

The articles took over the entire internet. No matter where

I went, there was another headline, another story, another person claiming Art had yelled at them or thrown a half-empty bottle at their head or just flat-out vanished after what had appeared to be a minor disagreement on the direction in which they were taking the game's narrative.

The *Bitter Mouse* team severed ties with him. Most of his new partners, who had been working on the game he had told me about, admitted they had been struggling to collaborate with him.

Art's silence was chilling.

I didn't tell my parents. I didn't know how to, and I didn't want to hear what they had to say. Thea sensed something was wrong, but I kept telling her it was just the pressure of senior year. I promised myself I would talk to her about it once I had a better grip on the situation. Soon enough, I thought, Art would speak up.

Not even a week after the allegations first broke, he was dead.

I raise my head. *You never even said anything.*

Art shifts uncomfortably. *There wasn't much to say.*

That's the biggest lie I've ever heard, I say, and he flinches.

A small part of me hates myself for hurting him. The rest of me wonders if I should be proud instead. I hurt Art Harris. He deserves it. Doesn't he?

I'm sorry, he says.

I don't need your apology, I say. *I just need the truth.*

But I already know the truth. Someone from his family announced he had passed away, saying he had struggled with substance abuse for years, found an escape in games and music, and expressed deep regrets over what he had done.

What he had done.

So it had been true.

In the days following the news, articles flooded every gaming site. The forums and groups I had joined were forced to enact rules around any discussion about him. Most of the people who had spoken out against him said nothing. Their silence, like his, drove me crazy.

I tried so hard to push down all my feelings about it. I was supposed to be focusing on history—and not Art Harris's history. The history that really mattered.

Except it sure didn't feel like history mattered. Nothing did, really. I didn't know how to feel about him anymore. I couldn't play the game, couldn't comment on discussions, couldn't listen to the soundtrack. He was the first person to have passed away since my uncle and grandmother ten years earlier, and the game and the team that had helped me to grieve were now the very things I was grieving.

One day, my mom found me lying on the floor. I could feel tears trickling down my face, running along my ears, but made no move to wipe them away.

Monika, she said as she knelt beside me. *I think we need to talk.*

I shook my head.

Monika. She reached for a tissue, but I shook my head again, harder. She let her arm fall back to her side. *I'm worried about you. I'm not going to leave until you tell me what's wrong.*

I don't know how long it took me to scrape the words out of my throat, but when I did, they hurt.

Do you remember the game developer? I asked quietly.

The one we met? she asked, crouching just to hear me. Her voice was guarded, as if she was expecting me to yell at her for refusing to let me go alone. He had turned out to be so nice, after all.

I closed my eyes. *He's dead.*

I curled into a ball, trying to contain my grief, to trap it in the confines of my body, even as my vision got blurrier and blurrier until everything was just one big mess.

What? my mom said softly. *What happened?*

I thought the story would spill out of me, leaking everywhere, soaking into the carpet like blood. But I could barely speak. Each word of my cobbled-together explanation was more painful than the last.

My mom said nothing for a minute. Then she said, *He must have had a lot of issues we didn't see. That doesn't excuse what he did to other people, but I think we can both be grateful to him for being nice to you and wish he could have been as nice to everyone else.*

She collected me in her arms. I was afraid she was going to call my dad in for a family discussion so we could all process things together, but she instead held me close and let me cry. Once I was done, she led me back to bed and tucked me in, as if I was a child again.

Have you told Thea? my mom asked the next day.

I shook my head.

Maybe you should, she said, her voice firm but kind. *She texted me earlier to ask if everything seemed okay with you.*

I didn't say anything. Thea was such a good best friend. I didn't deserve her.

Monika, my mom said.

I know, I said. *I hate when you're right.*

She smiled and left my room. After a minute, I picked up my phone and asked Thea if I could call her. She replied immediately, and soon, I was wiping away tears, telling her about the game and what had happened with Art. She cried with me. Not because she knew the characters or the person behind them but because I had cried, and that was all it ever took.

The next time we met up, before our summer classes began, she asked if I wanted to talk about it. I said I didn't, but I loved her. She said she knew. And she never asked about him again.

Everyone thinks I'm over it, I tell Art now.

He raises his head. *Over what?*

You. I slowly turn the plate. A piece of the croissant flakes off. I keep spinning the dish. *I could be sad about it for a while. Then I was supposed to move on, the way it seems everyone else has. But I can't. I think about that game all the time.*

He picks at his nails, his glasses slipping down his nose.

Then, not much later, my classmate died. I keep thinking the best way to work through my grief would be to play Bitter Mouse. *But again, I can't.*

I'm sorry, Art says.

Some other fans of the game play it all the time. Every few months. Whenever they feel lonely. I swallow. *Even the thought of it makes me sick.*

I'm sorry, he says again.

I fix my gaze on the window clings. One of the snowflakes looks like it's barely holding on to the glass. *It's like when people say, "The only one who could understand my grief, the only I want to talk to about this, is the person who's gone."*

I'm sorry, he says for a third time. *I don't know what to say.*

I don't either. I cross my ankles. *So I guess now's the part where you tell me you think I should choose you.*

He shakes his head. *There was no coming back from that.*

I sit up. *What are you talking about? Yes, there was. There IS. You could have done something. You could have changed. There were still so many projects you hadn't finished yet. What about all your songs?*

What about them?

I grit my teeth. *What do you MEAN, "What about them?"*

I made a lot of mistakes, he says.

I'm sick of hearing people say that. I'm so sick of it.

I did a lot of bad things.

I'm not saying you didn't, I say, and he flinches. *I'm saying you were silent. The entire time, you said NOTHING. And the next thing I know, you're—*

I clench my teeth. I can't talk about this anymore. Not without losing it completely.

I was a messed-up guy, Art says.

But you made beautiful things, I say.

That doesn't excuse what I did. And I was trying to get better. I was. But recovery from addiction is very similar to recovery from loss; it's rarely ever linear.

He could have put that in a game.

It would have killed me.

You could have said that, I say. *Any of that.*

I just did.

Back THEN, I say, barely resisting the urge to slam my palms on the table. *When the allegations came out. When everyone was saying things about you. When you said nothing day after day after day.*

He looks away. *I'm sorry. I know I let you down.*

Not just me, I say. *Even if it sometimes feels like it was. Even if it sometimes felt like I was the only one still waiting for you to speak. Even if it sometimes killed me to know you really had done all those things, and I still loved the game.*

He dips his head. *I'm—*

Sorry. I bite my tongue. *Yeah. So you've said.*

We stare at opposite walls. The mason jar of water on the table is still as clear as crystal, not a drop of condensation to be seen.

You know, I say, *one of my favorite parts of* Bitter Mouse *is when one of the side characters says she doesn't even know why she's so sad about what happened to the main character's best friend. She didn't know him well. She felt less like she was grieving the loss of him and more like she was grieving the loss of never getting to know him.*

Art hesitates. Yes. *I remember that part.*

That's exactly how I felt about my uncle. I breathe out. *I keep finding myself wondering what he would think of me. If he would give me advice on what classes to take or what to major in or where to go for college or what to take up as a career. My mom said he was into music when he was younger, and I thought maybe he would tell me not to quit piano after only a few years. Maybe he would teach me how to sing. Maybe he would like your stuff and show me the right chords. Because when I tried to play some of your songs, I had to look them up and practice them myself, and I STILL sucked. I never sounded as good as you.*

Art dips his head. *I'm sure that's not true.*

It is. I may not be a musician, but I know what good music is, and yours was good. I chew my lip. *And maybe in my wildest dreams, I thought we could team up someday. I could study coding or writing for video games and ask you if I could work with you, and maybe we could've made something really special.*

But now we never will. I look up at him. *Because you're gone.*

And there's a part of me that wants to bring you back. Even though I didn't come down here for you, even though you don't seem interested in returning, there's a voice in my head screaming for me to drag you back to life. But I can't do that. Because I have someone else in mind, sure, and because you don't want that—but also because part of me can't forgive you for the thing you did.

Which thing? he asks. Then, looking appropriately abashed, he says, *I guess that's my answer, isn't it?*

I don't respond.

Why are you here? I ask. *If you weren't going to beg me to bring you back to life, why are we sitting at this table?*

He hesitates. *Maybe there's a part of me, just as small as that part of you, that wants to try again. Wants to start over. The rest of me knows I shouldn't. I might make mistakes. I might cause more hurt. I might waste the opportunity. And, as you told me, you're not down here for me.*

I glare at the croissant, as if I think this is all its fault. All that flaky pastry around that tiny little treasure, gone too quickly to be enjoyed.

What am I supposed to do now? I ask.

Art blinks at me through his glasses. *I'm not sure. I don't think I'm allowed to have much of a say in what you do next.*

I wish he were yelling at me instead. I would even prefer if he were down on his knees, pleading with me to revive him. Seeing him like this, the way I remember him, awkward and sweet like Eli when I know this isn't the Art so many other people remember, hurts the most.

It's not too late for you, he says. *If you want to play music, or if you want to write stories for video games, or if you want to replay* Bitter Mouse *or never touch it again, do it. Do what you want.*

I don't know what I want, I say.

I think, Art says slowly, *part of being human is questioning everything.*

My breath leaves me in a long, stringy exhalation.

WHY WEREN'T YOU LIKE THIS AROUND EVERY-ONE? I want to shout. *WHY COULDN'T YOU HAVE KEPT MAKING GAMES THAT HELP PEOPLE? HOW AM I SUPPOSED TO FEEL ABOUT YOU NOW?*

Instead, I slump down in my seat, the iron back of the chair cold and unforgiving.

I really am sorry, Art says. *I'm sorry I couldn't be what I should have been. I'm sorry the memory of a game that once brought you comfort has been tainted.*

We're quiet.

I'm sorry too, I say at last. *I'm sorry for the people who had to endure your abuse. I'm sorry you didn't get the help you needed. I'm sorry I still don't know how to get over this.*

He looks over at the far wall, where a blank-faced clock hangs. *You should go.*

Okay. I get to my feet. My knees are shaking. I manage to make it about halfway to the door before turning back. *I'm sorry.*

I'm sorry too, he says. *To everyone I hurt.*

I nod, then continue my long trek toward the exit. I've been able to leave of my own free will these past two times, and though I should find it freeing, in a way, it's worse. I'm so tired of walking on my own two feet. It's so much easier to fall.

If I really wanted to, I could probably link my reluctance to *Bitter Mouse*. Falling off platforms is simple. Progressing is what propels us forward. What brings us closer to the goal.

But I don't feel like thinking that hard about anything. I'm just so tired.

I pause at the door and take one last look at Art. He's looking at me, neither smiling nor frowning. I hear my favorite song from his soundtrack looping in my head: *Wish I flew / home to you (ooh)*.

I lift a hand. He lifts his. We watch each other for a moment longer. Then I turn and leave him behind.

CHAPTER TWENTY-ONE
Most Morally Gray

FOR A GOOD few seconds, I swear my heart doesn't beat. I stare up at the ceiling of the tunnel, wondering if I'm dead. If I've joined all the rest of them.

After a pause, my heartbeat flutters beneath my fingertips. I hold my fingers to my neck for a little while longer, feeling that hummingbird beat, then ease myself up to a sitting position.

"Shiori?" I call out. "Shiori, can you hear me?"

Nothing. It's unnaturally quiet. I find myself tiptoeing through the tunnel because the sound of my footsteps seems deafening otherwise.

I start counting the seconds aloud. I don't know how much time has passed. Hours, probably. I'm afraid it may have been days, or even weeks, since Shiori and I first stepped inside. If it's been even close to an entire day, I bet Thea has already caved and told my parents, and they're sending out search parties and plastering my face across social media. If I do manage to come back, no one will ever let me live it down.

Of course, if I *do* return, there's a chance I won't be alone. Then I'll definitely be famous. And so will Shun. He'll receive even more media attention than Art, the internet clamoring over the boy who returned from the dead. It won't be like when Shun died, his life reduced to a mere mention in a school assembly or a memorial page with a handful of likes. He will be everywhere.

That's what I wanted when he died. I wanted something to reflect the way I felt. I wanted everyone to talk about it. I wanted everything, every newspaper, every website, to say something about him. I wanted the school to suspend classes. I wanted all the parents to create a support group for his mother. I wanted all the students to talk about nothing but him.

That's why I have to bring him back.

When I stumble across Shiori, she's sitting on the ground, her back ramrod straight. She faces away, her lavender hair obscuring most of her face. If I had taken a few more steps, I would've walked into her shoulder.

"Shiori," I say. "Are you okay?"

No response.

Frowning, I scoot around her. "Shiori?"

The sight of her makes me gasp. Her eyes are wide open and fully white, her pupils nowhere to be seen. Her breaths come fast, as if she's in the middle of a panic attack. Her hands, dropped onto her lap, twitch like she's being electrocuted.

"Shiori." I crouch beside her. I don't know if I should touch her or if physical contact would only make her lash out. "Shiori, wake up. Shiori, come on. Hey. Are you there? Can you hear me?"

She keeps hyperventilating, her chest heaving.

"Shiori," I say. I place my hands on her shoulders to shake her awake—

—but I just don't see why.

I blink, but my vision clouds. All I can see are smears of color: peaches and silvers and blacks and whites. I try to raise a hand to rub my eyes, but I can't move.

Can you explain it to me? a voice asks. I know it from

somewhere, but I can't identify the speaker. *I told you I'm willing to take you wherever you want to go. Within reason, of course.*

I know, a second voice says, *and I appreciate it. Really. I just want to be able to do some things on my own for once.*

Shiori. That's Shiori. I take a breath to call out to her, but every time I try to open my mouth, nothing comes out.

"For once"? the first voice echoes.

And then it hits me.

Shiori's mother.

You do a lot of things on your own. You eat breakfast on your own—

But you make it for me.

—and do your homework on your own—

But you checked over every single one of my problems and essays until I asked you not to.

A sigh.

Mom. Shiori has slowly begun to come into focus, the vaguest outlines now visible, but most of the scene remains hazy.

See? Shiori's mother says. I think she's pointing a finger in Shiori's face. *I hate that. "Mom." Children usually call their mothers "Mommy."*

Yeah. When they're, like, six. I'm almost eighteen.

Why does turning eighteen mean everything has to change?

It doesn't, Shiori says. *It's just—I need a little independence. I'm supposed to be going to college soon, and you can't—*

So you don't want me. That's what you're saying, isn't it? You're nearly eighteen, all grown up, so you have no need for your old mother.

The first time I referred to my parents as Mom and Dad, my mom cried a little. That's natural, though. It's part of life. Yes, a large part of being a parent is taking care of a child. But children grow up. That's kind of the point.

That's not what I mean, Shiori tells her mother. *What is it, then? Why are you doing this to me?*

Shiori exhales. *We've had this discussion before. Last year. You promised you would give me the space I needed.*

And I did. I let you stay later at school, even though there's no reason for you to be there once classes are over. I let you join your little club. I even let you choose your own clothes.

Discomfort pulls at my insides. The more time I spend with Shiori's mother, the less I like her. I don't know how she ever thought Shiori would be able to make it on her own when she was forced to rely on her mother for so much.

By now, most of the cloudiness in my vision has cleared. Shiori and her mother are sitting in the driver and passenger seats of the car. Shiori rests her hands on the steering wheel, the silver H shining even in the clinical lights of the parking lot. I sit maybe a foot or two away behind them, as if I've been placed in the backseat. I attempt to lower my head, but I can't move. I'm not even sure I have a real physical body in this vision.

Shiori, I try to say.

I still can't speak.

You told me you would let me drive home, Shiori says, struggling to keep her tone even. *I need night hours.*

Her mother sighs. *I didn't even want you to get your permit.*

But I did, Shiori says, her voice surprisingly loud. *I did, and you said you would help me.*

Shiori's mother doesn't respond. Her arms are crossed, and her eyes have affixed themselves to the gray wall of the parking lot. I think I've been here before. My dentist is in this building somewhere, but it's primarily known for its restaurants. Based on the clamshell package on Shiori's mother's lap, I'm guessing the two of them went out to dinner together. I wonder where Shiori's father is and why he didn't accompany them.

Then I realize it's probably better this way. I have a feeling I know what this memory is. And I don't want to see it.

Can we please just go? Shiori asks.

Fine, her mother snaps, uncrossing her arms just to toss them in the air. *Do whatever you want. That seems to be your new life motto anyway. Let's go, then. Come on. Did you buckle your seat belt?*

Shiori doesn't bother answering. Her mother can see she did.

Unease builds in my stomach as Shiori starts the car. Keeping her foot on the brake, she shifts gears and turns around. I wait for her to see me, maybe even scream, but she looks right through me, focused on scanning her surroundings for cars and pedestrians.

Shiori, I say to her in my mind. *Shiori, are you there?*

She keeps focusing on backing up, her eyes darting from side to side.

And it just had to be nighttime hours, her mother mumbles.

Shiori says nothing.

You have to ease the wheel a little to the left first, her mother says as they head down the ramp, *to make a sharp turn. Otherwise, you'll end up in the other lane.*

Okay. Nervousness rings around the fraying threads of Shiori's voice. *Okay. A little to the left first.*

Not like that, her mother says, remaining unexpectedly calm. *Not on this part. On the first part. You shouldn't do it the second time.*

Oh. Shiori frowns. *But Dad said—*

Don't listen to him. He doesn't know what he's doing. Shiori's mother gives her daughter a playful grin. *There's a reason his insurance premium is higher than mine.*

Shiori laughs a little. Her grip on the wheel eases just the slightest bit. *Really?*

Really. Shiori's mother cranes her neck. *The car on the lower level is waiting for you.*

Waiting for me? Shiori stiffens. *Why? What are they doing?*

Shiori's mother sets a hand on the top of the clamshell package and glances out the window again. *He's giving you space to pass. It's dangerous for both of you to go at once. So just drive—don't rush—and thank him as you pass.*

I take another look at Shiori's mother. I didn't think she would be so good at this. I was sure she would be the type to burst into hysterics and pump her invisible brakes every time Shiori so much as turned her head a little too much to the left.

Okay, Shiori says. *I can do this. Just drive, pass, and thank him.*

That's right. But if thanking him is too much for now, I'll do it.

Okay. Thank you. Shiori passes the other car and lifts her fingers in a half wave. Once the guy dips his head and continues on his way, Shiori exhales.

Her mother laughs again. *You don't need to be so panicked. It's just another driver.*

I know, but I always forget what to do when I see someone else in here.

You're still new to this. Give yourself a break.

I would lift my eyebrows if I could. I like seeing this side of Shiori's mother. I wish I had seen more of it.

I raise my eyes to the windshield. I can't see what time it is, the digital clock and the touch screen pixelated, but it's clearly late evening. The sun has almost disappeared below the horizon, oranges and pinks clawing their way across the sky.

How are you feeling? Shiori's mother asks as Shiori slows behind another car at the intersection. *Or would you prefer not to talk?*

I kind of like talking, Shiori says. *I need to have something to listen to. Voices or music or something. Otherwise, I get in my own head.*

Shiori's mother nods as the light turns green. *I'm like that too.*

I'm not so sure about that. In the memory of the festival, the car was as chillingly silent as the tunnel, before I found Shiori in her trance.

Or maybe I should say I USED to be like that, Shiori's mother says.

Can she hear me?

Are you listening? I think to her. I monitor her expression, but she doesn't even blink.

When did that change? Shiori asks her mother.

I'm not sure. Sometimes, I think it was after you were born. Everything was so hectic, having a new baby. I learned to appreciate the silence.

Shiori's fingers flex over the steering wheel. *Oh.*

Shiori's mother glances at her daughter. *That wasn't an insult. I don't care about the noise. You were worth it. Most definitely. You're the most important thing in the world to me. You know that. That's why all of this is so difficult.*

Shiori's shoulders relax. *I know. I'm sorry. I'm not trying to—*

Hey, Shiori's mother says, sitting up, her eyes on something on the road. *What does that car think it's doing?*

What? Shiori looks out the windshield. *Where?*

I have no idea how she doesn't know where it is. Even I can tell there's something coming, a blob flying down the road, the bass of the music blasting from the speakers making the car hop.

They're speeding, Shiori's mother says. Her grip tightens around the package. *Shiori.*

What? Shiori says, her voice high. *What do I do?*

The panic is palpable, filling the air with electricity. I stare at the door handle, wondering if I can pull it open and jump out. But I've been locked into this car. Locked into this body. Locked into this nightmare. All I can do is watch it play out.

The other vehicle starts to zigzag. When Shiori's mother shouts for her to do something, Shiori screams, *WHAT? WHAT DO I DO?*

The horn blares as Shiori's mother slams her palm against the center of the wheel, hard enough to leave an imprint on her palm. Lifting her deathly white face to the sky, Shiori twists the wheel to one side and hits the gas pedal. We swerve to the side, and though the other vehicle veers back into its own lane, Shiori's car starts spinning in a screeching circle.

Shiori shrieks, the sound long, high, and terrified. The tree slumping over the edge of the nearest sidewalk looms larger and larger until—

SHIORI! her mother screams, reaching for her daughter.

There's a loud *CRASH*, followed by ungodly crunching, metal bending and warping. I stare, silent, as the food in the clamshell package explodes out of its container, and marinara sauce splatters across the windshield.

Then everything goes dark.

CHAPTER TWENTY-TWO
Most Unexpected

YOU'VE BEEN SO intent on doing everything yourself, even when it's inconvenient to both you and those around you. You keep insisting you're growing up, as if that's something you want, but I just don't see why.

I struggle to focus on what's in front of me. It takes me a few seconds to recognize Shiori in the driver's seat. Her mother sits beside her, a food container on her lap.

Can you explain it to me? her mother says. *I told you I'm willing to take you wherever you want to go. Within reason, of course.*

A chill creeps up my shoulders as I remember the swerving car. The crash. The rivulets of red splashing across the windshield. This is the same scene as before. That must be why Shiori was so unreachable in the tunnel: She's stuck in a loop, reliving her mother's death over and over.

I glance over at her just as she says, *I know, and I appreciate it. Really. I just want to be able to do some things on my own for once.*

I know how this goes already. I don't want to see it again.

Shiori, I say, and though I don't actually expect anything to come out, her name rockets out of my throat, loud enough to startle me.

She jumps, and just like that, the scene freezes, Shiori's mother mid-blink. Shiori's eyes run along my face, disbelief turning her eyes glassy.

Monika? she says. *How are you here?*

I don't know, I say. *What's happening? How long have you been reliving this?*

She chews her lips, then bursts into tears. *I don't know. This whole thing keeps repeating. I regain control of my body once in a while, so I try to make her drive instead, or I wait in the parking lot so we don't see that car, or I take a different road, but every time anything even slightly different happens, it pulls me back to the beginning.*

I let out a breath. *I'm so sorry. That's awful.*

I don't know how to get out, she says, her bloodshot eyes searching mine. *What do I do? How can I save her?*

I'm not sure. I pause. *Can you get up?*

She frowns, then slowly unbuckles her seat belt. *I think so.*

Okay. I take a peek at my own surroundings. I seem to have just been dropped into the backseat with no seat belt. *Make your way out of the driver's seat. Take your time. Don't push yourself.*

I expect her to ask me what I'm planning on doing, but she just gives me a shaky nod and warily moves one leg, then the other. Once she's inched her way out of the seat and into the lot, she asks, *What are you doing?*

Driving, I say, getting into the front seat. *You don't have to come if you don't want to see.*

She wordlessly slides into the back.

I buckle the seat belt. I have no idea what's going to happen now. If I try to un-pause the memory, Shiori's mother is definitely going to notice something's wrong. But I don't have any other ideas, so I check to ensure Shiori's buckled up in the back, then set my hands on the wheel.

As if on cue, Shiori's mother says, *"For once"? You do a lot of things on your own. You eat breakfast on your own—*

But you make it for me, I blurt out.

Shiori startles. I would too, but I seem to have lost control of my body. I didn't even make the decision to speak. Shiori's past self is speaking through me. It doesn't care which person is in the driver's seat. It just needs a vessel.

How did you do that? Shiori asks, but I can't answer.

—and do your homework on your own—

But you checked over every single one of my problems and essays, I hear myself say in Shiori's voice, *until I asked you not to.*

That's really creepy, Shiori says.

I try to agree, but I still can't say anything on my own. Instead, I'm forced to recite everything Shiori did the first time, getting into the same squabble I heard before.

In the backseat, Shiori squirms. In the middle of a stilted silence, she says, *So I guess you've heard this whole thing already.*

I can't answer, but I have the feeling she isn't anticipating a response.

I didn't want to argue with her, she says once her mother has ensured our seat belt is buckled. *We had gone to dinner together, just the two of us, as a sort of truce. Things hadn't been the same since I'd started doing my own thing, getting my permit and making friends. This was supposed to fix everything.*

She looks out the window and swallows hard as my arm jerks out toward the gearshift.

But, Shiori says quietly, *that obviously didn't happen.*

I swivel around, just as Shiori did. My eyes try to lock onto hers, but I can't focus. After searching the area behind the car, I start reversing.

And it just had to be nighttime hours, Shiori's mother says, pouting.

Shiori's quiet for a while. Then, as we're trying to navigate past the other vehicle, she says, *She told me she would let me drive home. I thought that was her way of saying she trusted me. She loved me even though I wasn't her obedient little girl anymore. She was trying, and that meant so much to me.*

So, Shiori's mother says, *just drive—don't rush—and thank him as you pass.*

Was she just humoring me? Shiori muses aloud. *Did she think I was going to change my mind the moment I remembered how scary driving is?*

Driving *is* scary. I hate doing it. I'm lucky Thea enjoys it. She thinks there's a beautiful kind of freedom in it. When she's especially stressed, she goes on long drives with no destination in mind. I sometimes tag along, just cruising in the passenger's seat, talking to her about nothing in particular.

God, I hope I can see her again. Thea and my parents. I have so much I need to tell them.

Maybe I'm being too hard on her, Shiori says. *She ended up letting me drive, didn't she?*

Yeah, but only because Shiori insisted. She has had to fight for every little victory, and every time her mother gives in even a little, she guilts Shiori for it. I've always been grateful for my mom and dad, but the more time I spend in Shiori's head, the more thankful I am to have them.

Shiori doesn't speak for a minute, her eyes darting between her mother and the road. I wonder what she's feeling right now. I'm glad she isn't mad at me for stepping into her mind. She must have been going insane, this one memory playing over and over.

You're the most important thing in the world to me, Shiori's mother says. *You know that. That's why all of this is so difficult.*

In the backseat, Shiori has begun to sniffle.

I feel my shoulders dropping. *I know. I'm sorry. I'm not trying to—*

Hey. Shiori's mother straightens up and squints through the windshield. *What does that car think it's doing?*

Close your eyes, I try to tell Shiori.

But when I catch a glimpse of her in the rearview mirror, she's staring right at the car. All the color has drained from her face, leaving her pallid and ghostlike. Her hands wring the fabric of her seat belt.

I'm sorry, I try to say.

What? I say instead in Shiori's voice. *Where?*

Time itself seems to slow. Unlike the first time, all the details are painfully clear. There's the car, the dark dashboard like an inky lake. There's the bass, its *thump-thump-thump*ing pulling the vehicle down with it. There's the screech of tires as the other vehicle slides along the road, a prolonged scream of rubber and grit.

They're speeding, Shiori's mother says. Her fingers are white around the food container, all the muscles in her arm taut. *Shiori.*

What? My voice is squeaky. *What do I do?*

I want to close my eyes. I don't want to see this again.

The other vehicle swerves. Shiori's mother starts shouting. I shriek, my voice still Shiori's, while the real Shiori weeps in the backseat.

Then everything stops.

All the information hits me at once. The digital clock blinks in neon red: 7:44 P.M. Below it, typed out in white font on the touch screen, is the date. It's early January, just after most of us have turned in our college applications.

I raise my head. From here, I have a perfect view of the other vehicle. The way it's weaving, music pumping loudly enough to make my blood jump in my veins. I can even see the person inside, just one lone driver.

At the last second, I lock eyes with him.
Shun, I say.
Then everything goes black.

I DON'T KNOW which of us wakes up first. Maybe we snap out of it simultaneously, as synchronous as we were when I was in her body, speaking her words, performing her actions. The moment we realize we're back in the tunnel, we both collapse onto the ground. I listen to her uneven breaths as she tries to calm herself down.

I'm sorry, I try to say, but I can't get myself to speak.

"Monika," Shiori says quietly. "Can you hear me?"

I don't respond. My ears ring with the sound of my own silence.

"Monika. Monika, come on. Come back to me."

I don't want to.

She places her hands on my shoulders. "MONIKA."

It takes all my self-control not to push her away. Not because I'm upset with her but because I want to save her from the grief leaking out of me.

"Of course," Shiori mutters. "Of *course* I lose you right when you get me out. God, I hate it here. *MONIKA. CAN YOU HEAR ME?*"

"I can hear you," I say. Every word hurts a little more.

Shiori lets out a breath. "Thank God. You scared me."

I still can't look her in the eye.

"I can't do this anymore," she continues, releasing my shoulders and sitting back on her heels. "I really can't. If this isn't the end of it, what's supposed to come next?"

"I don't know," I say.

She's quiet for a moment. "Do you think it could be? The end?"

I hesitate.

I don't see how it could be. If I'm going to have to face everyone, I'm definitely going to end up talking to Shun. But I have no idea what else Shiori could possibly have to endure. This loop should have been the last step. Maybe it is, for her. Maybe her trial is over, and I'm the only one who still has to keep going.

Somehow, though, I doubt it.

"Okay," Shiori says. "I guess that's a no."

"I'm sorry," I say softly. When she doesn't respond, I turn my head and look over at her. "That crash—it wasn't your fault."

"Yeah, right." She lifts a hand to the ceiling, turns her palm over, and lets her arm drop to the ground. "'You didn't *really* kill your mother. You just got into the *crash* that killed her. That's totally different.'"

"You didn't mean to," I say. "It was an accident. So please. Stop thinking you killed your mother. You didn't."

Shun did.

I sit up. My head is spinning. I feel like I'm going to throw up, and while that isn't exactly a new phenomenon down here, it's different now.

I know Shun had been with friends that day, and I know they had been celebrating. But I also know he got home safely afterward. He didn't crash. He parked his car, went back into his house, and passed away that night. He probably never knew about the accident.

Hadn't he heard it, though? Hadn't he seen it happen in his rearview mirror? How could he have kept going, knowing what he did?

Shun may not have slammed into Shiori, but his actions caused the accident that killed her mother. The worst thing that has ever happened to her, the reason she's down here, the cause of so much pain—it's Shun.

I mean, yes, she could have handled things differently.

She could have swerved some other way, could have avoided the accident, but in the end, he was an inextricable part of it, and as much as I wish I could, I can't just turn a blind eye.

"I'm sorry," I say to Shiori. My foot twitches from the guilt of all the things I can't tell her. "I'm sorry about the crash. I'm sorry I had to see it. I'm sorry for everything."

Shiori gives me a look. "Why are you apologizing? It's not like it was your fault."

If it wasn't, why do I feel like someone just shot a hole through my chest? Like every time I try to touch the wound, it bleeds just a little more?

"Did you say something?" Shiori asks.

No. I'm panting so heavily, I couldn't say something right now even if I wanted to.

"When we were in the car, I mean. Did you say something when we were in the car?"

I can't breathe. "I'm sorry. I'm so, so sorry."

"Stop saying that. You're freaking me out." Shiori's eyes won't leave my face, burning my skin like she's etching the H on the steering wheel into my cheek. "What's going on? What did you say?"

I can't respond.

"Monika," she says. "What did you *say*?"

Say something. God. Say SOMEthing.

"I can't—I don't—" Breathe. Breathe. I need to breathe. "If I tell you, you're never going to forgive me."

She shakes her head like she's not sure she's hearing me correctly. "What are you talking about? What did you do?"

"I didn't do anything." I close my eyes. "Yet."

"Oh my God. Can you stop with the vaguely menacing talk?" She nudges me, trying to get me to smile, but I can't. "Hey. What is it?"

I exhale. My breathing finally returns to normal, but that somehow feels worse, like I've gotten over it already. As if I ever could.

"Do you remember the person in the other car?" I ask quietly.

She doesn't play dumb. "Yeah. And don't you dare pretend it was you or something just so I feel less guilty about what I did."

"No. I wasn't going to do that. It wasn't me in the car."

I purse my lips, hoping she'll piece things together so I don't have to say it. But she doesn't. Obviously. There's no way she could make the connection.

"It's him," I whisper. "The person I'm trying to save."

She's silent. Dead silent. Even more silent than when I was walking this tunnel alone. I can almost hear her heart breaking. Just a tiny hairline fracture at first. Then a rift yawning so wide, she's left with more hole than heart.

When she speaks, her voice is barely audible. "What?"

"I'm sorry," I say again, choking on the words. "I didn't know until right then, when I saw his face. But it was him. I'd know him anywhere."

Even when he's in a car, under the influence, swerving across the road, his eyes glazed over and his music pounding in my ears. I keep thinking he's lucky he didn't crash too, but does it really matter when he died that same night?

The obituary for Shiori's mother might have been printed in the very same issue of the paper as the one for Shun. And worse, people probably didn't even realize she was sharing a page with the very reason for her death.

Shiori sits up and turns her head away.

"Shiori," I say. "I'm sorry. I didn't—"

"I don't get it," she says, her voice startlingly steady. "I watched him speed down the road. He didn't slow down. He didn't stop. He didn't die there."

"No," I say. "It happened later that night."

She chews her lip. "It was an overdose."

For a second, I think she's read my mind. She's slipped into my body. Pulled together all the memories. She knows exactly how I feel.

Then I remember: I told her how he died, just like she told me. We just didn't know how much we had told each other until this very moment.

"I'm sorry," I say again. "God, I'm sorry. I didn't—"

The *zzzmmip* of her bag's zipper cuts me off. I look over just as she thrusts a water bottle out to me. "Here. Drink."

I shake my head. "I can't. I've—"

"Oh, please." She grabs my hand, her skin cold and her grip strong, and crimps my fingers around the bottle. "*Drink*. Then keep going. Just like me."

I shudder. "But—"

"We can talk about this when we meet up again. Because we will. We *will* meet up again."

I hesitate. Then, trembling, I uncap the water and take a sip. It's tepid, but I manage to swallow.

We get to our feet. She takes the bottle back and zips up her bag. I keep waiting for her to break down and cry, but she holds herself together, her jaw clamped and her eyes blazing with determination.

"Shiori," I say.

"Don't," she says. "I'm sick of the apologies. I just want to get this over with."

I'm sorry. I'm sorry. I'm so, so sorry.

"Okay." I clench my hand at my side. "Then I'll see you soon."

She gives me a curt nod. "See you soon."

CHAPTER TWENTY-THREE
Class Rebel

EVERY TIME I take a step, I'm half expecting Shun to jump out at me and pull me down into another hallucination. And every time my boot hits the ground, I find myself just a little disappointed. After about four minutes of lonesome walking, I slow to a stop.

"You know," I say to the emptiness, "I really hate this. If you're going to keep torturing us, you should make it a little less tedious. I mean, couldn't you at least throw in a fog machine or something?"

I tense at the sound of a quiet laugh. I whip around to find him in the corner of my vision, leaning against the tunnel wall like the stupidly cool guy he always seemed to be.

Sorry, Shun says. *I don't know why I found that so funny.*

My eyes instantly fill with tears.

Shun's T-shirt is too big, stretched at the collar, and his basketball shorts are pilly and worn. His socks are pulled high, but his cap is pulled low. He looks exactly as he does in the blurry photo I've seen online, the one posted on some sketchy site devoted to linking people on social media to obituaries printed in the news. I heard some of his family members tried to get the page taken down, but last I checked, it's still there.

I close my eyes. I don't want to cry in front of him, especially without getting out at least one sentence. I'd even settle for a single word.

When I open my eyes, he's right in front of me, his hands in his pockets.

I take a step back. He lets me. The muscles in his jaw tense, then relax.

I don't really know what I'm doing, he says.

I nod. Hard. In a scratchy voice, I say, *I don't either.*

Reaching up, he tugs at the bangs smashed down by his cap. *I think I'm supposed to take you this way.* He points down the tunnel.

I want to ask how he gets his instructions and if there's someone watching, but I can't bring myself to say much of anything. I was always shy around him.

Trailing behind him, I take a breath and try to say his name—but only the first sound manages to lift off my lips.

Shh, I say, as if I'm hushing him.

He doesn't respond. I'm not sure he even hears me. Before I can try again, the shadows lift to reveal two third graders seated at a shared desk.

Shun and me, of course.

Near the beginning of the year, when we were first seated together, he would scoot his chair all the way to the far end to put as much space between us as possible. His friends thought it was hilarious. My friends shot me sympathetic looks. The teacher, who had been the one to pair us together in the first place, pretended not to notice.

I can't pinpoint exactly when it was, but over time, he slowly let his guard down. He never invaded my personal space, but as the boundary between us blurred, he stopped slamming his hand down on his pencil any time it rolled anywhere close to my seat. He refrained from tilting his head back and groaning whenever I raised my hand.

He still caused trouble whenever he could, though. He would sneak his 'ukulele to school almost every day. Once, when another student got in trouble, he reached into his bag and started playing "Twelfth Street Rag."

What? he said when the teacher gave him a dark look. *It's background music.*

It's weird, right? Shun says now.

I glance over at him. There are two of each of us: the ones we were, sitting at that desk, so small and curious; and the ones we are, one dead and the other barely alive.

I mean, it's crazy to think we were ever that small, he says.

I turn back to the children sitting in the middle of all the shadows, their desk the only thing illuminated.

I don't find it that hard to believe. Sometimes, when I think of him, he's still that little boy with nimble fingers.

I remember, I say suddenly, *that time I asked you how you could play music so well.*

The children's silhouettes flicker once, then begin to move. The little Shun pulls his 'ukulele out of his bag, draws his tiny fingers across the strings, takes the kind of huge breath only children can, and starts to hum. His voice is sweet, each note perfectly placed. My third-grade self closes her eyes, as if she thinks that will let her hear better.

What a show-off, Shun says from beside me.

I open my mouth to say something but end up biting my lip instead. The tears start pricking my eyes again.

My third-grade self turns to little Shun. *You're amazing.*

I look away.

Little Shun laughs. The sound echoes and spins in the

nothingness, but I can still hear it in my head as he says, *It's just a couple chords.*

I could never do that, I hear myself say. *No one can play like you can.*

Unable to stand on my own, I crouch in the darkness, my head in my hands. If he touches me, I'll break.

It's really not a big deal, little Shun says, his fingers grazing the back of his neck. *I bet you could do it if you tried. It's just practice.*

Still, I hear myself say. *You're really talented.*

Not really, he says.

You were so humble, I tell him now. *Every time I tried to compliment you, you brushed it off.*

It was just music, he says.

It was never just music. Not when it came from him.

I close my eyes for a moment. When I finally manage to stand back up, the children are gone, and I'm alone with the only Shun I have left.

How am I supposed to feel about you? I ask.

He doesn't answer.

I pull my arms around myself, holding on too tightly. *You were mean sometimes. Never to me, at least after you got used to me, but to others.*

I know, he says.

There was that time you teased a girl for being fat. I can still remember the stunned look on her face and the way she kept tugging the hem of her shirt. *That time you made fun of the boy with a lisp. That time you said the recess attendant looked like an old witch.*

Again, he says nothing.

You could be cruel when we were little, I say. *You could turn anything into a joke. And the worst part was how funny you were.*

It felt like a crime, not laughing at something you said. If we didn't laugh, we had to wonder if we would be laughed at instead.

I was a kid. Kids are brutal. His eyes flick to me, then back to the void. *Aside from you, anyway.*

No. I had my moments of brutality too. I just never had the audience he did.

I wait for something to emerge from the darkness, another scene, but there's only that same old void. Following his gaze, I say, *By the time we were freshmen, you had turned your attention to the teacher. You told her how much you hated what we were reading and why. You once dropped your book on the floor and stomped right on the cover. I could see the mark of your shoe.*

He takes off his cap and runs a hand through his hair. *I don't remember that.*

Yeah, well, that's the last real memory I have of you. Your shoe on that book. I blink, trying to ward off the tears pushing at the backs of my eyes. *And isn't that sad? Isn't that pathetic? Isn't that the worst thing you've ever heard?*

I can feel his eyes on me. *What do you mean?*

Look at what we had. I gesture to the place where our third-grade selves once sat. *A few conversations about 'ukulele and how quiet I was and how funny I thought you were, at least when you weren't making fun of our classmates. A shared desk we left almost ten years ago. A few times you asked me for help on homework with this ridiculously earnest look on your face, like you really needed me, which, to an eight-year-old girl who had never been much of anything, means a hell of a lot.*

Then, I continue, *years later, we had an English class together. One that didn't meet every day and lasted all of a semester. One where the only time you ever looked at me was when I was answering a question.*

That's not true, he says.

I ignore him. *I, of course, found myself looking to you all the time. You always had something to add to the conversation. People could say a lot of things about you, but they could never claim you weren't paying attention. You kept up with assignments, even if it seemed like you only did it to ensure you could say you HAD read the chapter; you just didn't think there was anything worth talking about, what with the author's clumsy metaphors and nonsensical, self-righteous blathering.*

Every time Shun opened his mouth in that class, our English teacher would roll her eyes and curl her fingers around the edge of her desk, as if she had to physically brace herself for whatever he was going to say.

She liked him, though. I could tell. She much preferred the students who turned a critical eye to the text to the ones who mindlessly dragged their noses across the pages.

And that's it, I say. *That's all there ever was to us. At least from your perspective.*

Shun studies me. *From my perspective?*

The tinny clangs of electronic music drift over our shoulders. When I turn, we're transported to my room. My child self is lying on her stomach, her legs in the air and her fingers crimped around an old game console.

I grimace. *Don't look at me.*

Shun raises his head, his eyes sparkling. *What? Why not?*

I look all small and weird. Like an umeboshi.

His eyebrows shoot up as he starts laughing. *The pickled plum things? I like those.*

I wrinkle my nose, trying not to feel too proud of myself. Making him laugh always felt like an accomplishment.

He lets out a breath. *Do you remember those bento from Fujimoto Market?*

I glance at him. *Of course I do.*

Nestled on the basement floor of a small mall, Fujimoto Market is known to have the best bento around. Every time my mother took me to the doctor for my yearly checkup, we would stop by to pick up lunch. My favorite was the salmon bento, complete with a small croquette and a side of vinegar-soaked vegetables.

The umeboshi was my favorite part, Shun tells me now.

Really? I think I used to throw mine away.

He gasps. *Sacrilege.*

When I laugh, I have to twist my fingers behind my back to keep from crying. *Sorry.*

We don't speak for a moment. Then he says, *I miss those bento.* He pauses. *I miss a lot of things, really.*

My eyes flit over to him, then away, the acrid taste of vinegar clinging to the back of my throat.

After a few beats of silence, he turns back and crouches beside my younger self. *What are you playing?*

A game.

He shoots me a look. *Yeah. I got that.*

I continue winding my fingers around each other. *When I was little, I was obsessed with this farming simulator. You got to build and run your own ranch and interact with all the other villagers. You could even date and marry them, as long as you talked to them every day and gave them the right gifts.*

Oh, right. I've heard of those. He lifts his head, a cheeky smile on his face. *I didn't think you would like them.*

I was a kid, I say stiffly.

All right. He's still smirking, the jerk. *So what were you going to say about the game?*

I hesitate. *This is going to sound so dumb.*

It won't, he says, his voice so earnest, it's like a punch in the gut.

He waits patiently, more patiently than he ever did in life, as I take a moment to catch my breath.

There was this one character, I say. *He was the animal caretaker. When you first met him, he was constantly grumpy, doing everything he could to get out of talking to you.*

He takes another peek at my screen. *Is it this guy? The one with the*—he hesitates—*the, uh, baseball cap?*

I don't feel that requires a response.

Self-consciously thumbing his own cap, Shun sits beside my child self and watches as my character runs over to him with a giant plate over her head. Smiling, he says, *Curry, huh?*

It's one of his favorite dishes, I say through my teeth.

I could take it or leave it. His expression softens. *My mom loves it, though. Japanese curry is one of her favorites.*

I think of her standing beside her son's cross.

I miss her, he says. *My mom.*

Stop. Stop. Stop. I don't want to hear this.

More than you miss Fujimoto Market? I blurt out.

Unease creeps over us like mold.

That's how it always went. In the rare times when I dared to make a joke, it never landed right. Everyone thought our teacher had seated us together so Shun could learn from me, but I always found myself wishing he could teach me his ways instead.

Sorry, I say. *I should probably leave the jokes to you.*

He leans back on his hands. *I'm not sure there's room for jokes here.*

A flash of irritation sparks in my stomach. *Oh, so NOW you know when to stop kidding?*

He looks over at me, surprised.

I duck my head. *Sorry. I'm sorry. This is just . . . so much harder than I thought it would be.*

He tilts his head. *What is?*

My breath shudders through my body. *Everything.*

I bite my tongue, praying he won't ask me for details. I can't say anything further without tearing myself apart.

Hey, he says quietly. Still sitting beside my child self, he watches as I guide my character around the ranch. The stories in those games were never all that great, but I always fell in love with the characters. *Why are you showing me this?*

I don't know, I say. *Because it's easier than showing you anything else.*

He nods. *It's hard.*

I suck in a breath. *You have no idea.*

He raises his head until our eyes lock. *You could tell me about it.*

I don't want to.

I also know if I don't, I'll regret it for the rest of my life.

I like to tell people I didn't have a crush on anyone until I was in the eighth grade, I say.

Shun's eyebrows skyrocket, nearly disappearing under his cap. *What? The EIGHTH grade?*

I nod. *But now, I'm starting to wonder how true that is. Because sometimes, I think maybe I was just a little in love with you.*

His lips part, but he doesn't say anything.

I know, I say. *We barely ever spoke, aside from that one year in elementary school and that single English class years later. And we didn't know each other. Not really. If we had, you probably wouldn't have liked me.*

He blinks. *What do you mean?*

I'm not like you, I say. *I can't get everyone to like me in a matter of seconds. All my jokes fall flat. I break into a cold sweat whenever I have to talk to anyone with even a modicum of authority. I almost never break the rules. I don't know how anyone hears about parties because I have never, in my life, been invited to one, unless you count the ones Thea and I have thrown for her birthday.*

Shun blinks. His eyelashes are short and barely curl at the ends, almost sticking straight out. *Monika.*

I wasn't madly in love with you, I say, because if I stop now, I'm never going to be able to say everything on my mind. *Not ever, but especially not after elementary school. To be honest, for a while, I forgot about you. I didn't really think about you until we were in that class together in our freshman year, and even then, it's not like I fell for you all over again.*

I just—I take a deep breath. My eyes are burning. *I admired you. From the moment we met, I found you so interesting, in all these ways I never could be, and that made me love you, at least in some way.*

Thea would call it love at first sight.

But, I say, *you don't have to tell me you never felt the same way. I already know.*

How? he asks, his voice slicing off the end of my last word. He gets to his feet. Behind him, my child self plays on, completely oblivious. *How do you know I never felt the same way?*

Because, I say, laughing a little from the sheer ridiculousness of this whole conversation, *I was just some girl you had to sit next to.*

I liked talking to you.

Then why didn't you write anything in my yearbook?

He's quiet for what feels like a long time. In the background, my child self flips onto her side, using her arm as a pillow.

I looked at it the other day, I say. *I thought maybe, after everything we had been through, you might have written something. Even something short, like "Have a great summer" or "Hope to see you next year" or anything, really. But when I opened my yearbook, do you know what I saw?*

I—He hesitates. *I didn't write in it?*

Well, you did. You wrote your name. And a smiley face. And that's it. And I KNOW it's stupid to be sad over that, but that was the only real chance I had to get some kind of proof of the year we had shared, even if it had always meant more to me than it ever did to you. Something to look back on, years later, and smile about.

But you didn't say anything to me, I say quietly. *And granted, I have no idea if I wrote anything to you. But I feel like such an idiot.*

Don't, he says. *I don't remember what I was thinking when we exchanged yearbooks, but I never meant to make you feel like I didn't care. I did. I've always appreciated you.*

I close my eyes. Is this really him? Is he really saying this? Or is this just what I want him to say, a preprogrammed line triggered only by my giving him the right thing first?

Shun. The first boy I remember ever wanting to befriend. The one who challenged students and teachers alike. I can still see his scribbled smiley face in my mind, the eyes not dots, the way they're usually drawn, but long, a vertical equal sign.

Everything I've told him is true. For years, I forgot about him, just as I'm sure he forgot about me. But it all feels like such a slap in the face now. He's gone, and all I have to remember him by is that one mark in my yearbook. No notes. No pictures. Nothing.

Monika? he says softly.

How did we end up like this? I ask.

He doesn't reply. There is no way to program in an answer to that.

CHAPTER TWENTY-FOUR
Most Devastated

WHEN I MANAGE to raise my head, I see my child self has faded back into the shadows, and once again, it's just Shun and me. It hits me that we haven't spent this much time together, just the two of us, since we were in the third grade.

As the silence between us stretches on, something appears in the distance. I squint, watching it take shape.

A white cross.

I don't get it, I say. Shun turns to me, but I keep my focus on the cross. *What were you doing on the road? What were you thinking?*

He drops his hands into his pockets. *Would it be a cliché to say I wasn't?*

A cliché and an excuse, I say. *You caused an accident. Did you know that?*

He looks away. *No. I know now, but then, I had no idea. I was just so out of it.*

That doesn't really make it better, I say. He opens his mouth, but I just keep talking. *You shouldn't have been driving like that. I mean, you shouldn't even have been that inebriated in the first place, but to get behind the wheel after, it's—*

Unforgivable, he finishes. *I know.*

I cross my arms. I don't want to be here anymore. I want to slip back under the covers and forget any of this ever happened.

I'm surprised you didn't make fun of me for dropping the word "inebriated" into the conversation, I say quietly.

It caught my attention, he admits. *But you were always like that.*

I run my finger over the hairs on my arm. *Nerdy?*

Smart, he corrects. *I thought that for as long as we knew each other.*

Well, joke's on you. I pull at a hair, but it slips through my fingers. *I'm an idiot.*

Don't say that, he says. *You're not the one who—*

He stops. Which is, in a way, even worse than if he had finished his sentence. Now I'm coming up with a thousand ways to end it: *Who got his 'ukulele confiscated so many times, his friends wound up pooling their money together to buy ANOTHER so he could at least alternate between the two. Who narrowly avoided suspension after getting into a fistfight with some other kids over pudding cups at lunch. Who, in freshman English, armchair-diagnosed Holden Caulfield with "a bad case of being a whiny asshole, but a funny whiny asshole, which makes him kind of cool."*

Who celebrated the end of college applications by getting outrageously drunk and high. Who got in the car afterward and swerved along the road. Who caused a girl to crash her car.

Who got home, crawled into bed, fell asleep, and never opened his eyes again.

Just like my uncle.

Do you hate me? Shun asks softly.

Oh, right, I say, my voice startlingly sharp. *Yeah, for sure. You know me, chasing dreams and falling down rabbit holes and enduring psychological torture to get the slightest chance at bringing someone I HATE back to life.*

He removes his cap and flips it along his wrist. I remember when he used to do that. He could do all the things I couldn't, like perfectly whistle a tune and play the 'ukulele and, most infuriatingly, flick his cheek to imitate the sound of a water drop.

You didn't know about the crash when you came here, he says.

I open my mouth, then sigh. *Yeah.*

I didn't really believe you hated me before, he says. *I wasn't sure you liked me all that much either, but I didn't think you despised me. Now I don't know.*

It was stupid, I say. It was really stupid. That girl is going to have to live with that guilt for the rest of her life.

Unless she manages to revive her mother. But even if she does, it's not like all the animosity between them will fade away. Shiori will still hate herself for crashing in the first place. I have no idea what their relationship would look like if they were to reunite now.

I'm sorry, Shun says. *It was stupid of me. I was just—*He cuts himself off and shakes his head. *I don't want to make excuses. There aren't any. I'm just sorry.*

So am I, I say.

We lapse back into silence. The white cross glows.

If I stay in this tunnel forever, I say, *will I keep meeting people who have passed away? Is this, like, some kind of channeling chamber?*

He hesitates. *Monika. This isn't real.*

I know, I say, even though I don't. *And what does that mean anyway? How can this not be real? I'm having a conversation with you right now.*

He gives me a sad look. *But maybe it's all in your head.*

Maybe it is.

I had a full conversation with people I barely even remember, though, I say, desperation leaking into my voice. *They knew things I couldn't have.*

Unless you happened to overhear things. He sucks in a breath like he's pouring antiseptic over an open wound. *What if that's the reason they always look exactly the way you remember?*
That's not true, I say.
But even as I say it, I realize he's right. My faded grandfather. My nightgown-wearing grandmother. My uncle behind glass and Art at the café.
My breath is loud in my ears.
Pulling my fingers into my palm, I ask, *So what are you telling me? None of this matters? I'm just hallucinating wildly on my own? You and Art and my uncle and my grandparents, they're all fake? They're all meaningless?*
I never said that. He stuffs his cap into his pocket. *I just—I don't know.*
What? I say. *What were you going to say? You don't want me to get my hopes up?*
He doesn't say anything.
If I wanted to bring you back, I say, my voice so tiny in the tunnel, *would you let me? Is it even possible?*
He still doesn't say anything, and for a second, I hate him for it. I can't keep asking and asking and receiving nothing but silence.
What do you WANT? I shout.
He doesn't flinch. *To start over.*
I shake my head. *That's what everyone says.*
Maybe because that's what everyone WANTS. He runs a hand through his hair. *Maybe when we die, all we really wish is to get the chance to do things differently.*
It doesn't even have to be when we die, I say. *I'm still here, and I wish...*
I close my eyes. It shouldn't feel like such a huge change, keeping my eyes open versus closing them, when it's so dark in

here now. But it *is* a huge change. Even if all I ever have is one person beside me, one bright thing in the distance, it makes a difference.

I wish you had never died in the first place. I wish you were still here. I wish I could have had the chance to reach out to you at graduation. I take a shaky breath. *And you know what? Maybe I wouldn't have. Maybe I wouldn't have gone over to you and given you a candy lei and told you I hoped you had a good time at college. Maybe I wouldn't have even thought about you.*

But at least we could have had a chance. Because now I'm never going to know what we could have been, or even what we couldn't have been. I'm never going to know if YOU would have come to ME. If you would have said "Congratulations, Monika. We made it," or if you would have ignored me because you had forgotten me a long time ago.

I am never going to KNOW, I say, *and that just . . .*

His smile is mirthless. *Say it.*

Kills me, I whisper.

He nods. *What else do you wish?*

My attempt at a laugh sounds a lot more like a sob. *Does it matter?*

Doesn't it?

I open my mouth, close it, then turn away, my chest aching. *I wish I had gotten to know you better. I wish we hadn't drifted apart. I wish my last concrete memory of you didn't have to be from freshman English. I wish I had known what was going to happen. To you and me and my uncle and Art Harris and Shiori and her mother.*

I wish, I say, *you had celebrated turning in your college apps in any other way. I wish you hadn't lost control. I wish you hadn't gotten into the car. I wish you hadn't veered into Shiori's lane. I wish you hadn't fallen asleep. I wish you could have graduated with the rest of us. I wish I never had to see that thing.*

He follows my gaze to the white cross.

I wish, I say softly, *you would tell me if any of this is real.*

He doesn't meet my eyes. *I'm sorry.*

I don't really want to hear that anymore, I say. When I squint, I can just barely see the top of the tunnel. *How am I supposed to feel about you now?*

I asked Art the same thing. And, like Art, Shun doesn't have an answer.

Maybe they can't answer because they aren't real. Maybe they sound so similar because all these conversations are figments of my imagination. Maybe that's why my uncle reminds me of Art, who reminds me of Shun, who reminds me of my uncle.

In *Bitter Mouse*, one of the characters says we look for patterns in everything. It's human nature. Which, of course, is a funny thing for an anthropomorphic creature to say. That line, easily missed if you don't interact with the NPCs around town, ignited an entire online debate about whether the characters are actually all humans in disguise. Maybe the main character is hallucinating. Maybe it's a metaphor. Or maybe it was an oversight, or an inside joke, or a throwaway line meant to spark discussion.

I never asked Art about that line. I didn't want to know what the intention was. I thought there was something beautiful about leaving it up to interpretation.

But I want answers now. I *need* them. I can't keep doing this to myself.

Shun, I say.

He turns. *Huh?*

Are you okay? I ask.

He blinks at me, as if to say, *Well, I'm dead, so . . .*

Wherever you are, whether you can hear me or see me or

remember me or not, are you okay? I search his eyes. *Will you be all right?*

He watches me for a moment. His gaze softens as the realization dawns on him. *If you don't bring me back to life, you mean.*

My stomach drops.

Is that what I mean? Can that possibly be what I'm trying to tell him? After everything we've been through? After what *I've* been through, to get to him?

Shouldn't this be the end? The part where I take his hand, squeeze it once, and tell him *Let's go home*? Shouldn't he nod? Smile? Say *Now I can tell you all the things I never did in life*? *Who needs a stupid message in a yearbook when you've got the real thing*? Shouldn't I laugh, because God, he *always* made me laugh?

I close my eyes. *I don't know what I mean anymore.*

Yes, you do, he says, his voice so much kinder than it should be.

But I came all the way down here, I say. *I went through all of this and told the others I couldn't save them because I had to save you, and now I'm looking right at you, and I . . .*

He waits. I want him to say it for me, but I know he won't.

I can't, I say softly.

His smile is sad. *I know.*

How can he know? How can he know when I didn't? When I was so sure it would be him?

I was sure. Wasn't I? Wasn't that why I kept going? Because I needed to bring him back?

Or was it because I needed to see him? Because I knew the moment I did, I would understand exactly why I couldn't bring him back?

There are a million reasons why he can't come back: Because it's wrong. Because it's unnatural. Because he died, and that's supposed to be it.

Because *he* was wrong. Because he was drunk. Because he was involved in the crash that killed Shiori's mom.

Because he was mean. Because he was cruel. Because he took jokes too far, and I sometimes find myself wondering, years later, if his targets still think about the things he said, the way I do.

Because he's gone. Because he's been buried. Because his mother said, at our graduation, she finds peace in knowing he's in Heaven, reunited with his father, and it was never my right, or even my duty, to deprive them of that.

There's only one reason why I was going to bring him back. Because I wanted to.

And now, perhaps for the first time and most definitely for the last, I'm realizing that's not enough.

We stand together, his hands in his pockets and mine clamped around my elbows.

In a way, I say, *I hope this isn't real. Then at least I won't be letting you down.*

I let you down first, he says.

I look at him, but he's staring straight ahead, right at the cross.

I didn't say anything in your yearbook, he says. *I didn't reach out after the third grade. I didn't try to reconnect with you after that first semester of English. And I didn't tell you I liked you too. Romantically, platonically, whatever. I just know I did.*

Don't, I want to tell him. *Don't make this harder.*

But wouldn't it have hurt more if he hadn't said it? If I had spent the rest of my life wondering?

You asked me if I'm okay. He finally takes his eyes off the cross and fixes them on me instead. *But are you?*

My breath catches in my throat. *How could I possibly be okay right now?*

Fair enough. He takes one hand out and studies it for a moment. If I squint, I can see through it, to the ground beneath our feet. *WILL you be okay, then? Tomorrow? A week from now? A month? Someday so far in the future, you won't even remember my name?*

Tears spring to my eyes. *I'm always going to remember your name.*

Yeah? He smiles for a second, then lets it fade. *You'll be okay, Monika. You were always stronger than you seemed.*

I don't know how to respond, or if there's even a point in trying. Swallowing hard, I say, *I wish things could have been better.*

Me too, he says quietly.

I dip my head. Tears form along my lashes. When they spill over, they burn so badly, I have to bring my fingers to my face to ensure the tears aren't scorching my skin.

I swear my eyes are only closed for a moment. But when I open them, he's already walking away.

I remain perfectly still, his name caught in my throat, as he presses onward. His hands remain in his pockets. I try to keep my eyes on him, but the farther he gets, the brighter the cross glows, until soon, I have no choice but to look away. When I finally lower my hand, he's gone.

"Shun?" I call out, even though I know he's not coming back. "Shun, are you there?"

Silence rings around the tunnel as the walls and ceiling slowly sharpen back into focus. The white cross has vanished, but I find myself sleepwalking toward it anyway, like I think it'll come back if I just pray hard enough.

The cross doesn't reappear. But there's something in its place.

I crouch, taking my time, half sure I'm going to pass out

and wake up to the sound of the alarm I set to ensure I got to the Japanese Club brunch on time. On my hands and knees, I reach for the white square lying on the ground, then hold my breath and flip it over.

HAGS, it says, accompanied by a smiley face, its eyes two uneven vertical lines.

My ankles give out from under me. I fall hard onto my left hip, cover my face with one hand, and cry.

CHAPTER TWENTY-FIVE
Most Desperate

THIS TIME, IT'S easy to find Shiori. Because she's screaming.

Stumbling to my feet, I take off running. "SHIORI?"

She keeps screeching, her garbled syllables turning to mush when combined with the echo of the tunnel.

"SHIORI!" I call out. "WHERE ARE YOU?"

My sole skids along a pebble on the tunnel floor, my hands colliding with the wall. Taking a moment to catch my breath, I raise my head and call for Shiori again. Now that I'm getting closer, I can pick out certain words.

"—PROMISE," Shiori shouts. "I—I *PROMISE!*"

Pushing off the wall, I take a right, round the next corner, and stop dead.

The exit. She's standing right in front of the exit.

Packed dirt and ferns line the domed walls. Footprints mar the nearby ground, tiny rocks kicked up by merciless boots. Beyond the beaten path, the sky is an offputtingly beautiful blue.

"Oh my God," I whisper. "You found the way out."

Shiori whirls around, her boot knocking into the backpack she dropped at her feet. Her eyes are wild, her lavender hair in total disarray. Before I can react, she grabs me by the shoulders. "*YOU* did it, didn't you?"

"What?" I wince. "You're hurting me."

"Where is he?" She practically throws me to the side. "You brought him back, didn't you? Let me talk to him."

I brush my hair out of my face. "I . . . I didn't."

"You didn't." She purses her lips. They're so chapped, they're cracking. "You *didn't* bring that guy back to life. The guy who—the one who—"

"No," I say. "I didn't."

She shakes her head, hugging her arms to her chest. Her entire body is trembling. "Then why?"

"Why what?" I edge closer, afraid I'll scare her off. "What happened? What did you see?"

"My *mother*," she shrieks. "I saw my *mother*, and she kept telling me to *save her*, and when I woke up, I started running, and I got all the way here, and I was thinking, 'Oh my *God*. I actually did it. I actually did it,' and I got to the end, and"—she takes a frantic breath—"and *nothing. Nothing happened.*"

"Shiori," I say.

"Don't," she says, her voice low. "I've tried everything. I called for my mother. I told her I love her. I said I was sorry. I begged for forgiveness. I cried out to her and pled for the tunnel to bring her back. I even left." She closes her eyes. "I left without bothering to check if you were around."

"That's okay," I say, but she's not listening.

"I ran around outside. I thought I had to actually get *out*, like maybe she would be there, waiting for me, but she wasn't. I went back inside, but nothing happened then either, and nothing is happening now, and *God*, why isn't anything *happening*?" Her hands are squeezing white fingerprints into her arms.

I take another small step forward. "Shiori, what if this isn't real?"

"What if this isn't—what?" She shakes her head. "What?"

"What if there's nothing here? What if all of this really *was* just a rumor?"

She shakes her head again, faster. "What are you saying? How could it—But you *saw* it. You saw the memories and the—you *saw* it. Don't tell me you were just playing along this whole time."

"No, I—"

"*Don't*," she spits. "You were *there*. You were *right there*. When I was in the car with my mother, you were *there*. What are you trying to do to me?"

"I'm not trying to do anything," I say. Her eyes roam around my face, searching for meaning. "I'm just wondering if maybe this isn't what we think it is."

Her voice is raspy. "And what, exactly, do we think it is?"

"We thought going through the tunnel would give us the chance to revive someone. Or that's what I thought."

She gives me a dirty look. "You *know* I thought that too. And I *still* believe that."

"How?" I hold out a hand. A beam of sunlight hits my fingertips. "The exit is right there, and nothing is happening."

"Maybe it thinks I don't want it enough. Maybe it heard the things I told you about my mother, and maybe it's convinced I don't want her back, even though I do. I do, I do, I do, I—" She takes a deep breath and screams it: "I DO!"

I can barely look her in the eye. "Shiori."

She drops to the ground, pulls her knees to her chest, and covers her face. I'm just about to move toward her when she lets out the loudest, most desperate scream I've ever heard in my life.

My instinct is to clap my hands over my ears. But I move closer instead.

"Shiori," I say, and this time, when I reach for her, she wraps her arms around me. She sobs, her body shaking us both, as if we're one again.

I HOLD HER tightly until the trembling finally stops.

Even once Shiori has calmed down enough to sit beside me, her arms curling over her body like a pair of crisscrossing seat belts, she can't seem to catch her breath.

Lowering my head, I check my palm. Shun's note is still clamped between my fingers. I don't want to risk putting it in my pocket, just in case it disappears like my phone did. A part of me keeps hoping he'll appear, one hand on the bill of his cap and the other reaching out to us. The rest of me knows he's really gone this time.

"What did you see?" Shiori asks, her voice hammered down by grief and exhaustion.

I hesitate. "People I lost."

"Your classmate." She can't even muster the strength to sound angry.

"Not just him." I glance at her. "But yeah."

She nods, her face turned away.

"I'm sorry," I say. "He wasn't in his right mind. He shouldn't have been driving."

I press my lips together. I don't know if I can tell her he apologized when I still can't figure out how real any of this is. But I know I'm holding his message written with his humor and in his handwriting. That has to mean something.

"He said he was sorry," I say. "That doesn't make it better, though."

"No. It doesn't." She inhales. "But I can't put all the blame on him. I could have—"

"You can't keep thinking that way."

"Well, that's the only way I *can* think right now." She sets her teeth on her lower lip. "You know, I didn't want to keep arguing with my mother. I didn't want to have to fight for every tiny bit of freedom. I didn't want to disappoint her over and over again. But I couldn't stand the thought of being Mommy's Little Girl forever either."

"I get that," I say quietly.

"So there's a part of me," she breathes, her voice gossamer thin, "that was relieved when my mother died. So overwhelmingly relieved."

I open my mouth to respond, but she doesn't give me the chance.

"I *know* how disgusting that is," she says. "I *know*. And I love my mother. More than I can ever say." She closes her eyes. "But I also really hated her sometimes."

When she opens her eyes, she looks right at me, challenging me to look away.

I hold her gaze. "I think you have every right to feel the way you do. Your mother loved you, for sure, but she also showed some abusive tendencies."

She tenses at the word *abusive*. I knew she would.

"No," she says. "You're wrong. She wasn't like that at all. I mean, how would you have any idea? You spent, what, a minute with her?"

"Everything you just listed—"

"*No*," she snaps. "No."

She curls into herself. Manically tapping her finger against her kneecap, she presses her head against her legs.

"Maybe nothing's happening because the tunnel knows I'm a bad person," she whispers.

"Or maybe," I say gently, "you did everything you could, and things still didn't work out. And that's not your fault."

She starts rocking again. The toe of her boot presses into

the bottom of her abandoned backpack. I pull it closer and unzip it, extracting her water bottle.

"Here," I say. "Have a drink."

She shakes her head. "That's probably what it wants me to do. Maybe if I don't, maybe if I just never eat or drink again, it'll see how badly I want this."

"You can't do that to yourself." I hold out the bottle, careful to keep a tight grip on it, just in case she lashes out. "Come on, Shiori."

"No," she says, her voice fracturing. "You're trying to trick me. You're working with the tunnel. Maybe even with my mother."

She starts knocking her head against her knees.

"Shiori." I lift my eyes to the blue sky outside. "I think it's time for us to go."

"Go." She stares at the ground, her jawline sharp as she grinds her teeth. "You want us to leave the tunnel. Without having done a single thing."

"We may not have accomplished what we thought we would," I admit, "but that doesn't mean we did nothing."

She narrows her eyes. "How? What are you even talking about?"

"When we first got here, I didn't trust you as far as I could throw you." I tip my head. "And I'm sure you felt the same way about me."

"Please," she says through her teeth, "for the love of God, do not tell me the great lesson to have come out of this was *friendship*."

"No. Not only that."

"Oh, great. Not *only* that."

"I couldn't understand my own grief," I say, "and you couldn't admit there was a part of you that hated the way your mother treated you."

Her eyes flick around the tunnel. "That's not true."

"Shiori." I extend a hand. When she flinches away, I place

my palm on my knee. "All the things you saw, all the memories you've had to watch over again—they aren't meaningless. They're helping you heal."

"*This* is healing?" She rests her head on her knees. "If this is what it's like, I'd rather stay in denial for the rest of my life."

I give her a small smile. "I know. But even if it hurts now, it'll save you in the end."

"Who cares about that?"

"Me." I wait until she looks at me. "I care."

She rolls her eyes, then fixes her gaze on the exit. "So what are you saying? We get up, take each other's hand, and skip out of here?"

"No. We help each other up, then head home." I carefully place my hand on her arm. "You must be so tired."

She closes her eyes for a second. "What if this really *is* a test? What if we're failing right now? What if waiting just a little longer will bring her back?"

My hand instinctively slips into my pocket, even as I remind myself I haven't seen my phone since entering the tunnel. I pull my arm out so quickly, I don't even realize my fingers have brushed against something until it clatters to the ground.

Shiori jumps. "Oh my God. You scared the crap out of me."

"Sorry, sorry." I pick up my phone and scrutinize it, searching for cracks. "How did this get back here? Do you have yours now too?"

"Who cares?" she mutters, but after sliding a hand into her pocket, she nods. "Yeah. It's back. Oh, joy. Oh, happy day. I can't bring my *mommy* back, but I can bring back my stupid, worthless phone."

Tapping the screen, I bring my phone to my ear. As expected, Thea answers before the third ring.

"Monika?"

"I'm sorry," I say. "I know I freaked you out."

"You mean when you ran off and told me to cover for you, then disappeared? Where have you been?"

"Long story. Though in my defense, I didn't 'disappear' until this morning."

"How long has it been?" Shiori asks, still curled up like a bug.

I pull my phone away from my ear and check the time. "Under an hour."

"Who's that?" Thea asks.

"Shiori. She ended up in the tunnels with me." I take a breath. "Look, Thea. I'm sorry. I know I've already asked a lot of you, but if I send you my location, will you pick us up? And can you bring some snacks?"

"I don't need anything," Shiori says.

I ignore her. "Please? I'll pay you back."

"No, you won't," Thea says. "But when I get there, I expect you to tell me everything."

"I will," I say. "Thank you. I love you. I'll owe you for the rest of my life."

"Shut up and send me your location."

She hangs up. Not even five seconds later, a text pops up on my screen: **WHERE ARE YOU?**

"So what happens now?" Shiori asks as I send Thea my location. "Are you just going to leave me behind?"

"No. You heard me. We're taking you home."

Her eyes fill with tears. She knows now. Her mother isn't coming back.

Whipping around and nearly lashing me with her lavender hair, she leans forward until her forehead is resting against the wall. I can see her lips moving, a silent plea. I try to speak to her, but no matter what I do, she won't respond.

• • •

THEA ARRIVES A few long, silent minutes later, a canvas bag slung over her shoulder. Afraid to leave Shiori alone, I stay at the mouth of the tunnel and wave my arms to flag Thea down. She frowns but reluctantly approaches us.

"Don't come in," I say. "Just in case."

Thea's eyelashes flutter. "Just in case what?"

"I'll explain later." I glance at Shiori, who hasn't stopped to even take a peek at the newcomer, then turn my attention back to Thea. "Thank you for coming."

"Of course." She opens her bag. "I didn't know what you wanted, so I just kind of brought whatever I could grab from the pantry."

I reach for the bag, careful to position myself between Thea and the tunnel. "Thank you." After rummaging around for a moment, I pull out some peanut butter cups and hand them to Shiori. "Here. You like chocolate and peanut butter, right?"

She barely even turns her head. "I don't want it."

"You need to eat."

"You said it hasn't even been an hour."

"You're the one who said we need to keep our energy up. Besides, chocolate may not be able to fix everything, but it can help to ease the pain."

She rolls her eyes.

"Come on," I say. "I'm going make you eat it either here or in the car."

"I'm not going."

Taking a deep breath, I set the peanut butter cups beside Shiori's knee. I don't expect her to respond, and she doesn't.

I turn to Thea. "Could we stay here for a bit? I can catch you up on what's been going on."

Thea's eyes flick between Shiori and me. Her expression softens. "Sure. I've got time."

CHAPTER TWENTY-SIX
Most Supported

I MAKE NO effort to lower my voice as I explain everything to Thea. I've seen so much of Shiori's life. It only seems right for her to hear about mine. I have no idea if she cares, but at least she knows I trust her enough to let her listen.

Thea is silent throughout almost the entire thing, but when I mention what I saw near the end, when she looked me right in the eye and told me she had no idea who I was, Thea shakes her head. "I could never forget you."

"Well, it was a manifestation of my worst nightmares, so I guess—"

"I could *never* forget you." Her gaze is so intense, I kind of feel like she's glaring at me. "I *do* love you. And I *am* going to miss you."

"I love you too." I swallow. "And I'm going to miss you too. So, so much."

Rustling sounds come from Shiori's corner. Thea and I glance over to see Shiori opening the candy wrapper. We both turn back to each other just as Shiori lifts her head to ensure we aren't staring.

Thea and I make small talk as Shiori nibbles on the chocolate. Almost as soon as she finishes the candy, Shiori gets to her feet and turns to us, her eyes riveted to the ground. "Thanks. For the food."

"Sure," Thea says. "Are you ready to head out?"

My eyes flick to her, then back to Shiori. After a moment, she shuffles her feet, flicks her eyes to the entrance, and asks, in a small, heartbreakingly shaky voice, "Are you sure?"

I don't respond immediately. Then, leaning over and picking up her backpack, I say, "I think if there were a chance, you would've proven yourself a thousand times over."

Her jaw works as she fights back tears. I slowly approach her and ease the straps over her shoulders. Once the bag is securely on her back, she clears her throat and says, "Okay. Let's go."

We both stop at the mouth of the tunnel. Turning back, I say, "Thank you."

Shiori glances back over her shoulder. In a voice even quieter than a whisper, she says, "Thank you."

Then, without looking at me, she takes my hand. On our way out, I grab Thea's hand too. An unbroken chain of unbroken people, we leave the tunnel behind.

WE DROP SHIORI off first. I ask if I can accompany her to her door, and though she gives me a withering look, she doesn't argue. As we walk up her driveway, I tell her, "I feel like I should say something to you, but I don't know what."

"Yeah, well." She brushes her hair behind her ear. "We've been through a lot."

"That's for sure." I listen to the clink of our boots, then look over at her. "I know you aren't my biggest fan, and there's absolutely no pressure to ever reach out, but would it be okay if I put my number in your phone? So if you ever feel the urge to talk, or if you just want to know someone's there, you have me."

She hesitates. "What if I can't be there for you, though?

What if I'm not ready to give you my number and comfort you about your classmate?"

I glance back at Thea, who's fiddling with her car mirrors, entirely oblivious. "I have Thea. And I know you probably have people you feel you can count on too. I'm not saying you don't have friends. But you and I were the only ones in that tunnel."

Shiori hesitates, then unlocks her phone and hands it to me. "Fine. Put in your number."

"Thank you. And look, I know it's not my place to say, but for whatever it's worth, I think Natsuki would listen to you too."

She gives me a dirty look. "You have no idea what you're talking about."

"All right." I pull my mouth to one side. "He's nice, though, isn't he?"

She starts walking faster.

Once we reach her front door, I return her phone and look at the gold locks. It's strange to think I've been here before, in Shiori's body.

"Is your dad home?" I ask.

She nods. Her face has gone pale.

I frown. "Are you okay?"

She nods again. "I just don't know what to say to him. I mean, I didn't tell him about the tunnel, since he never would have believed me, but I just—I feel like I failed."

"You didn't," I say. "But maybe you can tell him you might need some support."

She scoffs. "Easier said than done."

"Do you want me to be there?"

"No. I don't need you to hold my hand through everything." She chews her lip. "Okay. Well, I'm going now."

"Okay. You can text or call me whenever you want. Or not at all."

"So you've said." She takes out her keys, but just before the teeth enter the top lock, she looks over at me again. "Look. I just—thanks. Okay? Thanks."

My eyes slip down to the golden locks. A fingerprint has been pressed into the side, a small, near-invisible *I was here*.

"Thank you too," I say. "And I'll support you. No matter what."

She opens her mouth like she's going to add something, or maybe just insult me. But in the end, she just gives me a curt nod.

I stand back as she unlocks the door and steps inside. A man on the couch looks up from his phone. At the sight of him, she relaxes just a little.

Taking small steps back, I swivel on my heel, return to Thea's car, and buckle myself in. As Thea sets her hands back on the steering wheel, she says, "I can't believe you really went into a magical tunnel."

I don't respond. I still don't know how magical it was. I probably never will.

She backs out of the driveway and steers us back onto the road, her movements fluid and easy. Once she hits the main road, she says, "Monika."

"Yeah?"

"You didn't tell me all those things bothered you. Your uncle and that game developer and even Shun. I mean, I knew you were sad. We all were. But I didn't realize how much it hurt you." She eases the car into a turn. "Why didn't you talk to me about them?"

I face the window and study the pale girl in the glass. "I don't think I even knew how much all those things impacted me until I was down there."

She presses her lips together. "What are you going to do, then, now that you know?"

I don't have an answer for her. So I just stretch out my hand. Without even having to think about it, Thea takes it and holds on. Then, when we finally reach my building, my legs shaking as I brace myself to get out of the car, she lets me go.

I push the door open and step outside. When I close the door behind me, she rolls down the passenger side window.

"You'll be okay," she says. "Won't you?"

I close my eyes for a moment, my fingers running along the paper hidden in my palm. When my eyelids lift, she's still watching me, her brow furrowed.

"Yeah," I say. "I think I'll be just fine."

Stepping back, I watch Thea disappear down the road. Once her white Honda has disappeared into the rush of traffic, I start making my way up to the apartment. It isn't until I'm alone in the elevator that I allow my fingers to uncurl, revealing the *HAGS* message, complete with that signature smiley face, sitting safely in my palm.

CHAPTER TWENTY-SEVEN
Best Surprise Appearance

BZZT-BZZT.

Setting my cup of water on the table, I pick up my phone and check the screen.

Where are you now? my mom's message reads.

I glance up like I need a reminder. My eyes snag on Thea first, that already-familiar pendant dangling from her neck. We bought them together, two silver heart necklaces. There is no BEST. No FRIENDS. No hearts split down the middle. There are just two wholes, perfectly matched, no matter how far apart they may be.

Running my thumb along the back of my phone, I turn to the other person at the table.

"What?" Shiori asks, one eyebrow raised like she's getting ready to take offense. One of her legs keeps bouncing, as if she's revving herself up. "What are you staring at?"

It took her a long time to text me. So long, I wasn't sure she ever would. But one day, my phone buzzed with a message from an unknown number.

hi. it's me. i don't know how serious you were about the corny "i'll be there for you" thing, but i figured you've already seen me at my worst, so what have i got to lose, right? so here's my number, if you need it. don't know why you would, but whatever.

I read the message once, then again. I had just saved her contact information when my phone buzzed again.

this is shiori, by the way.

"Sorry," I say to Shiori. "It's my—"

I stop.

"What?" She rolls her eyes. "Your *mom*? You can just say it, you know. I'm not going to have a mental breakdown every time someone brings up their mom."

Lifting my cup back to my lips, I take a small sip to hide the smile sneaking along my face.

Thea and I kept inviting her to hang out with us, but this is the first time we've actually managed to coax her out. I was afraid she would change her mind at the last minute, but when I texted Thea to ask how things were going, she responded with a picture of the two of them in her car, Thea throwing out a peace sign as Shiori shielded her face with one hand. Thea offered to pick me up too, and while I'm sure the three of us in one car would have led to some utterly delicious chaos, I had something I had to do first.

The evening I returned from the tunnel, I sat my parents down. I could tell they were bracing themselves for the worst: I was sad. I was pregnant. I was running away to join the circus. I was sad and pregnant *and* running away to join the circus. In a way, I think learning I had spent my day in an underground tunnel with either magical properties or hallucinogenic gas came as a bit of a relief.

They were still upset, though, first because I hadn't told them what I was doing, then because my mom didn't know what to do with all the apologies I had for her. She had trouble processing it all, but as I told her about the cigarette smell, about the day I wrote my name wrong, about the way my uncle had called me *kiddo*, I saw her slowly coming around.

Then, that night, when I screamed my way out of a nightmare, she helped me out of the maze of my memories, flicking on the light and holding me the way I had held Shiori.

It was real, I told her. *I was there.*

I know, she said. *I believe you.*

We visited her family's graves earlier today, armed with so many flowers, the car will probably smell like pollen all summer. When she asked me to give her a moment, I stepped away and let her speak to everyone she had lost, her words drifting through the cemetery like the last wisps of a dream.

She agreed to take me to the mall to meet Thea and Shiori afterward, but she warned me she would be sticking around. She had some errands she needed to run.

Is that okay? she asked, her eyes searching mine.

I thought of Art for a moment. How my mom had insisted on accompanying me, even when I gave her every reason not to.

I'm not going to hang OUT with you, she added. *I'm not going to embarrass you like that.*

I gave her a look.

Again, she added. *I'm not going to embarrass you like that AGAIN. Besides, that was different. I KNOW Thea.*

Yeah, yeah, I said.

Then I reached over the center console and squeezed her hand.

At the tables outside The Bean Jive, I type back to my mom now. Why?

On my way. With some people you're going to want to see.

I frown. Leaning forward, I type, ???

She doesn't respond.

Thea's humming again. This time, I know exactly what the song is. I fill in the lyrics in my head: *I just want to fly / back home to you.*

Thea's still working her way through *Bitter Mouse*. She only ever plays once she finishes one of the countless new books she picked up from the library or the bookstore, but considering how fast she reads, that's basically every day. I can tell the game hasn't touched her the way it touched me, but I didn't think it would. I'm just glad she's giving it a chance.

I'm also trying to give *myself* a chance. I've set up an appointment with my college advisor at the state university. When we meet, I'm going to tell her I want to study English and Communications so I can start getting into video-game writing.

I'm not expecting to make the next *Bitter Mouse*. I'm also not secretly hoping my interest in English will get Eli to fall madly in love with me. Thea, ever the stalker, has discovered he graduated from college and is now moving back from the East Coast. She's convinced he and I will run into each other one day, fall in love, and write romance novels together, but I don't think I want that. I just want to make things that hurt in a way that matters. In a way that heals. In a way that makes people realize there *is* a light at the end of the tunnel. Light and life and little things that keep us going, one foot in front of the other, until one day, we reach the ending we've always wanted.

"Monika," my mom says.

I turn.

And everything falls away.

In the corner of my vision, Thea brings a hand to her mouth, her gaze fixed to the two figures beside my mom. Thea looks back over at me as I push myself to my feet, my chair skittering along the cobblestones.

"Look who I found," my mom says quietly.

I take a step forward, my heart pounding as I slowly make

my way over. I don't know which of us starts crying first, but by the time I reach Shun's mother, my vision is almost too blurry to make out the boy shuffling his feet beside her.

"Is this . . . ?"

I can't finish the sentence.

Shun's mother nods. "Arata. Shun's brother."

I didn't even know he had a brother.

There's a sprinkling of spots on his skin, as if his neck has been flecked with paint, and there's a softness to his jaw that his brother never had, even when he was this young. But he looks so much like Shun, I find myself breathless.

"I was in line outside that Japanese curry place downstairs," my mom says, "and I just happened to run into them."

Concern weaves its way along her face, leaving a trail of unspoken questions in her eyes: *Is this okay? Are YOU okay? Are you upset with me for bringing them?*

I look up at Shun's mother. "Your son—"

But that's as far as I get.

Because what can I possibly say? How can I ever express everything Shun was? Everything I loved about him, everything I hated about him, everything I wish he and I and we had said and felt and done?

When Shun's mother wraps her arms around me, the aromatic smell of curry clings to my skin like a promise.

We get about five seconds of uninterrupted weeping before Arata, Shun's little brother, starts shifting his weight from foot to foot. "I gotta pee."

Laughing, his mother pulls away. "Okay, okay. Let's go find a bathroom." She places a hand on his shoulder and looks up at us, her eyes still misty. "It was really nice seeing you."

My throat is so tight, it's a miracle anything gets through. "You too."

Once she and my mother have given each other a hug, she takes my hand, squeezes it gently, then slowly lets me go.

I stand there for a minute, my arms limp at my sides. It feels like I just woke up in the tunnel again, my mind slow and foggy.

"Hey."

When I turn, Shiori's watching me, her eyes running along my face. Thea leans over and takes my hand, her fingers weaving around mine. Behind me, my mom places a hand on my elbow, as if to steady me.

"You're okay," Shiori says.

It takes me a moment. Then, nodding, I say, "Yeah. I am."

As I return to the table, tugging my mom with me, even as she tells me she's too old and uncool to hang out with us, I raise my eyes to the sky and smile.

I have a feeling I'm going to have a really great summer.

ACKNOWLEDGMENTS

I PROMISED MYSELF I would make this short.

To everyone who supported *The Lost Souls of Benzaiten*: Thank you. You made all my prayers come true.

Thank you to Savannah Brooks, Sara Megibow, Kate Schafer Testerman, and Andrea Somberg for taking a chance on me. I don't think you ever read this book, but I wouldn't have had the courage to write it if you hadn't believed in me first.

Thank you to Alexa Wejko. This book is so special to me. I couldn't be more grateful to have gotten to work on it with you. I also want to thank the stellar Soho team: publisher Bronwen Hruska, art director Janine Agro, cover artist Yuta Onoda, copy editor Erin Della Mattia, proofreader Joy Hoppenot, cold reader Atira Gali, managing editor Rachel Kowal, publicist Erica Loberg, and all those who brought this book to life.

To those of you who see yourself in this book—those of you who recognize anyone in these pages, those of you who knew them and were closer to them and hurt a thousand times more than I can even imagine, and those of you who didn't know them and hate the fact that you never will—may this book be your reminder that there's still hope out there. There's still light. So keep going. Keep walking. I'll be right there with you, every step of the way.